DEEPER
THAN TEMPTATION

EMMA ASHE

Deeper Than Temptation

A Single Dad Romance With A Dirty Talking Irish Accented Hero

———————

The Deeper Than Love Series, Book 5

———————

...

———————

EMMA ASHE

This is a work of fiction. Similarities to real people, places,

or events are entirely coincidental.

...

DEEPER THAN TEMPTATON

A Single Dad Romance With A Dirty Talking Irish Accented Hero

Third edition. November 18, 2019.

_____

_____

Written by Emma Ashe

emmaashe.com/books

ALSO BY EMMA ASHE

...

An Indecent Apposal Volume 1, Books 2-4

An Indecent Apposal Volume 2, Books 5-7

An Indecent Apposal Volume 3, Books 8-10

———

Get notified of new releases & free reads:

www.emmaashe.com/signup

CONTENTS

ACKNOWLEDGMENTS

This book wouldn't even be here without the encouragement of some of the finest writers I know. Thank you for cheering me on Skylar Hill and Cici Coughlin.

DEDICATION

_____

For Tony

CHAPTER 1 | Aiden

And now she knows I'm jealous, I realize, staring Parker down because I'm furious, but also because I can't help myself. It seems like when it comes to Parks, all I do is stare. I haven't been able to look away from her since the moment she became my twins' nanny. Right now though? I want to argue.

And undress her. Honestly, the reminder just pisses me off even more, but my anger is nothing in comparison to hers, and I can't really blame her. Minutes ago, my jealous inner fourteen-year-old escaped and I insulted her professionalism. It was a dick move.

Parker lifts her chin, dark eyes flashing. "You told me you needed me to 'handle things' because you didn't have time. Well, I'm handling them—and how *dare* you imply I was flirting with that guy!"

It's not funny, but I force myself to laugh anyway. 'That guy' is another kid's dad. He came by to watch Parker give a riding lesson to the twins because he wants to enroll his own kid in lessons, and after laying eyes on Parker, he wants her too. She has no idea how he was looking at her, how attracted he was.

But I do.

"You really don't know how he was looking at you, do you?" I ask.

She gapes at me. "Nothing was going on between Brandon and me. If you saw something, you're inventing it." She pauses, looking half a second away from tears, and it nearly rips me in half. "No one looks at me like that."

"I do." It's so quick it probably sounds like a line, but it's the truth— probably the biggest truth we've ever shared because I can't *ever* take my eyes from her. Call it instant attraction or lust at first sight or whatever, but I've wanted Parker since day one. It's totally out of line. I'm her boss. She's the twins' nanny.

And yet we can't seem to keep our hands off each other.

"In fact," I continue, "I look at you like that all the time, and you know it." Her breath quickens, and it pools heat in my gut. "And furthermore, I know you look at me the same way."

I also know it knocks the breath out of me every time.

Parks nods, and catches herself, eyes narrowing at me in annoyance. "Fine," she says at last. "I like looking at you. What of it? We have...a thing."

"We do," I whisper.

"Doesn't mean anything."

"Nope."

"Because it can't," she adds.

"Right."

"Exactly." We talk to each other like we're on the same page, and everything's fine. But my already small apartment kitchen suddenly feels even smaller. Everything is filled with Parker. She's doing that absent nod thing, blinking those doe-eyes the way she always does when she wants me, and I can't stop walking toward her. I can't stop until we're toe-to-toe, until she has to look up to meet my gaze. It makes her lick her lips, and I have to hold myself back from touching her.

"See?" I whisper, and she shivers. "You're doing it again: looking at me like you want me to kiss you."

"Maybe I do."

Shouldn't be possible, but I go even harder. My dick strains against my jeans, but I stay still. I'm never going to be the asshole who forces himself on a woman—let alone the asshole who forces himself on an employee. If she wants me, she's going to have to say it.

And without me uttering a word, the realization dawns in her eyes. She licks her lips again.

"So kiss me," she says, and my mouth goes dry. "Because I'm wondering if it's worth it."

A challenge. Christ, I love that. I love how she gives as good as she gets—and she's about to get everything from me. I bend to her, hands taking her face, fingertips brushing her hairline. For a heartbeat, I hold my lips millimeters from hers, and then I fit myself to her. She feels just as good as I imagined she would. Parker's all heat, all softness, and it nearly takes me to my knees.

I tease her—hell, tease both of us—by keeping the kiss deliberately light. I want her to want this as much as I do, and she's almost there. Her hands are all over my chest—exploring me, *learning* me—and I hiss against the corner her mouth. She doesn't feel as good as I imagined. She feels *better*.

And just as she's about to melt into me, I pull back an inch, feel her ragged breathing. "Worth it?"

"Maybe."

I laugh, wrapping my hand into her hair and tugging her head back for a harder kiss. She gives into me so sweetly, but it makes me want more. I deepen our kiss, my tongue sweeping her mouth and setting our rhythm. It makes her sag into me, turns her softness even softer and her heat even hotter. She enjoys me taking the lead.

Which is exactly how I like it. The realization jerks me out of the kiss. I pull away, grabbing the hem of her T-shirt.

"This doesn't count," she pants, helping me yank it over her head.

Doesn't count? Briefly, I'm confused, and then I realize she's talking about last month's decision to keep our hands off each other. That was some ridiculous bullshite on our parts. That was back when I thought I could keep my hands off her, back when I thought this was just attraction.

Back when I thought I could keep my feelings in check.

I lift her, wrapping her legs around my waist. "Doesn't count."

"Means it won't happen again."

Even through her jeans, I can feel the heat of her pressing into my dick, and my head spins. I tighten my grip. "Then I better do everything I've been wanting to."

And I grind once against her, watching her expression as I slide over that sensitive place between her legs. It makes her gasp. I rub her again, and she moans.

"I like that," I tell her, unable to stop my grin. I've wanted that moan for weeks. I've *dreamed* of that moan. "Do it again."

But I don't give her the choice to deny me. I thrust once more, and her head falls back, breasts lifting up and begging for attention. I lick my lips. I'm ready.

I put her down, and she staggers, eyes fluttering open in confusion. "What's"—she swallows—"Is something wrong?"

"God, no. I'm just trying to decide where to start." I run my fingers along the band of her sports bra. "Take it off."

Shyness creeps into her expression. She reaches for me, but I step back. "Ah ah. Take it off."

Color flares in her cheeks. Parks *is* shy. She had an asshole husband who did a number on her self-esteem, but I've seen moments of the real Parker—the woman who's confident and self-assured. The woman who can put me on my knees with a look. She has no idea what she does to me, and I want to show her.

Still blushing, Parker pulls the sports bra over her head, revealing small, but perfect breasts. The nipples are already hardened, and it makes my mouth water.

All the things I'm going to do to you, I think, taking her in both of my hands and rolling the tightened peaks between my fingers. Squeezing. Pinching. Torturing both of us until—

9

"Please," she whispers, and I'm undone.

I flip her around, pressing her ass into my shaft as my hands go to her jeans' button. I tug it loose, and shove everything—panties, jeans—past her knees. She gasps.

And I bend her over the kitchen table.

I slide my hand down her bare spine and over her bare ass, finding that tender spot where cheek meets thigh. I stroke her for a moment, watching goosebumps climb up her arms. "I've been thinking about this for ages," I say, squeezing her with both hands, spreading her until she's pinned.

She whimpers, making my dick throb. Hard. "Thinking about what?" she whispers.

I laugh. God I love how she plays. "I think you know," I say, fanning my thumbs across her ass. I can't decide if I want to kiss her or spank her. "I think you just want me to tell you."

And saying it out loud makes me realize how much it's true—and how much I want it. I *want* her to talk to me. I *want* her to tell me all the dirty things she needs from me.

So I can give them to her.

I wrap my hands around the backs of her thighs and listen to her hiss. "Tell me," I say lightly.

"Tell you what?"

There's a teasing lilt to the question and it makes me laugh again. I can't help it. Forget the kissing, I give her an open-handed slap across her ass and she jerks, struggling against the table's edge. No good though. She's pinned and I can do what I want—and when I push her forward another inch, she goes still like she's suddenly realized that.

Is that going to be okay? I wonder and lean over her, pressing my chest into her back. "Is this what you want? Because I can stop—"

10

"Don't you dare."

And just when I think my raging hard-on can't get any worse. Three little words and she's nearly bent me in half. I shift my weight, enjoying her heat as my dick brushes against her. She's slick already, and it takes every ounce of self-control I have to keep from thrusting into her.

"Tell me," I whisper, and feel her shiver underneath me. "Tell me you want to hear how I've been fantasizing about you."

Her breath catches. "Have you?"

"Every damn day."

"Fantasizing about what?"

"You're   soon   to   see."

CHAPTER 2 | Aiden

I pull back, running my hands down her shoulders and across her arms. I flatten her to the table, and then curl her fingers around the edge, squeezing them for a heartbeat so she understands she's to stay put.

I've wanted her like this for ages, and I want to enjoy every damn minute of it. I straighten and pull off my clothes. Parker fidgets, and I know I should say something, but the sight of her—bare for me, on her tip-toes, bent over, *pinned*—has left me damn near speechless. I have fantasized about her for months now. I have imagined her in every way possible, and she still leaves me in awe.

She trembles and lifts her head, starting to look around for me.

"Ah, ah," I say, hearing how my Irish accent has grown thicker, harder. It always does for her. "This is for me."

I drag my fingers through her wet folds, and my eyes nearly roll back into my head. She feels fucking fantastic. "I could look at you like this all damn day, do you know that?"

She inhales like she wants to answer and I caress her again, rendering whatever response she had into mindless whimpering. I grin. I like that. I'm going to have to do it again.

"Waiting on me with your perfect ass in the air," I continue, sliding my fingers back and forth, "getting wetter and wetter as I play with you."

And she is. Dirty talk turns Parker even wetter. She's getting frantic against my hand, needing more pressure, but it feels like I've waited forever for this and I want it to last.

"Please?" she manages. She tries to push back and slips. *Beauty of this position*, I think, not stopping. She can't get purchase—she's up on her toes, and her arms are too far ahead. All she can do is enjoy, and I want to give it *all* to her.

Up and down. Up and down. I find her clit with one knuckle and rub her over and over until she's moaning.

"I love how you melt for me," I whisper, backing off before she can come. I slide my knuckle to her entrance and begin to play again. It makes my brain scramble. "You give so sweetly," I manage.

She growls. "I'm not going to be sweet if you keep playing with me like this."

"Aren't you?" I push in one finger, and she gasps. I push in another, and she squirms, making small noises of delight. I stroke her, setting a rhythm that I know will madden her. It already makes my eyes want to roll back in my head. "Because I think this is exactly what you need."

"I *need* an orgasm," she mutters, sounding irritated—or rather trying to sound irritated. She's melting for me again, relaxing into me and letting me take the lead. *Damn*, I love that.

"Oh, you'll be getting your orgasm." I scoop my fingers, and she cries out, growing wetter in a rush. She enjoys our games, and knowing she enjoys them nearly makes me come on the spot. "But right now, you need this."

"I don't—"

I stroke her again, reminding her who's in charge and she gives to me. She sinks into the table, letting me have her until she's close. Too close. I want to take my time with this. I want to enjoy every *second*.

I nudge her legs farther apart, and she lets me take them wide. "Christ, yes," I whisper, pulling out my fingers and replacing them with my thumb. I find her clit with my fingertips and she arches hard against me, giving me the perfect opportunity to slide my free hand under her.

I cup one breast and then the other, playing her nipples like I did before: twisting them, pulling them. I play until she cries out, going wet and hot against my hand. She's desperate for this.

13

We both are.

Doesn't take away from this being wrong—we both know it—but I'll deal with that later. Working for me might have been what brought us together, but the attraction between us is bigger and *better* than anything I've experienced. Up until now, we've denied ourselves. I want to show Parks why that's such a bad idea. I want to prove to her this could be more than just complicated.

"I love how sensitive you are," I tell her, still playing with her breasts. I run my thumb over and over the hardened peak, enjoying how she squirms helplessly under me. "Would you like my mouth on them?"

She whimpers, and I smile.

"Good," I say. "Because I want my mouth on them too. I'll be enjoying that later as well."

"Enjoy it now," she moans.

"No. I'm enjoying this."

"Aiden?" Lust and worry snake underneath my name. I go still as she peeks over her shoulder, eyes wide. "Why are you doing this?"

The question could mean so much—*why do I want her, why am I taking her*—but somehow, I know it's *why am I teasing her?*

I grin. I can't help it. "Because it's the only time I ever see you soft, and I know it's *because* of me. It's *only* for me."

And then I slide my fingers to her clit, and pinch.

Her mouth falls open in shock and pleasure. She screams, arching her back. Her eyes are wide and pinned to me. Now *she* can't look away, and I have to will myself not to spill all over her.

"Again," I whisper, and my fingers stroke her twice as my thumb slides forward, tapping that hidden place inside her that I know will shatter her and it does. She falls forward, bucking against my hand as her orgasm takes her in wave after wave.

"Mmmm," I breathe, pulling her off the kitchen table. She fits beautifully against my chest as I settle both of us in the closest chair: her back to my chest, her legs draped on either side of mine. It's another position I've fantasized about, and now I get to have her.

I run both hands down Parker's sides and tug her knees wider apart. She shivers. My dick has pushed up between us, and I can feel her scalding heat. It makes my breath catch.

"Christ, I don't think I've ever been this hard," I mutter, keeping one hand on her hip while I pull on a condom with the other. "Are you ready?"

She goes still, and I can't tell what she's thinking. I don't like that. At all.

"Parks?" I whisper, lifting my hips so my dick skims across her clit. "Are you okay?"

"Don't you *dare* stop."

It's even more frantic than before, and I catch myself grinning against the back of her neck. *Hells yes*, I think, and lift her, the head of my dick prodding her slick entrance. "Yes, what?" I ask.

"Yes, *please*."

And I pull her down, feeling her gasp as she stretches around me. I pump her once and hold her tight, a stream of curses escaping me. "You are fucking *perfect*."

She is too. Hot, wet, and sweet as hell. Parker stays tight against me, but her shoulders have gone rigid. I get it. To be open and exposed like this for me, it has to be intense for her. It's what makes it so good for me.

But more than anything it has to be good for *her*.

I give her a gentle pump, and find her breasts, teasing her nipples and kissing her neck. "Stay with me."

A tiny moan escapes her, and my hands tighten. I spread my knees wider, taking her legs even farther apart. Her skin goes hot, but I can tell her brain is working overtime. "Stay with me," I add, "or I'll bend you over the table again."

She gasps, eyes flying open to meet mine. I don't look away. I hold her gaze until her focus narrows just to me. Only to me.

"Stay with me," I whisper, "and I'll do this for you."

And I pump her once, feel her pussy clench around me. Pleasure makes her whole body slacken, relax. It feels so good, I nearly come. I *knew* she'd be like this. I *knew* it would be this good. Her head falls back, dark hair tangling around me. This is what she needed.

What we've both needed.

"That's right," I tell her. "Just enjoy." I lift her and then slide her down my cock, lift and slide. She feels fucking amazing. She's perfect like this. I could take her all night.

"More," she moans, and my fingers clench around her hips. I should make her wait. I should make her *beg*. But I'm already lifting her, already increasing our pace because she needs it and I can't help but obey.

I bounce her harder, and she gasps, going softer and softer in my arms. "Yesyesyes, like that," she whispers, head whipping back and forth as I drive her toward another release.

"Again." I grip her ass, pumping her up and down as I slide my other hand around, finding her clit. She jerks against me.

Sensitive, I realize. *So sensitive she probably doesn't think she can come again.*

I'll need to show her otherwise.

"Come for me, Parks."

She squirms, shaking her head as tension begins to climb her spine. *Losing her*, I think and grab a handful of that dark hair, pulling her backward until she's arched over me, impaled and trembling and *needing* because by my taking control like this, she's gone even hotter. She's burning alive for me.

And I'm burning for her.

I thumb her clit once, twice. "Come for me, Parker. Come for me *now*."

She does. She comes hard, seizing my forearm and biting down until it smothers scream after scream. It works. She *is* quieter, but I can still hear my name on her lips. It rolls through me like honey and lights me up like gasoline.

CHAPTER 3 | Parker

He barely lets me catch my breath before he pushing me for another release, another wave of pleasure. I knew Aiden would be demanding, and I knew I'd enjoy it. I just didn't realize how much. My body responds to him like it was made for him.

Like he owns it.

The realization spikes pleasure through me again, and Aiden tightens his grip. I'm pinned to him, but I feel like I'm flying. Soaring. The chair squeaks under our combined weight and he pumps me hard.

It drives a gasp from me. I love it. Love. It. All that teasing, all that soft *soft* play, and it's only made him as wild as it made me. My pussy clenches around his hard length, and now *he* gasps. His breath coasts along the back of my neck, the skin of my spine. I feel him everywhere and it makes me moan.

"Never going to get tired of hearing that," he mutters, fingers flexing against my hips. "Never."

And I love hearing him say that. It turns me frantic, hungry. I ride his shaft, letting it satisfy me in a way that his fingers and thumb never will. I thrust my hips back and he hisses. I grind down...

And he comes.

He swears under his breath. The words are quiet, but I still catch a few—things like *you're perfect* and *beautiful, so beautiful*—and it makes me feel triumphant. I don't remember the last time I felt perfect, let alone beautiful, but right now Aiden makes me feel that way.

He also makes me feel incredibly sexy. Which is kind of hilarious since we're still in his kitchen and I'm still straddling his lap, legs apart and back arched. Before, my head kept wanting me to think about how exposed this position left me—every dip and curve on me was on display—but now, I love it. I'm spent, relaxed. We might be in his apartment, but I feel a thousand miles away.

Aiden is a mini-vacation, I think, and nearly giggle.

He shifts underneath me, and carefully, withdraws. I start to sit up, expecting him to put me away, but he pulls me back, keeping me tight against his chest. It makes our breathing match. In and out, in and out, and ever so slowly I come back to myself.

Reality leaks in: the refrigerator's hum, the moonlight stretching across the floor. Somewhere outside, a horse neighs and I can hear the faint pounding of hoofbeats as they play in the night. It all comes back—and then I feel Aiden. He's *trembling*.

I did that to him, I think. It would make me smile, but suddenly I realize I'm shaky too. Our chemistry is like nothing I've ever experienced. The power nearly knocks me breathless.

"Are you okay?" I whisper.

He rubs his warm hands up my arms. "I'm fucking fantastic."

The force behind the words startles me. It's so raw, so...honest. I glance over my shoulder, taking in Aiden again. The shadowy kitchen light throws his usually blue eyes into darkness, but his blond hair looks almost white. After two months of taking care of the twins, I'm used to beautiful Aiden, smiling Aiden, the man who pretty much looks like sunlight incarnate.

But the Aiden I'm looking at now is nothing like those Aidens. He's straight out of every indecent fantasy I've ever had. The shadows turn his already sharp cheekbones sharper and throw his already hard jawline into something razor-edged. He looks like something I could cut myself on, and then he smiles and his whole expression turns relaxed. He's almost boyish looking as he studies me, smiling at me like everything is perfect.

Gotta admit it certainly feels pretty perfect. I've never come like that before.

"Parks?" He palms my hips, and in spite of the fact that we've used him hard, I can feel his shaft stir. "You okay?"

He's grinning at me like he can't stop, and that makes *me* grin. How did we go from something so intense to something so...light-hearted? I laugh because the whole thing feels ridiculous, but the laugh comes out all shaky. "Yeah, it was fun."

"Only fun? Is that a challenge?"

Heat swirls through me, and I go still. He's teasing, but my body responds like it's been beckoned.

The power he has over you, I think, searching for any pang of nervousness or unease at this realization and...not finding any. That's kinda crazy.

Or maybe it isn't.

When I divorced my ex, it broke me. I'd been so in love with him. I'd followed him clear across the country, leaving my family and friends behind. And he'd taken advantage of that. I'm not the same person anymore. Maybe enjoying Aiden like this is something the New Parker does.

In fact, I want it to be.

I give him a slow smile, feeling how his body instantly tightens against me. *You can have this*, I remind myself. *You can have him.*

Then I say, "Definitely a challenge. Try again."

***

An hour later, I'm coming down again. This time, we're in Aiden's bed and it's probably the softest, best thing I've ever felt. I know that's the sex talking, but I'm struggling to keep my eyes open. Aiden's hard and warm next to me and I can practically feel the smug radiating off him. He's really pleased with himself. With other guys, it would be annoying, but this makes me smile. He loved satisfying me, focusing on me.

And you loved it too, I think, smiling wider. Maybe I should get back to our original argument, the one where he got jealous of Brandon talking to me, but I want to enjoy my bliss right now.

Might as well. After all, I just slept with my boss. There *are* consequences to this.

And just like that, *there's* my twinge of discomfort. I watch the shadows seep up the bare, white walls and tuck my pillow closer to me. We both know my job as nanny to his sister's kids isn't going to be forever. The twins have been living with Aiden ever since he moved to the States, and while they're amazing, they're also holy terrors who were recently thrown out of school for inciting a small riot during class.

That's where I came in. They needed stability. I needed a job. And Aiden? Aiden needed—and still needs—wins at international competitions, not a girlfriend. I frown. Wait. Strike that. I am not his girlfriend. I'm...whatever this is. I'm not sure.

And for a second—okay way more than a second—my body remembers his and it's entirely okay with 'whatever this is.' In fact, it would put up with a lot to have him again.

I shake myself. Get a grip. Aiden's in the U.S. for work, not for play. He rides jumpers for Caleb Reese, owner of Jacks or Better stables. They travel to all the major East Coast competitions, and even though he's only been here maybe six months, people are already whispering about how he's sure to take gold at the next Olympics.

He's getting his life on track, which I totally understand. I'm getting my own life back on track after marrying my boyfriend straight out of high school, moving across the country to help him with his business, and making him my world.

This is dangerous enough with normal people, but my ex was—*is*—a narcissist and I walked away with nothing just to get away from him.

And now you're sleeping with your boss, I think, listening as a horse neighs again in the distance. *Typical of you to make such bad decisions.*

Which unfortunately is the biggest truth about me: I made a terrible decision to marry Matthew, and now I don't trust myself not to make the same mistake again.

I've had these sorts of feelings before—well, almost. Sex with Matthew was never this good, but those butterfly stomach twirls I get when Aiden looks my way? How my heart double-thumps when Aiden gets closer? I know now those are warning signs. I like him too much. I let my feelings override everything.

Like when you rode him on the kitchen table, and then he took you *against the wall, and*—I mentally slap myself. The sex isn't the point. The point is I can't trust my feelings.

The idea makes me sigh, and suddenly Aiden's curving me closer to him. My back fits his chest, and for a moment, all I can think about is how perfect he feels against my shoulder blades. He holds me like he's trying to soothe me, and it threatens to lull me straight to sleep. I shouldn't. I should get up. I should go. But it feels so right to *stay*.

This is more than just lust and crazy attraction. Lying in his arms, I feel safe—and that's really saying something for someone like me. I feel like I've been walking on eggshells most of my adult life, but Aiden and I always talk freely. It's one of my favorite things about us.

There is *no us*, I remind myself, and as I drift off I promise myself there never will be. To protect myself, I need to keep him at arm's length, keep my heart firmly out of reach.

Even if I know I won't be able to resist having him again.

CHAPTER 4 | Parker

Two months ago...

"WHAT DO YOU KNOW?"

I've been studying the job-search question headline for the better part of twenty minutes, mentally scrolling through all my options. According to the online job search site I've been reading, I should have dozens and dozens of answers.

And I don't.

I pull my gaze away from my phone's screen and study my surroundings for inspiration. Yeah, nothing there either. It's standard issue elementary school office—beige carpet, beige walls, beige plastic chairs—populated with one pot-bellied dad in khakis and a receptionist who keeps giving us the stink eye. I gotta say, of all the places I thought I would end up this morning, I never considered this, but such is life when Ellie Lenox is your best friend.

"Only a few more minutes," Ellie says, dropping into the plastic seat next to me. She's wearing barn clothes—black riding breeches and a black Twelve Oaks Stables polo shirt—and when she crosses one lean leg over the other, her tall, black boots gleam under the overhead lights.

To me, she looks like Ellie, Olympic Hopeful. To the dad and receptionist, I'm sure she looks like Helga, the Dominatrix.

I nudge Ellie with my knee, and whisper, "You sure you want to keep Caleb? Because buddy over there looks like he'd love to spend some quality time with you."

Ellie turns in the dad's direction and he gives her a creepy eyebrow wiggle. "I have whips," she tells him, "and I know how to use them."

He pales and scoots a little further away, pretending to suddenly be *very* interested in a *Southern Living* magazine. The school receptionist *tsk*s and I grin.

"Tactful," I murmur. "You know how that sounds to people who don't own horses, right?"

A wry smile. "Of course, I do." Ellie lifts one shoulder in dismissive shrug. "Can't help it though. Something about being back in school brings out the surly side of me."

I get that. Even after *years* of being out of grade school, sitting in the principal's office makes me feel guilty. I have the urge to chew my gum too hard and twist the ends of my hair around my finger.

I crane my head, trying to see through the glass windows and down the school's main hallway. It's trophy cases and posters about doing your best as far as the eye can see. Definitely no sign of the twins Ellie's here to pick up. I twist back around, wondering for the billionth time what they did.

When the school receptionist called, she didn't give her much information other than it wasn't a medical emergency, but it *was* serious and Ellie would have to meet with the principal.

"Can you believe this?" Ellie had asked me when, in true Ellie form, she'd called me as soon as she'd hung up with the receptionist. "Caleb so owes me."

"I don't get how this is your problem." At the time, I'd been sitting at Starbucks and applying online for jobs. "Wait." I'd sat back in my chair, trying to make sense of her predicament. "Are these *Caleb's* kids?"

"Lord, no." Her snort of laughter had barreled down the phone line. "They're Aiden's, Jacks or Better's rider—the new guy, the one from Ireland—and they're not really *his* kids, they're his sister's, but he's their guardian and I don't know. Aiden asked Caleb to ask me to stand in as an emergency contact while they traveled down to Wellington."

In any other world, this would sound super strange, but among the horsey set it makes perfect sense. Caleb Reese, Ellie's boyfriend and heir to Jacks or Better Stables, has been in Florida for the past week, taking advantage of the winter show season to look at sale horses. Caleb's been in the horse industry his whole life, but he doesn't ride professionally, and always brings one of his top-notch staff riders with him.

Okay, it probably *still* sounds super strange. Bottom line, the twins' real guardian was out of town and Ellie had agreed to step in. She's lovely like that.

"Want to come?" she'd asked me. I could hear her slamming her truck's door as she spoke. "Are you busy?"

I'd looked from the newspaper want ads spread across the tiny table to my laptop opened to another job hunting site. I'd just applied to my twentieth retail position and odds were decent I wasn't going to get it. "Not busy at all."

"Thank God. I'll pick you up," she'd said and disconnected.

Thirty minutes later, we were at Chattahoochee Hills Elementary School, sitting in the waiting room and getting eyeballed by the receptionist.

Still better than another Banana Republic application, I think, going back to the job search article. *What do you know?*

Honestly? I have no idea. I don't trust my judgment. Not anymore.

The waiting room's glass doors open and Ellie and I both turn, expecting to the see the twins. No such luck. A brown-haired kid with missing front teeth runs up to the dad and as they turn to leave, the kid notices Ellie.

"Why are you dressed like a lion tamer?" he asks her.

"Ssssh!" the dad hisses, whisking him away.

The doors swing shut and Ellie admires her boots. "I do sort of look like a lion tamer," she says before twisting toward me. "What are you doing?"

"Reading up on career advice." I pass her my phone so she can read the job search article too. "I'm supposed to think about all the things I know and then extrapolate possible jobs from there."

"Any luck?"

"Not yet."

"Have you considered a job where people use 'extrapolate' in a sentence?"

I grin. Okay, I *do* know one thing without a shadow of a doubt: I have the world's greatest friends. My shattered marriage took a lot from me: my finances, my house, and pretty much all my confidence. Matthew and I had been together since high school and he'd seemed so perfect...and then he wasn't. I made a huge mistake marrying him. The biggest decision of my life? I blew it on a guy who cheated on me and then said it was my fault.

The worst part is I think I believe him.

"I don't know *what* I know anymore," I say at last, taking back my phone and exiting the article. Ellie gives me a look halfway between pity and confusion, but before she can say anything, the receptionist looks up from her computer.

"Principal Rooney will be here any minute now."

"Great!" Ellie gushes.

The receptionist glares at us like this is the farthest thing from great, but my best friend keeps her smile plastered on.

"I don't think you're supposed to sound happy," I whisper.

"How should I know?" Ellie whispers back. "I don't have kids."

I pocket my phone. "I'm suspicious of how you got roped into this. It's almost like Caleb knew something was going to happen."

"No kidding." Ellie and I both slouch lower in our seats. She's been with Caleb for a while now, and he makes her crazy happy—although I might say right now, he's just making her crazy. Ellie's twitching like some sort of prairie dog as she waits for the twins.

"How old are they anyway?" I ask.

"Five or six, I think."

Oh, wow. That's young to have a guardian who works as much as theirs must. The horse industry is demanding. "Who stays with them at night? They have a nanny or babysitter or something, right?"

Ellie frowns. "They do, but she isn't taking my calls."

"That's not good."

"Nope, I don't—there they are!" She bounces to her feet, grinning like this is some sort of happy occasion and not, well, whatever *this* is.

Please don't let them be expelled, I pray. Caleb's out of town for another week. If Ellie gets stuck supervising children during school hours, she'll probably put them to work mucking stalls.

I pause, thinking this over. Actually, it might be a great deterrent. Nothing like heavy-duty, manual labor to make you decide playing nice at your elementary school is a better idea.

The glass doors swing open again, and a tall, redheaded man guides a blond set of twins into the waiting room. Between their enormous blue eyes and equally enormous sweatshirts, they look bedraggled and adorable.

How could someone so cute be in trouble? I wonder.

"You can come through with us," the man says to Ellie and me, hands resting lightly on the children's shoulders. "We can discuss the matter in my office."

There's something about the guy I instantly dislike. Maybe it's the pompous tone. Maybe it's the way he looks down his nose at us.

Maybe it's because he's male, I remind myself, following everyone into the principal's office. This is a fair assessment, and I like to think it's perfectly understandable. After all, I've only been divorced for a month and a half.

"Principal Rooney," he says, sticking out his hand first for Ellie to shake and then for me. His palm is warm and damp and I have to resist the urge to wipe my hand on my jeans. "Please sit down."

The twins slouch into a set of chairs along the wall and Ellie and I take the squishy armchairs in front of desk. The office is small, beige as the waiting room, and smells a little like window cleaner.

"I must say, Miss Lenox," Principal Rooney begins, "this is rather unusual." He glances down at the papers on top of his desk. "I see here that you're the emergency contact, not the caregiver."

"Their father is out of town," Ellie explains. "We wanted to be prepared in case anything happened, and I guess it did, huh?" Her laugh is forced. "So, uh, what did they do?"

Principal Rooney's whole body quivers. He leans forward, hands flat on his desk. "They incited a riot, Miss Lennox. They conspired with the other students to act out against the teacher."

My skin goes cold. That sounds serious. I glance at Ellie and her eyes are deer-in-headlights-wide. She swallows once and asks, "What kind of riot?"

"Every time Mr. Shepherd turned around, Mr. and Miss Macken had the class *hum*."

There's a moment of silence while everyone takes this in. I look at Ellie. Ellie looks at me. We both look at the twins.

Good Lord, they're cute, like blond cherubs come to life. The boy gives us a smile that belongs to toothpaste commercials and the girl raises one brow like she's daring us to say something.

"You got the whole class to play along with you?" I ask Bridget. She nods like this is no big deal, like maybe next she'll teach her classmates to jump through flaming hoops.

28

Good for you, I want to say. Unlike me, you're not going to fall for anyone's bullshit. This is the first time we've met, but I'm already beginning to like her. I wonder what that says about me? Probably nothing good if I'm siding with the riot inciter.

"That's not exactly a riot," Ellie says carefully. "It's getting a bunch of kids to hum. Maybe it shows leadership skills?"

Principal Rooney runs one hand over his slicked down hair, and I suddenly realize why I disliked him on sight: he looks like a bulldog with a comb over. Matthew loved bulldogs. "This is not a laughing matter, Miss Lenox," he says.

"I didn't say it was—"

"There will be consequences. I can't have insubordination in my school."

"Of course you can't," Ellie says in the same soothing tone she reserves for obnoxious horses and clients who are freaking out. Unfortunately, Principal Rooney doesn't seem to respond. Even his nose hairs twitch with indignation.

"How do you even know they were behind it?" I ask.

"Good point," Ellie says, nodding vigorously.

Rooney's expression flattens. "They admitted it."

"It's true," Bridget says, still looking a bit bored. "I did it."

"And I *helped!*" Her brother points his finger at us like a politician running for office and I have to squash the urge to giggle. I really am a terrible person.

"It's important to take credit for the things you do," Bridget adds.

I consider this. "I don't think that's quite the sentiment you're going for here," I tell her, and she narrows her eyes. I narrow mine right back.

"Regardless," Principal Rooney interrupts, leaning back in his chair until it creaks. He steeples his fingers like a Bond villain. "The infraction has earned them a week of expulsion, *and* I expect a formal letter of apology from both of them."

"Sure thing," Ellie manages. She sounds breezy, but I know inwardly she's freaking out. Ellie doesn't have a week to babysit two tiny terrors. She has horses in training, a barn to run, and clients to take care of. This isn't going to work.

"Good," Principal Rooney says, leaning forward. "Now get out."

CHAPTER 5 | Parker

Outside the elementary school, it's another gorgeous winter day—robin's egg blue skies, sunshine, and a faint nip to the air. As a southern girl, this is how I prefer my cold: faint. One could even say barely noticeable. Even so, I zip my jacket a little higher.

Ellie stands next to the doors and thumbs through her cell's contacts. "I tried calling your nanny earlier," she says to the twins, "but she isn't picking up. Did she have an appointment or something?"

She glances up, just in time to see the kids exchange another tiny glance. Her eyes narrow to slits. Something's going on and she knows it. "What happened?" she demands.

"She quit," Brody says flatly. "Had herself a right shite fit too."

"Don't say 'shit,'" Ellie hisses. "When did this happen?"

"This morning."

"And she didn't *tell anyone?*"

They shrug.

"Who dropped you at school?" I ask.

"We take the bus," Bridget says, inspecting her fingernails and looking closer to twenty-five than five. "We're not babies."

"You're something, alright," I tell them, and turn to Ellie. Her eyes are still bugged out of her head. A freak out is fast approaching. "We can't stay here," I tell her. "Let's take them home. We can figure something out."

"Like *what?*"

"You know...something."

Ellie makes a tiny huffing noise and spins around. She stomps toward her work truck, a shiny Ford emblazed with the Twelve Oaks Stables logo on the sides, and we follow. As the twins climb into the backseat, she tells them, "You know you're cleaning stalls for the next week, right?"

"Fine by me," Bridget says, buckling her seat belt. "I like cleaning stalls."

"I hate horses," Brody announces.

"No, you don't," his sister says.

"Yes, I do!"

"No, you don't!"

Ellie slams the door and we both watch as the twins begin to fight each other, muffled cries of anger leaking out. "This must be why someone animals eat their young," Ellie says, watching the truck begin to rock. "I cannot handle this right now. I cannot."

I smack my palm against the truck window. "Knock it off," I tell them. To the twins' credit, they do. Bridget hurls herself to one end of the truck's bench seat while Brody takes the other.

Ellie looks at me. "I'm going to need combat pay if I have to take care of them until Caleb gets home. I have clients coming in tonight and tomorrow. I have horses shipping out. I need to *work*. What are we going to do?"

Now, this is the part where normal people would ask 'What do you mean, 'we?'' but I'm probably the farthest thing from normal *plus* I adore Ellie. I wouldn't ditch her to deal with this alone.

There's also the not so tiny fact that I live with her and Caleb at the moment too so if she's taking care of the little monsters, I'll need to help. When I divorced Matthew, I took the fastest way out I could: I gave him everything. Well, everything except my dog, Wookie, my clothes, and my laptop. At the time, I'd just wanted my freedom and I was willing to pay for it at any cost.

Which I did.

I'm pretty much broke. I'm still glad I did it though. If I'd asked for my half, Matthew would've dragged the proceedings on for as long as he could, trying to squeeze anything and everything from me. It would have been awful, and I knew I wasn't up for it. I wanted to start over.

"I wish Holly were here," Ellie said, passing one hand over her dark hair. "She's really good at this stuff."

"Wrangling children?"

"Making people behave."

I grin. It's true. Even when we were teenagers, Holly always had a knack for handling our meanest teachers. It prepared her well for the New York fashion scene when she went to work for Scott Ricio, a style darling and all-around ass. And that probably prepared her for coming home and working as Beau Kent's personal assistant. His antics are legendary, or rather they *were* legendary. As far as I can tell, now all he does is grin adoringly at Holly. I only saw them together a few times before she went back to New York for work, but they were gaggingly sweet.

"What do we *do?*" Ellie asks.

"I don't know yet," I tell her, tugging at my jacket again as a chill breeze swirls around us. "But we'll figure it out. I promise."

She nods and we climb into the truck. The cab is blissfully warm from sitting in the sun and I melt into the seat, barely budging as Ellie cranks the engine and pops the truck in reverse. She guns it out of the parking lot with a bit more enthusiasm than necessary, but I get it. She's stressed.

"Is this the part where I'm supposed to say something?" Ellie whispers to me as we merge onto the highway.

I stare at her. "What?"

"Is this the part where I'm supposed to impart wisdom about not turning to a life of crime?"

"Oh, totally time for the wisdom." The truck's heaters kick on full force, blasting me with skin-peeling levels of heat. "Bring it," I say, adjusting the vents so the air blows right on me. "I want to hear this."

"Me, too," Bridget announces from the back.

Ellie shoots both of us a filthy look. "They started a riot, Parks. Pretty sure this is how soap opera villains get their start."

"Well, I mean, it was a *small* riot."

"It was Bridget's fault," Brody adds.

"Wasn't!"

"Was!"

"Wasn't!"

I twist around in my seat and lean toward them, dropping my voice to barely above a hiss, "Knock. It. Off."

It's the low, menacing voice I used to use on naughty ponies, and again, to my utter shock, it works. The twins actually *do* knock it off. Bridget huffs and crosses her arms, Brody mutters something I'm pretty sure sounds like 'shite' under his breath, and silence resumes.

Ellie eyes me, hands flexing on the steering wheel. "You're good at this."

I shrug, turning back toward my window and watching the south Atlanta suburbs surge past us. Gorgeous, old, tumbledown homes share fence lines with swanky, new developments. It's pretty much a builder's dream around here. Matthew would've loved it.

I bite my lower lip until my eyes sting with tears, and in the silence, my career homework comes rushing back to me: *What do you know?*

For a miserable second, my chest wrings tight and my brain fizzles. I don't know anything, not any more—wait, no. I do know one thing: I want to kick something. Hard.

I let out a long breath instead, concentrating on a new neighborhood going up on our turn off, and then suddenly it comes to me: what do I know?

I know I have the greatest friends in the world.

I know I had a terrible marriage.

I know I'm swearing off relationships.

I know I need a job.

"Ell," I say, turning the idea around and around in my head. It's not half bad. "What if *I* took the job as their nanny?"

CHAPTER 6 | Aiden

Of all the things you want to hear *just* as you settle into the saddle of a seven-figure, Grand Prix showjumper, 'Your kids' school is calling' is undoubtedly the last.

"Can you get that?" I ask my boss, tightening my saddle's girth. Normally, I'd have my mobile on me and I would answer it myself—this is the *twins* we're talking about here—but taking calls on eleven-hundred pounds of flight animal is beyond stupid, and 'you break it, you buy it' is pretty chilling when the asking price is a cool two point five million so Caleb always holds my shite while I'm riding.

"Is everything alright?" the horse's owner asks, eyeing Caleb and then me. She's done business with our farm, Jacks or Better, before, but she always acts like she's doing my boss a favor. Thankfully, he rolls with it way better than I would.

"It's fine," Caleb tells her, answering my mobile in one smooth movement. He listens for a moment, and then says, "We'll get back to you," before hanging up.

"The hell was that?" I ask, tightening my girth as the young mare dances around under me. I can't wait to try her over the outside course. She already feels amazing, and judging by the breathless expressions on the spectators' face as they crowd the arena fence, everyone agrees she *looks* amazing too.

Caleb clears his throat. "Seems the twins had...a moment at school. Everything's fine, but they've been sent home for the week."

The mare jigs to the right, and for a second, my whole world swings around. She's powerful and impatient. We need to get going, but my stomach's down around my feet. "What did they do?" I ask Caleb.

"Something about 'insubordination?'"

I scowl. No surprise there. "What kind of—"

A murmur ripples through the crowd and I glance toward them, spotting a short older man in a tweed cap weaving between the spectators. Murdock Kelly. He's the current coach for the Irish Showjumping Team and has been watching me on the sly ever since I arrived in Wellington last week. It's not a big deal—he might just be interested in the horses we've been trying—but my heart swings into my throat anyway. I've dreamed my whole life of riding for my country and now, thanks to Caleb, I'm one step closer to everything I want.

The mare dances sideways, and I turn my attention back to her. Caleb's cell rings, and he checks the screen. "One second," he says to me, lifting the mobile to his ear. "Hey, babe, did the school call you?"

I know without even having to ask that Ellie, his girlfriend, is on the other end. She's standing in as my emergency contact and is no doubt knee deep in the twins' bullshite. My niece and nephew are bright, hilarious, and utter monsters when they put their minds to it.

Which is pretty much all the time these days.

"What's going on?" I ask Caleb as the mare bounces in place.

He glances up at me, still mid-conversation with Ellie. "It's handled," he tells me, putting one hand over the receiver. "Promise. I'll explain later. Go enjoy your ride."

For a moment, I don't know what to do. My family's in turmoil, but my boss has basically told me to get back to work. I like Caleb. I'd even say we're friends. But neither of us is going to be cool with the twins deciding to, well, be the twins when we're weeks away from one of our biggest competitions of the year, and in the middle of our biggest buying trip of the year.

Gritting my teeth, I nod and turn the mare toward the middle of the arena, weaving her around brightly painted practice jumps, soothing her until her nervous, bouncy walk turns long-strided and panther-like.

Slowly, I pick up my reins, feeling my way around her as we trot and canter through various warm-up exercises. Ring attendants adjust the fences to my specifications, but it still doesn't feel right. The mare's tense. I'm distant.

No, correct that. I'm distracted as hell, and after about thirty minutes, I call it quits and ride back toward Caleb and the owner. Worrying about the twins screwed the trial ride, and we all know it. I snatch a glance at the crowd, and I'm not sure whether to be relieved or disappointed that Kelly's nowhere to be seen now.

Caleb watches us approach, expression unreadable. "She's quite lovely," he tells the owner at last. The woman rolls her eyes as if this is the most obvious thing she's ever heard and snaps her fingers at the waiting groom. The guy leaps forward to take the mare's reins from me as I dismount.

"And?" she asks Caleb.

"And I'll be in touch." He gives her a thousand-watt grin and she practically melts for him. "But right now, we have some farm business to handle." He looks at me. "You ready?"

I nod and follow him toward the barns, pulling off my helmet and running my fingers through my sweaty hair. Even in winter, Wellington temps can top the mid-eighties and I'm feeling every bit of it—not that I'm complaining. The heat feels amazing. It's hard to believe that in two days, I'll be back to wool jumpers and heavy coats. Georgia is a long way from Ireland's chill and damp, but it still gets cold.

"Sorry about that," I say as Caleb passes me my mobile. We dodge a groom coming through with four polo ponies and turn for the parking lots. "I told them how important this trip is. I don't know what gets into them."

"Don't sweat it. It's handled."

"What?"

Palm trees stud the walkway, and Caleb stops under a wedge of shadows. He shows me his phone's screen. There's a text from Ellie saying she has everything worked out.

I glance up at him. "Already? How?"

An uneasy shrug. He thumbs his keychain fob and our rental SUV unlocks. "Ellie works in mysterious ways."

"Should I be worried?"

"You aren't already?"

Honestly? Yeah. I worry all the time—and not just about the twins getting thrown out of school. I worry about them growing up, and I worry about making a living, and I worry about getting seen by Murdock Kelly.

I worry *a lot* about what to tell the twins when they ask me again where their mother is and when she's coming back.

"Let's get out of here," I say. I grit my teeth, getting ready for what's coming, and we leave the horse park—and everything I want—together.

***

To Caleb's eternal credit, he chartered us a private flight home that night. I felt like shite about it. We were supposed to stay another week—there were some other sales horses I was supposed to try and I'd wanted to follow up with another client who was in Wellington for the show season—but Caleb wouldn't hear of it.

"Don't sweat it, man," he'd told me as we drove to the airport. "Family's important. Believe me, I get it. The Reeses have their own issues."

Doubt it, I thought, watching the highway whip past us. My family's issues start with 'not enough money' take a hard left into 'egomaniac father' and finish up with my sister.

Who ran off with a guy and ditched her kids with our parents.

Who then sent them to me.

Not that I intend to tell Caleb about any of it. I'm sure he's guessed enough. When we started working together in Ireland, I was childfree and single. When he offered me a job, I suddenly had two six-year-olds.

"Well," I manage at last. "I appreciate the ride home. It's more than I can ever repay."

And isn't that the damn truth of it? Caleb comes from millions. I...do not—and if I can't get the twins to behave and get my career on track, it's never going to get any better.

"Don't sweat it," he repeats. "Seriously."

I hate taking the favor, but I bite my tongue and let it go. Honestly, flying home might not be entirely for my benefit. His lovely girl, Ellie, has been watching the twins since lunchtime. Considering I've seen Ellie handle Caleb, obnoxious horses, and even more obnoxious clients with tact and style, I'm not too worried.

Then again, I've also seen Brody make a grown man day drink.

The grown man was me, by the way. In my defense though he poured an entire bottle of dish detergent down the back of our toilet and then flushed until the foam was countertop high. It took *days* to clean everything up. I smelled like Dawn for a month.

"You, uh, need anything?" Caleb asks, glancing at me as, hours later, we coast up the Jacks or Better driveway. In the winter dark, he looks even more tired than he usually does. I'm sure I look just as bad. We've been burning the candle at both ends for weeks now. "Like any...help?"

"Absolutely. Come on up and babysit for me. It'll be grand."

Caleb wheels us into a parking spot and stomps on the brake. He's gone completely white. I grin. "I'm joking, man. It's fine." I open the SUV's door and slide out. "I'm sure the whole thing is one big misunderstanding."

Caleb nods. "Totally."

Because it's entirely possible to misunderstand when the principal says your kids started a classroom riot, I think, grimacing. I shut the SUV's door and wave as he drives off then shoulder my bag and head inside the barn.

This time of the evening, it's blissfully quiet. All the grooms are gone for the day and the horses are munching hay in their stalls. If I didn't need to go upstairs and figure this out, I'd linger.

What the hell am I going to do? I wonder. Yeah, I'm the twins' guardian, but fuck if I know what to do with them. After Anna took off with some bloke who wore boat shoes (but didn't own a boat), our mam packed the kids off to me.

"They need a father figure," she'd told me—over the phone, mind you, because she'd already dropped them off at my apartment while I was at work. "I can't give that to them, poor, wee mites."

Poor, wee mites, my arse. The twins are holy terrors and will probably be running the country before they're ten. God knows, they're already running me. We've all been living together for just over a year now, and we've been in the States for almost six months. Which, I'll grant you, is a lot of change. I was hoping things would settle once we arrived at Jacks or Better, but so far I'm on my third nanny and the last of the Irish whisky I brought from home.

I walk up the darkened stable aisle, heading for the tack room and the staircase to my place. We live on the stable's second floor in a small, but comfortable apartment that overlooks the courtyard and pastures. I reach for the tack room's doorknob and hear someone screech from the floor above me.

"You're a dead man, Brody!" Bridget screams. She's muffled, but not by much. Her brother must've really gotten to her.

"God give me patience," I mutter, letting myself inside and weaving past the rows of saddles. I take the spiral staircase up and kick off my boots on the landing. The door wrenches open and Ellie grins at me.

41

"Well, hello there," she says, an unholy glint in her eyes.

I swallow. "Having fun?"

"You could say that." She grabs my arm and drags me into the kitchen, both of us stepping over moving boxes. I really need to get around to unpacking.

Somewhere on the other side of the apartment, either a herd of elephants has decided to race around or Bridget is chasing Brody with intent for bodily harm. "You know, Aiden, when you asked me to be your emergency contact, I thought you were just being a good uncle, but now I'm pretty sure you *knew* something would happen."

Not half wrong, I think, dropping my overnight bag by the table. "I'm really sorry, Ellie."

"Oh, no you're not. Not yet." That grin widens and it sluices ice through my veins. I know that look. It's Ellie's 'You are on my shite list' grin. It's usually something she saves for Caleb.

"Ellie—"

"Aiden!" Brody screams, hurling himself across the kitchen. He hits me square in the stomach and all the air whooshes out of me. "So glad you're here! It's been utter shite since you left."

My left eye twitches. Shite and asshat are Brody's favorite words these days. I've given up telling him to knock it off. I figure he'll get tired of them as soon as he learns others.

"Hi there, little man," I say, hugging him. "I heard you got up to some trouble at school."

Brody frowns like he's just now remembering this and is trying to decide what he's going to use as a defense. It makes him look so much like Anna I feel like I've been hit in the stomach all over again.

I ruffle his blond hair. "We'll talk about it tomorrow. It's late. You should be in bed."

"I'm not tired. I'm hungry."

No surprise there. I sigh, suddenly feeling about a million years old. Brody's always hungry. He's like a bottomless pit.

"You *just* ate," Ellie says, wide-eyed.

"I'm growing," he tells her. "I can feel it. Do you want me to be stunted?"

She arches one brow like she's deciding what she *does* want, and odds are good, none of it will be good for Brody.

"I'll get you something, mate," I assure him, looking around the kitchen. My stomach sinks through my feet. Place looks like a bomb went off. It isn't just the moving boxes. There are dirty dishes overflowing the sink, something green on the counters, and I'm pretty positive dried Play-Doh caked to the cabinets. "Just give me a minute or...ten."

"Or a miracle," Ellie mutters. She nudges me with her elbow. "Hey. I want you to meet someone."

"What?" I turn, spotting a slight, dark-haired woman walking into the kitchen with my niece at her side. Bridget runs to me, plowing into my stomach with the same enthusiasm as Brody and I barely feel her.

"Aiden," Ellie says. "This is Parker."

At the sound of my name, Parker's eyes meet mine. She smiles and something inside me pitches over.

And cracks.

The hell? I feel unsteady, like someone's sucked all the air from my lungs. Parker's a bit taller than Ellie and a good bit thinner—too thin, honestly. She looks as if she's been sick. Even so there's something fluid about the way she moves, something gut-tightening about the way those brown eyes look me up and down.

She's lovely, I think, and suddenly realize I'm staring at her like a creep.

"Nice to meet you," I say, offering her my hand. "Aiden Macken."

"Parker Waye." Her hand slides into mine, and lightning forks across my skin. My palm tingles and my breath leaves me all over again. Damn. Just holy damn.

"Parker's going to be your new nanny," Ellie announces, hands on hips. "She's going to need a raise too."

I blink. "I'm sorry...what?"

"She's going to be your new nanny."

"I *have* a nanny."

"Not anymore," Bridget mutters.

I give her a sharp look and she pretends to be suddenly *very* interested in the hem of her sleeve. "What did you do?"

"The woman quit," Ellie says, sliding in between Bridget and me. "I called her a bunch of times, but she won't call me back. Maybe you'll have better luck reaching her."

Doubtful, I think. *Bridget and Brody strike again.* For a moment, I'm so tired I want to collapse. This is the fucking limit. I'm exhausted, I'm overwhelmed, I have jam-packed schedule for the next month, and now I have to get a new nanny up to speed?

I take a deep breath, praying for patience. It doesn't come so I take another deep breath. Still nothing. Jesus. I want to go to bed and not get up—not an option when you have two little ones.

Especially two little ones like Brody and Bridget.

I rub one hand over my eyes and look at Parker. "How long have you been nannying?"

"Oh." Her cheeks pinken beautifully and I shouldn't notice, but I can't seem to *stop* noticing. "Um...this will be my first time actually."

Alarm bolts through me, but Ellie speaks up before I can utter a word: "She's really good with them, Aiden. *She's* the reason the barn is still standing. They've been out of school since before lunch. I would've been lost without her. She's a natural."

For a few seconds, all I can do is stare at Ellie. I was wrong. *This* is the fucking limit. Exhausted, overwhelmed, jam-packed schedule, and now I have a new, *inexperienced* nanny to get up to speed.

One who's still blushing.

Not that I'm noticing. I clear my throat. "Yeah, okay. Fine. Seven forty-five work for you?" I ask Parker.

She nods, eyes briefly dropping to my mouth. "Perfect."

"Great!" Ellie hooks her arm through Parker's and eyes me like I'm an employee she might have to fire. "Okay, well, we'll leave you to it. She'll see you in the morning, right?"

I hesitate. "Right."

Parker gives me the tiniest smile. "Looking forward to working with you, Aiden," she says—and is that the tiniest bit of anticipation under her tone?

Christ, I can't tell.

I hope there is. I *really* hope there is.

"'Night," Ellie adds, dragging Parker toward the door. She closes it behind them, and I can't stop staring. What is going *on* with me? Is it exhaustion?

It's something else, I think, touching my fingertips to my palm. I can still feel her warmth. It heats the rest of me.

CHAPTER 7 | Parker

Right. So. First day as a nanny. This is going to be good—no, great. It's going to be great. I lean closer to the mirror as I swipe on my mascara. The girl who looks back still kind of surprises me. I'm thinner than I used to be, the dark circles under my eyes won't go away, and I need a haircut.

Actually, I've needed a haircut for almost a year, but I never bothered getting around to it. Technically, that's a bit of a lie. I never *thought* about it. I was so consumed with Matthew and his cheating and our divorce, it was the last thing on my mind.

Until last night, when I met Aiden Macken and suddenly I could feel every, single, tiny thing that was wrong with me. Shaggy hair? Check. Frumpiest clothes I own? Double check. But the way he looked me over? The way his hand felt when we touched? I nearly fell over. My long-absent libido reemerged with a vengeance and it took everything I had not to stammer.

Over on my bed, Wookie whines. He's ready to go out and I'm taking too long. "One second, buddy," I tell him, stuffing my feet into socks and then into boots.

Wookie hurls himself off the bed, hitting the floor with a gigantic *whomp*, and trots to the bedroom door. His whole butt wags as he waits for me. We're up early, but it's still not early enough to catch Ellie. By the time Wookie and I pad down the hallway, heading for the stairs, she's long gone, probably already saddling her first horse of the day. Caleb's out too. Like Twelve Oaks, Jacks or Better Stables begins their day well before seven and those two like to be in the thick of it.

Matthew was the same way. In the last couple years of our marriage, he was gone all the time. He'd assured me it was because of work, but odds are good it was because of her.

Accomplished, confident, blond, and beautiful, Lell Winters is everything I'm not. I'd tried so hard to be the wife Matthew wanted, and in the end, he went with someone entirely different. Now, I don't know who I am or who I want to be.

But I'm going to figure it out.

Downstairs, the house is quiet as Wookie and I make our way to the kitchen. Mary, the housekeeper, is busy at the stove. When I moved in with Ellie and Caleb, I had a bit of a hard time getting used to someone taking care of me—actually, that's not true, I had a *really* hard time. I've never lived with this kind of wealth, but Mary can make anyone feel comfortable and now it's like coming downstairs to another friend.

She looks up when we come in and smiles. "Well, good morning!"

I grin. "Good morning to you too."

I open the back door and Wookie surges outside, making a beeline for the patch of lawn reserved for him. Gotta give the dog some credit. He doesn't sit, stay, or stop barking unless he feels like it, but he is extremely good about keeping his business contained. I lean against the doorframe, watching him through the window and waiting for him to circle back to us.

"Come eat," Mary says, sliding a plate of pancakes onto the marble-topped breakfast bar. "That dog isn't going anywhere when there's food to be had."

She has a point. Wookie is a walking appetite. I sit down on one of the stools and pull the pancakes closer, taking a deep breath of vanilla and maple syrup.

"Now where are you off to today?" Mary asks, pouring herself a cup of coffee and then one for me.

"My new job," I say around a big bite of pancake. "I'm a nanny now."

"Oh, that's lovely, dear." Her stirring begins to slow. Stops. "Wait. Who are you nannying for exactly?"

47

"Aiden Macken." Just saying his name makes my cheeks pinken. "Well, technically, for his niece and nephew."

Mary pales. "Dear, do you have experience being a nanny?"

I nearly laugh. She asked me in the same tone one might say, 'Dear, do you have any experience with rabid monkeys?' It's funny, but it's not. I know this isn't going to be easy.

"No, no experience." There's a bark at the door, and I get up to let Wookie in. He bounds across the kitchen and scarfs up the bowl of dog food we keep by the fridge for him. "I was studying for my real estate license before I left Seattle, but I rode horses for years. I can't imagine it's that different."

Mary's mouth forms a perfect O. "Well, for starters, you can't lock children in a stall when they're being naughty."

I grin. "I'm sure I'll think of something else."

Mary arches one brow like 'You'll need to.' "You wanted to do real estate?" she asks.

"Not really, but it was useful to my ex-husband's business. Nannying will be a nice change of pace while I figure out what I *do* want."

"Oh, definitely." She's nodding like this all makes perfect sense, but there's terror in her eyes. I guess Brody and Bridget have made themselves known around the farm.

Still not scared, I tell myself.

"Thank you for breakfast," I say, taking my last sip of coffee as I grab my coat from the countertop. Wookie clumps along next to me, ears pricked even if his eyes are pretty much buried in brown fur. "I really appreciate it."

"You don't always have to thank me," Mary says. "It's my pleasure—besides, you're the only one who appreciates my cooking. Ellie's always running off and Caleb's always running after her. They're utterly useless, those two." She's smiling though and I can tell she's happy he's found someone. "Besides," she adds, "you could use some feeding up, and I could use the challenge."

At the rate I went through Mary's pancakes, I doubt there will be much challenge to it. I wave goodbye and walk Wookie out to my car—well, technically, it's Holly's car, a bright, orange, mid-seventies Bronco. Holls is in New York at the moment so she told me to use it whenever I needed something—which is pretty much all the time now, because my car was in Matthew's company's name and I had to leave it behind.

"I still don't understand why you gave it to him," Holly had said when I told her. "You were married. You were entitled to half. You helped build his company."

I'd nodded, shame and regret tangling up in me. I've known Holly my whole life. She wasn't criticizing. She was genuinely confused. Honestly, it *is* confusing to anyone who hasn't lived with a narcissist. Why would I leave like that? Why would I screw myself over?

Because I didn't want to fight Matthew on every dime. Because I wanted him out of my life. Freedom was more important than my bank account. Of course, now I'm dealing with the fallout.

"Not bad fallout though, right, Wooks? We're making it." Wookie cocks his head and wags his tail and I decide he's definitely agreeing with me. "Alright, let's go." I open the driver door and he heaves himself inside, hopping clumsily into the passenger seat. I follow. Getting behind the huge, leather-covered steering wheel gives me flashbacks to high school. The Bronco was Holly's first vehicle, and we all learned to drive stick on it.

I crank the engine, catching a glimpse of myself in the rear-view mirror. I still look perky—remarkably perky considering this may have been a very bad decision. The girl in the mirror presses her mouth into a thin line.

You're not losing to a pair of six-year-olds, I tell myself. *You need this job. You can make it work.*

49

CHAPTER 8 | Aiden

The stove clock has just clicked over to 7:40 A.M. when I hear Parker pull into the stable yard. That orange monstrosity of hers backfires, startling me and momentarily distracting the twins from trying to kill each other. They run to the wide windows that overlook the yard and peer out.

"She came back," Brody says, sounding surprised.

I take another sip of my coffee and wish it were something harder. "Brody, swear to Christ, if you run this one off, I will ground you until you're thirty—until you're dead, understand?"

Neither of them turns around. If anything, they press their noses closer to the glass, leaving smears and watching Parker with interest. "Thirty's already dead," Brody says at last.

My left eye starts to twitch again and I press my thumb to it, going back to making the twins breakfast. I flip some scrambled eggs onto a plate and will my nerves to stand down. They don't.

You should ship the twins back to Mam, I think, digging another plate out of a moving box. *There's no way this is going to work.*

I mean, it can't, right? Bridget and Brody need someone experienced caring for them, someone like a teacher...or drill sergeant. I wait for the sense of relief that should accompany the idea of sending them home and it never comes. I don't want to give them up. They make me crazy and I love them and I don't want to send them away.

I can't decide if that makes me selfish or suicidal.

My second round of scrambled eggs begins to burn and I yank the frying pan off the burner. *Yeah, because it's the twins you're really worried about*, I tell myself, dumping what's still edible onto another plate. *What a load of bollocks.*

It's true too. Last night, I couldn't stop thinking about Parker and that alone should've made me pick up my mobile and ring Ellie. I should've told her it wasn't going to work.

But of course, then I wouldn't see Parker again and I wanted to.

Want to.

I shove the thought away and go back to concentrating on breakfast. No one's done dishes since before I left so I have to search for forks. Not that box. Not that box either.

Ah. Here we go. I grab a handful of silverware, toss two forks on the kitchen table, and hurl the rest into the closest drawer. There. That much closer to being moved in and settled.

"Breakfast," I yell to the twins. "Get in here!"

Couple minutes later, they drag themselves in and climb into their chairs. Silence descends. Probably the only silence I'm going to get all day so I'll take it. I pour myself another cup of coffee and down half, feeling a little better as the caffeine begins to hit my system. Those...feelings I had last night? They had to be the effects of exhaustion and stress. Yes, I need a nanny, and yes, this one is wildly unqualified and probably going to get eaten alive by my niece and nephew. But she's all we have.

Exactly, I tell myself, taking another gulp of coffee and watching as Bridget holds up a forkful of egg. There's a worrying glint in her eyes as she examines it closely. "Bridge," I warn.

Too late.

She bends back her fork and catapults the egg into Brody's face.

"Bridget!" I set down my coffee mug, ready to make her apologize, but Brody holds up one small hand.

"It's fine, Uncle Aiden. I can handle this." He wipes a bit of yellow from his cheek and looks at his sister. "Now you're never getting it back."

"What?" I demand, but neither of them answers. Bridget hurls herself at Brody, Brody flings himself backward and runs for it, and Parker...well, Parker walks right into the middle of it and my throat funnels shut. I can't take my eyes from her.

And all those feelings? They come rushing right back.

Looking at her is like being punched in the chest. Parker's eyes are saucer-wide as she takes in the chaos, and for a moment, all I can think about is how those eyes studied my mouth last night.

You're in trouble, Macken, I realize. The right thing to do is to call it off. Right here. Right now. Tell her something came up. *Anything* came up. I can find another nanny. I can figure this out. It's the smart decision. The responsible decision.

Or you could stop acting like a hormonal teenager and keep your distance, I think. The idea makes me pause. That could work.

And you need *it to work*, I remind myself. It's not like nannies are easy to come by—especially ones that have met Bridget and Brody and have agreed to come back.

Only as soon as Parker takes another step into the kitchen I know I'm kidding myself. I'll make this work because I have to—Bridget and Brody need this—but just looking at her? It licks something inside   me.

CHAPTER 9 | Parker

You've got this, I tell myself. But I'm not really sure I do because I can hear screaming as I climb the spiral staircase to the Macken apartment, and I'm barely into the kitchen before the twins run past.

"How dare you!" Bridget bellows, her feet pounding as hard as a pony's against the floor. It makes the apartment floor sound like it's about to cave in, and I stop dead, feeling my eyes bug out of my head. Brody feints right, left, and then streaks down the hallway, Bridget hot on his heels.

"Give it back!" she screams.

Give what back? I wonder, and then realize I'm going to have to find out. Lucky me.

"Morning."

An electric charge rides up my spine, scattering my thoughts. Oh God. Aiden. In the light of the morning, I'd hoped my body would find him less attractive, but clearly not. I catch my eyes wanting to linger on the breadth of his shoulders and the hard cut of his jaw and...well, the rest of him. He's almost pretty. I know guys aren't supposed to be pretty, but he *is* and—

Get. It. Together, I tell myself and lift my chin. "Morning," I manage.

He quirks one brow, and heat climbs my cheeks. So much for getting it together.

And when his eyes drop to my mouth it only gets worse. My face...body...*all of me* goes hot.

Aiden clears his throat. "Coffee?" he asks, turning away.

"I'm good. Thanks." I follow him deeper into the cluttered kitchen. There's half-eaten breakfast on the table, moving boxes on the floor, and most of the cabinet doors are wide open. That level of chaos alone is bad enough, but the twins sound like they're trying to kill each other (again) and Aiden doesn't seem to notice (again).

"Yeah," Ellie had said last night when I mentioned how Aiden seemed oblivious to their behavior. "I think he might've given up his will to live. I would too if I were in his shoes."

Honestly, at the time I thought she'd been joking, but as the children run past, screeching, Aiden takes his cell and some paperwork from the countertop like this is *normal.*

"Glad you're here," he says, pocketing the phone. "We didn't get much time to talk last night so I thought we could get on the same page."

"Sounds great," I say, and *ohmygod* does it *ever* because his accent is toe-curlingly delicious. I never knew I had a thing for Irish accents until now.

If he dirty-talked to you in that voice, you would explode, I realize and then mentally slap myself because inappropriate much, Parker? Ugh.

I nod encouragingly, like my mind is on work and not on him. "What do you have in mind?"

I take a step forward, and he takes a quick step back, eyes on his paperwork like it's suddenly fascinating. He takes a pen from one of the drawers and scribbles some note to himself.

"So the twins are off this week, yeah?" he asks.

"Yes."

"What do you have in mind for them?"

"Apology letters for starters. Principal Rooney is requiring them."

Crash! Something's pitched over in the living room, but Aiden doesn't look up from his note-writing.

"Good luck with that," he says. "Right. So. You'll have to be here until late. I have four horses to ride this morning, and some potential buyers flying in later. I doubt I'll be done before eight tonight."

The twins streak through the kitchen again, shrieking at full volume. Bridget looks like she's going to murder Brody if she gets her hands on him, and judging by how fast Brody's moving, he thinks so too. Aiden steps to one side as they fly past him.

"Staying late is fine. I can make arrangements," I say, thinking of how I'll coordinate taking care of Wookie and cancelling dinner with Ellie. She'd wanted to go out tonight, but I know she'll understand. "It's not a problem."

"Are you sure?" For the first time, Aiden looks at me—really looks at me—and I can't help but think there was the tiniest bit of hopefulness to his question.

I don't understand. Does he not want me here? Does he think I'm not up to the job? Probably. He did ask if I had any experience and I did tell him the truth so...I pull my chin up and give him my best 'I got this' look. "It's no problem."

He takes a deep breath. "Okay then. I pull long hours. You'll be responsible for meals, bedtime, driving to and from school—assuming, of course, that they don't get expelled again." His face pales as he contemplates the very real possibility of this happening.

Basically, I'm responsible for everything, I realize. Surprise settles over me, quickly followed by relief. Judging from the indulgent way he looks at the twins, I'd assumed he would be more involved, and while I wish for Bridget and Brody's sakes he were, I know for my sake it's best that he's not. We're at least four feet apart, but my skin prickles with goosebumps like he's right next to me.

Like last night, Aiden's wearing riding clothes again—a thin, wool V-neck sweater pulled over a T-shirt, carelessly half-tucked into fawn-colored breeches—and he's owning the hell out of them. The breeches hang loose on his hips and somehow still highlight the hardness and length of his thighs. They make my mouth go dry.

"It's allowance time too," Aiden adds, taking his wallet from his back pocket. He pulls out two fives and puts them on the counter, sliding them toward me. It's nothing. It *is*...and yet I feel like he's keeping distance between us.

That's because he is *keeping distance between you*, I realize, and now I'm embarrassed all over again although I'm not entirely sure why this is happening. Can he tell I'm attracted to him?

My stomach knots. *Oh, God, I really hope not.* Then again, I can't be the first woman who's looked at Aiden and lost her breath. He must get this all the time. Surely, he doesn't think I'm going to jump him. I mean, I have *some* restraint.

Although when he's around, I keep wondering where it's gone.

Still, I *am* an adult, and if he can do this so can I.

"Anything else I should know?" I ask him, smoothing the five-dollar bills and pocketing them.

"Uh, don't take them to the library. It never ends well—and don't let Brody touch the dish soap." Aiden's starting to look a bit overwhelmed and wild-eyed. "Oh, and there are fire extinguishers under the kitchen sink, in the bathrooms, and in their bedrooms."

I blink. Okay, forget the 'bit.' He's definitely overwhelmed. What have I gotten myself into? "Um, emergency numbers?"

"On the fridge." Aiden still doesn't move, but he does look at me again and the intensity of it sends heat spiraling through my stomach.

And lower.

I walk over to the refrigerator, pulling off the contact sheet and fastening on a smile like everything's fine—because it *is*, right? I'm fine. He's fine. No one's ever going to know I have a thing for him. Only, when I glance up from the emergency contact papers, I catch Aiden staring at me.

His eyes have dropped to my mouth again, but before I can decide what that means, he spins on his heel and walks out.

CHAPTER 10 | Parker

It shouldn't be possible, but as soon as Aiden closes the door, the twins get *louder*. They skid into the kitchen, and Bridget chases Brody around a table still crowded with breakfast dishes.

"You'll never catch me, asshat," Brody sing-songs and takes off, his sister in hot pursuit.

I snatch her up as she passes me, pinning her under my arm. Talk about a distraction from Aiden. My libido takes a nose-dive as she kicks madly against my side. "Enough," I tell her.

So she screams again. It's loud enough to make my eye twitch and my ear drums ache.

"Hey!" I swing her up and around so we're eye to eye. "Enough. What's the deal? Why are you acting like this?"

She blinks. "Because."

"Because *why?*"

Another blink. "Because he hid my dog from me."

Dog? I wonder. I didn't think they had a dog.

"Not a real dog," she tells me, catching up on my confusion. Her mouth twists exactly like her uncle's. "My stuffed dog."

"Oh." I pause. "Why don't we find it together?"

"Why don't I make him tell me?" She squirms to get down, and I have no doubt in my mind how she plans to 'make him.'

"No way," I say, setting her down, but keeping a firm hand on her shoulder. "It wasn't right that he took your dog, but it wasn't right that you tried to pummel him either."

"I hit him with eggs. I did not pummel him...yet."

"Still not right."

More blinking. I'm not sure which part Bridget's confused about, but I have her attention so I'm going to rack it up as a win. "Brody?" I call.

No answer.

"Brody!"

After a moment, the boy drags himself out of his bedroom and peers down the hallway at us. "What?"

"Bridget shouldn't have hit you with eggs, but you have to give back her dog or give up something of yours."

Both the twins startle. They spend a moment studying me, no doubt trying to figure out if I'm being serious. "I'm not kidding," I tell him.

Brody sucks his teeth for a beat, looking for all the world like a little old man, and disappears into his bedroom. He comes back out with a battered stuffed dog. He passes it to Bridget by holding it with two fingers, like it's infected with disease. She snatches it back.

"Say you're sorry," I tell Brody.

More teeth sucking.

"Brody!"

"Sorry."

It's almost inaudible, but it's there and I'll take it. I nudge Bridget. "Say you're sorry."

"Why?"

"Because you were trying to beat him to a pulp. C'mon guys, I know your uncle doesn't let you do this to each other."

Their blue eyes lift to me, holding my gaze until I realize he probably *does* let them. Something tells me Aiden's not really in control much around here. *Okay then*, I think. *Going to have to work on that.*

"We're not moving until you apologize," I tell Bridget. "I can stand here all day; do you want to do that?" They stare me down, but I hold fast. Honestly, I would hate to stand here all day, but I'll do it to prove a point. I can't back down. If I do, it's all over.

"Sorry," she finally spits out.

I blow out a breath, and all of us take a second to size each other up. I see a pair of twins who are adorable even when they're furious, and they see...I have no idea. In fact, I'm quite sure I don't want to know.

This is going to be way harder than I'd thought, and I *already* thought it was going to be hard. Still, I've learned one thing: they're not used to being heard. Not really surprising considering Aiden is so busy. Maybe listening to them will help—it seemed to a few minutes ago.

I suck in another breath. I'm all knotted up and anxious already, and if listening to them doesn't help, I might have to use something stronger, like Valium.

For *me*.

"Okay," I say, looking around the kitchen. Moving boxes are crammed here, there, and everywhere, and that's not going to work for me. If I'm going to handle 'everything' for these kids, I better start by figuring out where the pots and pans are. "So here's the deal: we're starting fresh. I'm new to you, and you're new to me, but we're going to be spending a *lot* of time together so let's make it work." I cast another glance around the small kitchen. "I'm guessing most of your moving boxes are still waiting to be unpacked, right?"

An unwilling nod from both of them.

"If you help me organize the kitchen," I continue, "I'll help you unpack your rooms. You're living here now. Let's make it feel like a home."

I have no idea if that means anything to them. Maybe it does because they settle in to help me. I let Bridget pick where the silverware should go, and Brody collects all the pots and shoves them into a lower cabinet.

"That's great," I tell him. "You'll be able to get them easily."

"Why would I get them?" he asks.

"Because I'm going to teach you how to cook. You're six, right? You can do plenty of stuff in the kitchen." *Including burning it down*, a little voice in my head reminds me. I brush it away, and face Brody. He's watching me with interest.

"You'd let me cook?"

"With supervision, yes."

"And me?" Bridget pipes up.

"Yes, but *with* supervision."

The twins look at each other for a beat before turning back to me. "Well, shite," Brody says, nodding with appreciation. "I like that."

"Ah ah." I shake my head. "No more swearing. New rule: every time you swear, you have to pay the Swear Jar."

"What's that?" Bridget asks, pulling the sleeves of her enormous sweatshirt over her hands.

I glance around for a suitable container, and finally, find something in a box shoved into the corner. "This," I say, holding up a plastic Tupperware jar. "Every time you swear, you have to pay twenty-five cents."

Brody plucks at his lower lip. "But I can still swear."

"Sure, if you're willing to pay the price." I pause, letting them think it over. I hadn't planned on a Swear Jar. It was a spur of the moment thing, but the more I think about it, the more I like it. Do the crime, pay the time...or pay the quarter, whatever.

"Does Uncle Aiden know about this?" Bridget asks.

"Uncle Aiden left me in charge. What I say, goes."

Brody heaves a sigh like I am the most irritating person ever. "Fine," he says.

"Fine," Bridget agrees.

I   grin.   "Fine."

CHAPTER 11 | Aiden

I finish up at the barn around six and head for the apartment. Technically, six is early for me and I feel more than a little guilty about leaving my grooms to finish up what I should be helping them with, *but* it's Parker's first day.

And the apartment is still standing, I think. Is that a surprise for other parents? Because I'm not entirely sure. Either way, I want to check in with her, make sure everything went okay.

Is that what you're calling it? an amused little voice in the back of my head asks. *Because it seems more like you can't wait to see her again.*

Or better yet, touch her.

Which pretty much makes me a first-rate asshole since the woman works for me.

"Are you okay? Caleb asks, falling into stride next to me. "You keep staring off into the distance?"

I clear my throat. "Yeah, fine. It's nothing."

We walk into the tack room together, my boss going to the desk by the window and me turning for the spiral staircase. "Just enjoying my last moments of freedom before going upstairs," I tell him.

Caleb drops some paperwork onto the desk and gives me a 'no shite' look. "Ellie said Parker's your new nanny?"

I nod and clear my throat again. It's a testament to how perverted I've become that the mention of 'nanny' and 'Parker' and 'yours' threatens to give me a hard-on. It's a job, and my dick wants to treat it like a poorly written porno. "Today was her first day. Figured I should see if there's going to be a second day."

Caleb leans his hip against the desk, thinking this over. Thanks to the winter dark, all the lights in the tack room are on, gilding the fixtures and saddles with a syrupy gold. The grooms have been cleaning again, and the smell of expensive leather and polished wood relaxes me even more than a shot of whiskey. Jacks or Better is the finest place I've ever worked. Just walking in here makes me feel like I've arrived.

I will not throw this opportunity away because I can't get my life under control, I think, but even I'm not sure if I mean Parker or the twins or me.

Caleb runs a hand over his jaw. "I gotta say, man. Those two kids are hell on wheels. I don't know how you're going to balance everything."

I pause, trying to decide if there's something veiled under the comment that I need to address. Caleb is a friend, but he's also my boss. Even more importantly, he's the reason I'm riding for Jacks or Better. His reputation is on the line too. I fuck up, the splatter will hit him as well, and distractions like Brody and Bridget *cause* fuck ups. I have to get on top of it.

"It's handled," I tell him.

"Let me know if you need any help."

"You offering to watch them?"

"God no." His shudder is almost comical. "But I know a few good boarding schools."

He would too. It's no secret Caleb and his father have never gotten along, and apparently, things got even worse after his mam died. They're trying to reconnect now, but it's a lot of history to overcome. I can't imagine being sent off to boarding school. It's not just a money thing—although we didn't have it. It's a separation thing. Yeah, true, there's no love lost between my da and me, but my mam and I have always been close, and I considered my sister, Anna, my best friend. It's part of the reason it gutted me so much when she ran off. It's also part of the reason I won't ditch the twins. They've lost everything. They won't lose me too.

But you can't explain that sort of thing to people on the outside—much less explain it to someone like Caleb who values professionalism above everything. I say good night, leaving him to his paperwork and coffee, and head upstairs. The door's unlocked and I let myself into the kitchen.

I really need to do something in here. We've been living at Jacks or Better for months now and the place still looks half-deserted. The white walls are blank. I unpacked our table, but only got around to adding two of the kitchen chairs to it. Most of our pots, pans, and dishes are still in their shipping boxes, and yeah, I'm guilty of fishing out what I need and leaving the rest. There hasn't been a lot of time.

I toss my keys and work gloves onto the countertop, and just as I'm pulling my cell from my pocket, I hear a low growl. From the corner of my eye, I spot something *huge* lumbering my direction.

"The hell?"

"Don't swear, Uncle Aiden," Bridget tells me, wandering into the kitchen. Her braids are loose and her clothes are dirty, but she's in one piece.

"What *is* that?" I ask, pointing a finger at the dog/pony/Yeti standing in my kitchen. It growls again, and Bridget pats it.

"It's a Wookie," she tells me.

"Who does it belong to? You better not say us."

"He's Parker's."

"He's bloody enormous."

"You've been warned." Bridget holds up a plastic container scribbled over with markers and crusty with glitter. "That'll be a quarter."

I blink. "What will be a quarter?"

"You swore. You have to pay the swear jar now."

"Since when do we have a swear jar?"

"Since Brody decided the s-word was his favorite," Parker says, walking into the kitchen with an armful of empty boxes. She's wearing baggy sweats and her usually tight ponytail has drooped, loosening dark wisps around her face. It makes my fingers itch to brush them back.

"You're making them use their allowance?" I ask, stepping out of her way.

"Yep, or they have to pay with chores." She stacks the empty boxes by the kitchen door and brushes off her hands while Wookie dances in delighted circles around her. "Brody ran out of allowance around lunchtime, which is why your living room is now unpacked."

She brushes past me and I catch the faintest scent of her soap. It's sweet and lemony, and when I try to take a deeper breath, the scent is already gone.

Stop it, I tell myself. *Get some distance between you.*

But even when Parker's three feet away, I feel awareness of her creeping through me. That's not good. This morning, I was confident I could keep a handle on everything. Now...not so much. Her ponytail looks silky. Her baggy sweats are perfect for getting my hands underneath. The very thought of it makes my dick stir.

Fuck's sake, Macken. I've wanted women. I've had women. I have never reacted like this. *It's love at first sight.* The voice in my head is now my mam's. She would laugh herself silly if she saw me now.

Honestly, this isn't love at first sight. It can't be. This is lust—and it's not backing down. My body remembers Parker's electricity. Another thing I've never experienced, and I want it again.

What would it feel like to touch her again? Hell, what would it feel like to kiss her? My whole body tightens at the thought, and I mentally kick myself. She's the twin's nanny. I'm her employer. Anything between us is all kinds of off-limits.

"You're home earlier than I thought you would be," she says, turning to me.

My ears go hot. There's something about her tone that makes me feel like she knows what I'm thinking. Christ, I hope she doesn't.

I clear my throat. "I thought you might need the help, but you seem to be doing all right—I mean, most people struggle and you're...not."

She gives me a small, amused smile and takes another box to the backdoor. "The morning wasn't exactly like licking a rainbow, but we're figuring each other out."

The thought of Parker licking anything almost bends me in half.

"Did you hear about the Swear Jar, Aiden?" Brody bounces into the kitchen and gives Wookie a pat. "It's the best damn thing ever."

"And now you get to wash the windows," Parker says without turning around.

Brody shrugs. He's about as bedraggled as his sister. There are dirt smudges on his face and a patch of his hair stands straight up. "Did they tell you about it? 'Cause the rules will apply to you too."

"Just heard."

"You're home early." Brody's tone wavers between accusation and curiosity. "What gives?"

"I wanted to make sure you three were settling in." Which is true and simultaneously some of the biggest shite I've ever come up with. I *was* worried about the twins—and Parker—but now everywhere I look everything's...fine. We're more moved-in. Bridget and Brody seem happy. *Parker* seems happy.

And you get to see her again, that little voice in my head is back, and it's right. Lust for Parker lives under my worry for the twins and I can't let it interfere.

She walks into the living room and I nudge Brody. "Did you have a good day?"

"Grand." His face lights up. "I like her."

Something twists behind my heart. "Really? That's...never happened with another nanny."

Brody scratches his nose. "Well, she's a bit inflexible on creative speech, but Grandma says we all have our faults."

I smother a laugh. "I'm sure she does."

"She says you do especially."

"She's not half wrong."

"What?"

"Nothing."

Parker comes back in with Bridget hot on her heels. "Parker says I can help with dinner," she tells me and my stomach drops a few inches.

"Uh, that's not a good idea. She could—"

Parker flashes me a smile and my words dry up. Christ, she's lovely.

"I promised them they could help me and I promise *you*"—if anything that smile widens—"that we will be careful." She turns for the fridge and then turns back to me. "Why don't you hang out with us? You can cut up the tomatoes. You'll actually have somewhere to sit now."

For about three seconds, I'm confused and then I realize Parker has also unpacked my other kitchen chairs. I'd only put up two—enough for Brody and Bridget—and had been eating all my meals at the counter.

"You can sit together as a family now," she adds, returning to dinner prep like this is no big thing, and it isn't. Or it shouldn't be.

But it *is* because I suddenly can't stop thinking about how the twins have lived with me for almost a year—six months of it here—and I've never shared a meal with them.

And you think this is better than shipping them off to boarding school? My stomach goes sour.

"Thanks for unpacking," I manage. "I've been meaning to get to that."

"Sure." I can hear the smile in her voice, but she doesn't turn around. I'm glad too because I'm not sure what she'd see. I watch the twins join her at the stove, noticing how they're not trying to kill each other and how Parker's hand guides Bridget's and I feel something in me relax.

Maybe for the first time since the twins arrived.

Love at first sight, my mother's voice whispers. I ignore it. This isn't love, but it is *something* and I'm going to find out.

CHAPTER 12 | Parker

Well, it's official: being around Aiden turns me painfully stupid. Pointing out the kitchen chairs like that? I don't know what I was thinking.

Wait. Actually, I do. I was trying to help him, make things more like a home and less like a place to crash, and now I'm worried I made the whole thing sound like he wasn't doing a good enough job, which was so not the case. He knows that...right?

I watch Aiden from the corner of my eye as I adjust the stove's preheat setting. He hasn't stomped off. He hasn't said anything cutting in return. He hasn't fired me.

He *is* watching me though, but when I look up, he looks away.

What's up with that? I wonder, opening the refrigerator and scanning the shelves. And, furthermore, what is up with *me?* I didn't used to overthink everything I said and now I am.

I blame Aiden's gorgeous face.

And his gorgeous shoulders.

I even blame his gorgeous abs, which I have not seen but I'm sure are absolutely perfect under those thin sweaters he wears.

Brody finishes mixing the salad I've given him and passes me the bowl. "This is boring. Can I go color?"

"Adulting is boring, isn't it? Yeah, you can color." He starts to spin away and I grab his shoulders. "Paper. You can color paper. Nothing else, okay?"

His little body sags and I know I've headed him off. "Brody?"

"Yes, only paper."

"Can I color too?" Bridget asks.

"Definitely. Same rules though."

They trot into the living room and I figure I have about twenty minutes to get dinner on before they start fighting.

So, I think, *dinner. We have a salad and...*

And nothing. I've only gotten as far as salad. There's soup simmering on the stove, but I'd rather give them that for lunch tomorrow and I need something more substantial for right now and I can't come up with an idea for substantial. My brain keeps stalling out. I can't think of a single thing.

Not entirely true, I realize. I can think *plenty* about the butterflies in my stomach, and even more about how Aiden's a bit to my right, leaning against the countertop and watching me. Everywhere he looks, my skin burns.

Which makes me linger in front of the open refrigerator a bit longer than necessary.

Maybe way longer than necessary.

"Can I get you anything?" He steps around me, heading for the sink, and his hip brushes my side. My face goes all kinds of red, and my mouth goes all kinds of hot.

"Oh, no! I'm good!" My voice is sing-song high, like Minnie Mouse on helium. *Get it together*, I tell myself, pretending to be very interested in a jar of tomato sauce. *Stop acting like you're twelve!*

"Parker?"

I whip around. Brody has padded back into the kitchen. Sleeves tugged over his hands and eyes big as saucers, he says, "I'm so hungry."

I blink. "I just fed you"—I glance at the wall clock—"an hour ago. Are you serious?"

"So hungry," he whispers.

"Okay then. Spaghetti it is," I tell him. "It's fast, but you're still going to have to give me a minute."

Brody sighs like I've asked him the impossible, and Aiden grins at him, tugging something deep inside me. It isn't the usual 'The man is gorgeous' response, it's something new, something a lot more like 'he really loves his niece and nephew, but he's totally drowning.'

It makes me like him even more.

"Great," Aiden says, turning to me. "I love Italian."

"I don't know that mine is exactly the best representation," I say, carrying dishes from sink to stove to sink again as Brody wanders behind me, opening and closing cabinet doors. "Dinner in ten, Brody, I swear."

Of course, that means I actually need a pot to go with my pasta and sauce. I duck into the pantry, surveying my options. I know I put a soup pot in here somewhere.

Brody was asking for a cracker, I think, mentally stepping myself through the earlier afternoon, *and Bridget was complaining and I had the pot in my hands and...*there *it is.* On one of the shelves above my head, I can see the edge of the soup pot poking out.

Fantastic, I think, my mind already winging away to pasta and butter and maybe some onions to go in the sauce, and will the kids actually eat sauce with onions it because I haven't asked them, and some children are funny about that, and—

I'm not paying attention. I don't notice how the pantry door has opened, and I definitely don't notice Aiden's slipped in behind me until I turn, and he's *right there*, reaching for a box of pasta just as I'm leaving with the oversized pot.

I dodge right and he dodges right and we collide. My breasts brush his chest, and even though I have my plainest, padded bra on, my nipples stand up. They tingle as if they've been rubbed with silk.

"Sorry!" I hurl myself backward, bumping into the shelves. His hand finds my elbow and he steadies me with a squeeze.

"No, I'm sorry. I didn't mean..." He swallows, staring at my mouth.

Which only makes me look down at his mouth, and now *I* can't stop staring.

I've never thought about men's lips before. They were always just sort of there, but Aiden's are different. They're fuller than most and set into a hard jaw covered in two days' worth of stubble. The way one corner tilts up in a smirk makes my knees shake and my thoughts go...somewhere—somewhere that definitely isn't here because I'm still gaping at him, and I don't have a single thing to say.

"Hi," I breathe, and it does something to his eyes. They darken as a tremor runs through him.

"Hi," he whispers, leaning ever so slightly closer.

Close enough to touch...

Or kiss.

He's in my space now, his warmth pouring over me, the hardness of his chest evident through the thinness of his polo, the skin of his throat moving as he swallows. My arms tighten around the pot, fingers splaying against the cold metal as everything in me thinks about my fingers splaying across *him*.

"Aiden?" I whisper, and that tremor rushes over him again. I'm not imagining it. It's like I have...power over him. The idea makes my breath shallow.

"Uncle Aiden?" Bridget appears behind him, pushing her way into the pantry and pushing Aiden even closer to me. Our bodies brush, and where five seconds ago, I would've combusted on the spot, now my stomach sinks.

Inappropriate much? I have *got* to get a hold of myself. He's my boss, and the kids' uncle and—

"What're you doing?" Bridget asks, peering around Aiden's hip at us.

"Getting pasta." He waves the box at her, and her little face lights up. I guess her appetite is as voracious as her brother's.

"Do you want to help me make spaghetti?" I ask, and she nods vigorously. The three of us emerge from the pantry just in time to see Brody dumping cereal into his mouth straight from the box.

Aiden scoops up both kids, one under each arm, and hauls them into the living room, leaving me with dinner. I'm so glad, so *grateful*. I need a minute to get myself together.

Maybe more than a minute.

I concentrate on filling the pot with water, but I can't shake my brain from the two new things it now knows:

Around Aiden, I feel everything.

Around   me,   I   think   he   feels   the   same.

CHAPTER 13 | Parker

After dinner, I run for it. Call me a coward. Call me an idiot. It's probably all accurate—especially the idiot part. It's not like I haven't been around good-looking guys before. Matthew was also bordering on the beautiful, and while I was pretty dumb, I didn't...react quite like this.

And thank God too, I think, boosting Wookie into the Bronco and hopping in behind him. I slam the door hard. If I had, it probably would've taken me even longer to leave him.

I reverse out of the parking space and turn onto the farm drive, taking the loop around until it veers off toward the main house. By now the winter dark is all around us, and it makes the gorgeous antebellum mansion look especially white and pristine in the moonlight.

Wookie whines in excitement as I drive around the back and leave the Bronco next to Ellie's truck. I'm kind of shocked she's home so early. When I cancelled dinner, she'd said it wasn't a big deal because she needed to stay at the farm for a bit longer anyway.

Hope everything's okay, I think, turning off the headlights and killing the engine. Wookie and I get out as the wind picks up, dragging the faint scent of the Chattahoochee River around us. I pull my jacket closer and hustle toward the house. Wookie gallops past, nearly taking me down in his haste to reach the door.

"What gives, you big—" There's a peal of laughter coming from inside and my heart leaps. *Holly*. That's Holly.

Wookie and I charge up the back-porch steps and burst through the door, surprising Ellie and Holly. They're sitting at the kitchen island, halfway through a bottle of wine, and they both shriek when they see me.

"Parks!" Holly jumps up and lunges for me, but Wookie gets to her first. They dance around, dog fur and slobber getting all over her gorgeous clothes.

"Ugh! Sorry! Wookie!" I admonish, tugging at his collar. I don't think he even feels it and Holly waves me off.

"It's fine. Don't worry so much. I'm so glad to see you!" She hugs me hard, but I hug her harder. I knew I missed my best friends while I was gone, but I didn't know how much until I came back.

"You're home early!" I say when we finally break apart.

She grins, a thick strand of blond hair falling across her eyes. "Sort of. I'm not really home. I'm visiting. Mom has Bunko this weekend, and the last time Beau took her, he nearly got jumped by a bunch of little, old ladies."

I whistle low. Even before I left, Holly's mom's Bunko Club was almost famous—or rather infamous. Once a month, one little old lady hosts the rest of the little old ladies at her house. They drink, smoke, and do not ever actually play Bunko. "Let me guess, he's never going within fifty feet of them again, huh?"

Holly laughs. "Nah, he'd do it if I asked, but I'm saving my favors for when I really need them." She hooks her arm through mine and drags me to the kitchen island. I drop onto a bar stool and Ellie passes me a glass of white wine.

"Here," she says and then pushes a platter of snacks toward me. "And eat something, or you won't be able to keep up with us."

I snort, but it's true. I barely ate anything today because I was chasing after the kids and suddenly I can feel every second of it. I swipe a couple cheese slices off the plate and chow down while Holly finishes telling Ellie some story about an intern accidentally gluing Holly's favorite boots to the floor.

"But who cares about boots?" Holly announces, swiveling toward me with wide, bright eyes. Too bright. I know what's coming, and for a second, we aren't in our twenties at all. I flashback to high

76

school sleepovers and whispering secrets and making promises. "Tell me about Aiden," she says.

Butterflies twirl through my stomach. Ugh. Even his *name* makes me silly, but I manage to keep my face blank as I say, "I don't know. He's tall?"

The girls exchange a smirk. "C'mon," Holly says.

"I'm serious," I say, praying to God I don't begin to blush. Just talking about Aiden threatens to unravel me. It's all kinds of ridiculous. "He's my boss."

"Doesn't mean you can't ogle him." Ellie takes a sip of wine as I stare at her. "What? Just because I love Caleb doesn't mean I'm blind. I can't think of any straight woman I know who wouldn't take Aiden home in a heartbeat. He's gorgeous—and *nice*. Seriously."

"Is he?" I ask.

"You haven't noticed?" She frowns, a vengeful look entering her eyes. "Wait. Has he been rude?"

"No no no," I assure her. I love Ellie, but she's totally the friend who will defend your honor by burning down someone's house. If she thinks Aiden is being rude or weird, she will fly up to the stables on her broomstick, and he hasn't been either of those things.

Well, keeping all the distance between us and not looking too closely at me *is* a little a weird.

And you should be grateful for it, I remind myself, *because if he did look straight at you, you'd probably self-combust.*

"Earth to Parker?" Holly nudges the toe of her boot into my calf. She's grinning. "Are you okay?"

"Oh, gosh. Yeah." And there it is. *Now* I can feel heat climbing my cheeks. "Fine. Sorry."

"Stop apologizing." She's still grinning, but the admonishment stings anyway. "You do that all the time these days."

"Sorr—"

"See?"

"Yeah." I concentrate on my glass, swirling the wine in faster and faster circles. It's another leftover from Matthew. I never knew what would set him off, and he was always finding fault, and I started apologizing for everything. The girls are watching me, waiting for an explanation, and I can't bring myself to do it. Not yet. "Aiden's not rude," I say at last. "He just seems really...overwhelmed."

Which is true. I can tell he loves the twins, but I can also tell he has almost no idea what to do with them.

"Not surprised." Ellie leans across the island to refill my wine glass and then hers. "And how are the terrible twosome?"

"Are they really that bad?" Holly asks. She puts some grapes and apple slices on a napkin and pushes them toward me. "I mean, they're six, right? How awful can they be?"

Ellie pretends to shudder. "Let's just say that after spending the afternoon with them, I now understand why some animals eat their young."

I laugh and nearly choke on my wine. "Okay, yeah, you have a point, but honestly they're not *that* bad. They're more...challenging."

Holly laughs. "How incredibly tactful of you."

"You like that?" I ask, forcing myself to relax a bit. The awkward earlier moment has passed, and I'm not going to hold onto it. Dwelling on Matthew will only ruin the evening for me and I'm not going to do it. I shoot her a wry smile. "Because in addition to calling them 'challenging' we could also call them 'spirited.'"

"'Strong willed,'" Ellie adds.

I point at her. "'Filled with leadership potential.'"

She cracks up and it cracks me up and now Holly is staring at both of us like we've lost our minds. "I gotta meet these kids."

78

"They would love you," I tell her.

Ellie wipes tears from her eyes and says, "I'm glad you took the job."

"Me too." And you know the surprising thing? I am. That's not being tactful or polite or putting a happy clappy spin on it. I find Brody and Bridget pretty funny. They're inquisitive and smart and, yeah, they're exhausting as hell, but then we have moments like today where I think I've found something I'm good at.

It's been so long I almost don't recognize the feeling.

I glance down at my wine again. Thanks to Ellie's prompt refills, I'm not sure if I'm on my second or third glass. My edges feel tingly and my body's hot.

Fuck it, I think. *Just tell them*. I blow out a sigh. "Okay, so I was holding back. One? Aiden is gorgeous. Like, makes me go stupid, he's so gorgeous. And two? He's weird around me."

Holly leans forward. "Weird *how?*"

"He seems nervous. I don't know, like he's always keeping space between us. I can't figure it out. Maybe I smell?" The thought hits me like a freight train, dropping my stomach around my feet. "Holls? Do I smell?"

"No," she says and lifts the wine glass from my hand. "And that's enough for you. Clearly, you need to eat more."

Ellie smirks, looking down at her own glass.

"What?" I demand. "What're you thinking?"

Now her cheeks are pink. "Uh, well, I was thinking about when I had the same problem with Caleb and Holly told me to, uh, get him out of my system."

Holy shit. I look at Holly who shrugs. "I did. It's true—but look how well it worked out." She takes a careful sip of wine, eyes flitting around the room. "Maybe you should try it, Parks."

"I've sworn off relationships." The reminder emerges so quickly it should ward off any dirty thoughts of getting Aiden out of my 'system,' but it doesn't. Images of me straddling him suddenly override my brain.

And Holly smiles like she can tell. "Yeah, you should definitely think about it."

"He's my boss," I say weakly.

Another shrug. "This isn't going to be your job forever—it isn't even going to be a move-up job. Why not enjoy yourself?"

I open my mouth, close it, and open it again. It's an absurd idea—an *inappropriate* idea—and also impossible. Just because I want Aiden doesn't mean he wants me.

And then my body remembers the way he responded in the pantry and I go wet in a rush. He's not immune to me. He's not. I try to swallow and suddenly can't. "I've sworn off relationships."

Holly laughs. "It's not a relationship. It's...friends with benefits. Or a fling. Or whatever you want to call it. You should think about it. It would be fun."

Except I don't have to think about it. I already know it would be amazing. I clear my throat and change the subject—asking Holly all about New York—but I can't get her idea out of my mind. I could have some fun.

I   could   have   Aiden.

CHAPTER 14 | Parker

And a week later, I'm *still* thinking about how amazing it would be to jump Aiden. The twins are due back in school the next day and forcing them to write their apology notes should've been enough to squash my libido for good, but the moment Aiden walks in the door, my entire body pricks to attention.

He leans one hip against the counter, watching as Brody and I argue it out (again) about whether he's going to take a bath. "Brody," I say, trying to keep my voice even and my brain on our argument and *not* on the fact that Brody's uncle is five feet away and looking like a Ralph Lauren model. "You could plant potatoes under your fingernails. They're filthy."

"I like them that way."

"But no one else does."

"You're not supposed to care what other people think of you."

I pause. Well, he's got me there. "You better care what I think of you or no allowance."

It's petty, but it's also all I've got. We stare each other down until finally Brody relents. His little body sags and he gives his uncle a scowl. "This is cruel and unusual punishment. What did we ever do to you?"

The tiniest flicker of a smile. "You dumped dish detergent down my toilet, threw lit matches into the air vents, tried to cut your sister's hair off, took—"

Brody gives him a withering look and spins on his heel, stalking down the hallway toward the bathroom he shares with his sister. He slams the door with enough force to rock the apartment and Bridget screams for him to be quiet.

I smother a giggle and snatch a glance at Aiden. He's looking at me. Our eyes meet, and this time, he doesn't look away. "You're so good with them," he says.

God, that accent makes my insides curl. I swallow. "It's like a staring contest. You can't blink."

He smiles, nearly taking all the air from my lungs. "Can I walk you out?"

"Sure," I manage. I grab my purse from the kitchen table and Aiden follows me down the spiral staircase. We walk side-by-side up the darkened barn aisle, the horses drawing closer to watch us.

Probably more like watch him.

I can't blame them. There's an easy grace to the way he moves, something I've always noticed in high performing athletes. They use their bodies differently than the rest of us.

I wonder how he'd use his body on me, I think, and it's all kinds of pathetic, but I can't seem to help it. He still keeps a careful distance between us. Not that it matters. Even two feet away, I can feel him. It's like he turns the air around me into velvet.

"Where on earth did you find that car?" he asks as we step outside into the moonlight. Holly's Bronco, usually bright orange in the daytime, looks especially dark and intimidating in the shadows.

"It's Holly's," I say. "She's our—"

"Friend. The blonde, right?" Aiden pivots to face me and it puts the moon at his back, dips in his face in dark. "We met a few times. Lovely girl."

I smile. "She is. She's in New York for another month so she lent it to me."

"Do you like it?" he asks, edging around the Bronco and peering in the darkened windows.

"How can you not? It's huge, and temperamental, and yeah, it leaks oil so you suck fumes the whole time, but it's fun to drive."

"Interesting. I would never have guessed you'd like it."

"Interesting. You think you know me."

We both pause, our breathing unsteady in the dark. I'm not exactly mad at myself that I said it. Aiden *doesn't* know me. Why would he have a clue what I'd like to drive? I'm more alarmed at the way I said it: light, teasing, *flirty*.

And Aiden heard it. He scrapes a little closer and I shiver.

"Tell me you're not cold," he says, amusement in his voice. "This is nothing."

I pull my jacket tighter around me. "Thirty degrees is not 'nothing.'"

"In Ireland, we wore shorts in this weather."

I laugh. "Well, in Georgia, we wear sweaters and gloves and long johns." *Long johns?* I think, heat suddenly surging over my face. *Did I seriously just mention the most unsexy underwear in existence to him? Ugh. This could* not *be worse.*

Even in the shadows, I can see Aiden quirk a brow. "'Long johns?'"

"Never mind."

His laugh is a short bark. "Thank you again for being willing to stay late."

"Sure. It's not like I have anything going on." Ugh, that was stupid of me. More heat climbs my cheeks, and I try to wrench the conversation around: "I mean, it's part of the job, right? I take care of them when you can't—like when you're at work or on a date or...whatever."

Nope. Now *it's worse.*

Aiden leans back against the Bronco and looks up at the stars. "I haven't actually dated anyone since I came over."

"Really?" The shock in my voice is almost as embarrassing as my earlier babbling. I am useless with this man. Useless. "That's surprising."

He grins, still studying the stars. "I can tell."

"Sorry. I'm not myself."

He drops his chin and looks at me. "I'm not either."

Three little words and yet I'm pasted to the spot. This feels like something...more.

Aiden tilts his head, considering me. "I have to be honest with you, Parker. I find you distractingly beautiful."

My breath dries up. "That's funny because I find you distractingly beautiful as well."

The silence between us stretches thin and sweet as pulled taffy. For the first time in the seven days I've known him, Aiden looks unsure of what to do, and for the first time, in the twenty-three years I've been alive, I know *exactly* what I want: "Maybe we should do something about that."

His inhale is sharp. "What do you have in mind?"

The question strokes me. *What* do *I have in mind?* For starters, I like how I'm in charge of this. I've never had that in a relationship. Matthew always called the shots, but Aiden puts the power in my hands. I grin. "I'm not sure how much I'm ready to admit, but there's a *lot* I've thought about."

It earns me another laugh, this one's half-strangled. "Me too."

The admission makes my heart double-thump. Shouldn't this be the part where he comes closer? But Aiden isn't moving, and I realize I'll have to make the first move.

I get to decide how this goes, I think, and it rolls heat down my spine. I take one step and then another. He goes still, and now we're in each other's space again. It makes my bones hum.

"I've sworn off relationships," I say.

Still no moving. Still watching me.

I lick my lips and tell myself to be brave. "This is unfortunate because just being around you makes me realize I haven't had an orgasm in...forever. I want one." I am so impressed with myself right now. I sound incredibly matter of fact and put together—especially for someone whose mouth is *this* hot because Aiden is *so* close.

He considers me, the shadows making his cheekbones sharper and turning his eyes into smudges. "Just one?"

My laugh is a sputter. It's nerves and want tangled together and it makes him smile.

"We shouldn't, Parks."

I shiver. Parks. It's what everyone calls me, but Aiden makes it sound indecent.

"I'm your boss," he adds, sounding half-pained.

It pulls me tight. "I know, but that means you can bend me over your desk."

CHAPTER 15 | Aiden

"I know, but that means you can bend me over your desk." Parker looks up at me with those huge, dark eyes, speaking in her sweet, matter-of-fact tone, and I...

I now have a raging hard-on, I realize. My mind's in overdrive, picturing *exactly* how I'd bend her over my desk and pull her panties down. I'd want to tease her until she was soaked, until she was begging for it.

"I'd love that." My voice cracks and I clear my throat, clear it again. "But we can't."

"Why not?" Her cool hand finds my cheek, and I should pull away, but she's so damn soft, I linger. "This could be fun."

"It would be better than fun," I say, and have to shift from foot to foot to accommodate my dick. *I* might have concerns about this, but he doesn't. "But it wouldn't be right."

Her thumb skims my cheek...the corner of my mouth...the seam of my lips. It feels as if she's learning me and suddenly I *have* to taste her.

I seize her wrist and suck her thumb into my mouth, swirling my tongue around it and watching her dark eyes fly wide open.

"Aiden," she whispers, swaying a little on her feet as I suck her thumb harder, showing her exactly what I'd do if I had her tits bared to me. She gasps. "Aiden!"

And steps to me—her hips pressing into my hard-on, her breasts brushing my chest. She pulls her thumb from my mouth and yanks my head down for a kiss, fitting her lips hungrily over mine. Our teeth bang together and she nips me, hot little hands all over my chest, fumbling with my belt buckle.

It's *exactly* what I've wanted. I flip us around, pinning her to the Bronco's driver's door and taking control of the kiss. My hands find her jaw and I tilt her up for me, slowing our pace even as her hands go frantic.

I pull back an inch, making sure her eyes meet mine before lifting her up and wrapping her legs around my hips. "Again," I whisper and take her mouth again, grinding my hard-on against her heat.

Her arms tighten around my shoulders, slide up to my neck. Her hands shove through my hair and grip, making me hiss. She feels amazing, like everything good in the world. She sucks my tongue into her mouth and my eyes roll back in my head. She's fucking perfect.

For everyone. The realization turns me cold. She might be perfect for me, but she's even more perfect for the twins. I can't mess that up. I *won't* mess that up. This has to stop.

I rip myself back a step, putting her down and holding her at arm's length. We're both panting.

"Aiden?" She sounds lost and I've already taken a stride toward her before I realize I've moved.

"Sorry." I sidestep and pace in a tiny circle, trying to get it together. "I shouldn't have kissed you. We can't...we can't do this."

"Why not?"

I stare at her. Honestly, at the moment, I really can't think of a reason. I just know I shouldn't.

Parker touches her fingertips to her lips like she can still feel me. "This job isn't forever."

I pause. She's right. I hadn't thought about it, but yeah, it isn't forever. She'll find another position—something more in line with what she wants—and that will be the end of it.

"That's true, and when you leave, I'll wish you well, but right now I count on you, Parks. The twins...they really like you. You're incredible with them. I can't risk it."

And I can't risk myself. It's a small, but vicious thought. Whatever this thing is between us, it undoes me.

"You think whatever happens between us I would take it out on them?"

"No! I think..." I run one hand over my mouth. It's still damp from hers and it's like a punch to the chest. "I think it's a bad idea."

No, stopping this is a bad idea. The voice in my head is speaking straight from my dick and it's right. It's *so* right.

Wait. No, it's not. I shake myself, taking a deep breath of winter air. "Look, you're the best thing that's happened to us since we got here. And the kids? They haven't had a lot of good things. My sister ditched them with our mam, Mam shipped them to me, and now I worry they're going to think everything's temporary. That *everyone* goes away."

"Everyone does go away, Aiden."

I hesitate, my chest suddenly aching for her. It's such a small statement, but it reveals way more about Parker than she probably realizes. "Yeah," I say at last, stuffing my hands in my pockets so I don't reach for her. "But I want them to be older before they have to understand that."

Her sudden smile is a stripe of white in the dark. "I do too."

I open my mouth and stop. The admission warms me with a different kind of heat. I don't quite know what to make of it. I know I want her even more.

But I also know I won't risk the twins' happiness to have her. This is for the best.

I swallow hard. "Promise to keep our hands off each other?"

There's the briefest hesitation and then, "Agreed."

CHAPTER 16 | Aiden

My cell goes off at five in the morning, waking me from an excellent dream about Parker bent over my work desk in nothing but a flimsy pair of panties. As if that isn't bad enough, I know even before opening my eyes my mam's ringing me. No matter how many times I explain the time difference, she swears she doesn't get it.

More like she doesn't care.

Actually that's not entirely true. My mam's incredible, but she also can't stand that I'm out of reach. Last farm I worked for, I was about thirty minutes away and she could show up at any time. Which she did.

She was particularly fond of rousing Sunday morning wake-up visits—even more fond of them when she'd wake me from sleeping off the night before.

I slam my hand around on the nightstand until it connects with the mobile, and then put it to my air. "Mam," I mumble, exhaustion threatening to pull me under again. "It's bloody five AM."

"Is it?" Two words and that Dublin accent brings me racing home. I roll over and stare at the ceiling. It's smooth white plaster—nothing like what I grew up sleeping under back home—but for a moment, I'm back in Ireland. "Ach. Well," she adds, "it's good that you're up then, isn't it?"

I pass one hand over my face, and grin. "You're shameless, you know that?"

"I wanted an update on the twins."

My grin slips. I groan and sit up. The bedroom is still mostly dark, the stack of moving boxes and the armchair I've been using as a dresser like black blobs. "I'm not so sure you want an update."

"What happened?"

I grunt, swinging my bare feet to the hardwood floor. The cold bites my soles, and suddenly, I'm fully awake. "More like *they* happened. Kids are bloody nightmares."

Instantly, my hand goes to my hip where my wallet would normally be. Gotta pay the Swear Jar, and then I realize what I'm doing and scowl.

She makes a *tsking* noise. "Don't swear. What did they do?"

"The short version is they started a riot and got suspended—oh, and their nanny quit. I've a new one already lined up though." Just mentioning Parker makes heat roll through me, but there's nothing like talking to your mam about your wayward niece and nephew to crush any feelings of lust. I clear my throat. "They were out of school for an entire week."

Another tsking noise. "Put them to work. That'll fix them."

"Mam, first of all? I'm fresh out of fields to make them shovel and hoe. Secondly? That was bloody awful."

Swear Jar, my brain announces and I scowl.

There's a faint rustle from her end of the line, like she's moving my da's newspapers around. "And it made an impression, didn't it? You didn't go joy-riding with your brothers again now did you?"

"Can you call it joy-riding when it's a Rover 800?"

Mam's tone turns dark: "You *stole* our neighbor's *car*, Aiden."

"I prefer the term 'heavily borrowed.'"

Her laugh is short, and then it begins to grow...and grow...and now I'm laughing too. It's funny now. Back then though she'd been furious. She'd clenched her teeth so hard she'd looked close to bursting a blood vessel. She'd sentenced my brother, Francis, and me to work in the back garden. Putting it like that didn't sound so bad, but 'back garden' was the better part of ten acres and we'd cleared it by hand. It took weeks. I still have the callouses.

"Before we get back to the twins, and I forget to ask, how'd the buying trip go?"

"Fab." I pause, thinking back to Wellington's sunshine and heat and horses. We were surrounded by multi-*multi*-millionaires and Caleb treated it like it was nothing. Course for him it probably isn't, but for me? It was a culture shock. It isn't just how the other half lives. It's how the one percent of the one percent lives. People didn't bat an eye at million-dollar jumpers. It was so far beyond where I came from, it was almost laughable.

Almost.

I remember thinking, if I can make it here, I will have arrived. It was everything I wanted. Not necessarily the flash and the money, though I'd be lying if I said that wouldn't be nice. It's the security of always having owners to work for, and even more importantly, it's the horses that can make you a household name. I want that. I want to make the team. I want a gold medal. I want it all.

"It's nothing like you can imagine," I add, stuffing my feet into some socks. "Let me take you next year."

"That would be lovely that would."

But we both know it won't happen. She rarely leaves our family farm anymore. Some of it's due to age. Farm life is hard. The wear it puts on a body makes a forty-year-old feel more like a fifty-year-old, or *older*. But most of it's my da. The man's no help. In fact, he's never been any help, but she won't leave him. The Church may not be as powerful today as it was in years past, but Mam and Da grew up with it. When they said 'til death to us part, they meant it.

But while a few weeks in Wellington may never happen, she did promise to visit Atlanta (and us) at the end of the month. She'll be just in time to see me compete Praise in our first Grand Prix, the Longines Masters Cup.

"I've so much to show you," I say at last, trying to focus on the positive—and God knows getting her to agree to even a quick visit had been difficult enough. "Your experience and eye for horseflesh would do well here—plus the Yanks love the accent. It makes you instantly more believable than an American sales agent."

"Pish, I don't know anything about anything. We've just been lucky is all."

"Not true," I say, but I let it go. When it comes to horses, luck is something you always need, but Mam's success stemmed from meticulous bloodline research and an eye for diamonds in the rough.

I grope around on the armchair until I find a jumper to pull over my T-shirt. Even after my laughter, the apartment is still quiet—and thank God for that because I need coffee before I begin wrangling the twins.

Wait. Wrangling. Who am I kidding? There is no wrangling. Wrangling would imply I eventually manage everything, and it couldn't be farther from the truth. Parker has them handled. I'm mostly along for the ride.

And like she somehow knows the direction of my thoughts, my mam asks, "How are you, Aiden? Really? No lies."

I sink down on the bed, exhaustion overtaking me once more. "I'm struggling. I'm in over my head, and you know what's even worse?"

"What?"

"The two of them know I'm in over my head."

"Well," she says, and I can hear a smile in her voice, "I'll admit you have a problem there. Parenting is nothing but a game of chicken, my son. You can't flinch, or they'll have you."

"Too late."

"It's never too late. You just have to put the fear of God in them."

"I'm not going to have some terrifying priest lecture them about fire and brimstone. It'll give me flashbacks."

"Ah, you're a cheeky one! I'll have you know you were a terrible little. I had to do something, or you'd end up on the news—and not in a good way."

I smile. It's true. We didn't make it easy on her. Three boys, one girl, and all four with our da's temper.

"If you won't put the fear of God into them, son, at least find yourself some leverage."

"Mam—"

"I'm dead serious. If we can't get them to behave because they want to, make them behave because otherwise they won't get what *they* want."

"What parenting manual did that come from?"

She makes a derisive noise. "Mine."

I shake my head. I don't want to resort to bribery. I think it's a slippery slope. So I give Bridget riding lessons and all goes well until she wants a car.

Considering it's Bridget, I realize, *she'll want a tank.*

Or minions to do her bidding.

"Listen, Aiden...they're going to struggle. You have to know that." She hesitates and I have the horrible suspicion she's trying not to cry. "Their mother is gone. We don't know where Anna is and we don't know when she's coming home."

If she's coming, I think. No need to say it though because I know Mam's thinking the same thing. Francis would say it, as would my other brother, Michael. But Mam and I have never been like that. We keep going. We fix things.

I'm just not sure I can fix this.

"I know with you around, they'll get on board again."

"Only because I'm fast enough to catch them."

Another snort of laughter. "True enough. They were wonderful babies. They'll be wonderful children." She pauses. "Eventually."

The grim note actually makes me smile. "Look at the optimist."

A truck engine rumbles below my bedroom window and I peek out the curtains. Light hasn't even begun to edge the horizon, but the grooms have begun to arrive. I need to get down there. I don't like asking people to do things I haven't demonstrated I'll do myself.

Whump!

Something hits the wall between my bedroom and theirs and Bridget lets out a furious war cry.

"What the devil is going on?" Mam asks. "It sounds like Brody set Bridget on fire."

"If he did, he won't survive it. She'll take him down too."

"Truer words were never spoken. She's a fierce little thing. Have you give any more thought to riding lessons?"

Only my mother like mine could carry on a conversation while children tried to kill each other in the background. Some of it is temperament: nothing can shake that woman. The rest of it is a lifetime of raising the four of us.

Maybe the twins are my karmic payback.

"No riding lessons until they behave themselves," I tell her.

"But—"

"No lessons."

Another furious cry.

"Well, carry on then," Mam tells me breezily, "but do think about contacting a priest, Aiden, my love. It sounds like you're going to need   him."

CHAPTER 17 | Parker

I've been sitting in the Bronco for the better part of five minutes, staring up at the apartment windows. My mouth is dry. My body's strung tight. I masturbated in the shower until I came—twice—and I'm still desperate for more.

Actually, that's not quite right. I'm still desperate for Aiden.

It's not that I disagree with his reasons for stopping us. He's absolutely right. It's that my body clearly disagrees with both of us.

Get it together, girl, I tell myself, but it's no good. My nipples actually ache. This is ridiculous.

Or maybe not because I've only ever slept with Matthew, and we stopped having sex two years before our marriage ended so that makes...

I gnaw the skin next to my thumbnail, doing the math in my head. *Good Lord*, I think, the numbers finally hitting me. *It has to be* at least *thirty some months since my last orgasm.*

My stomach goes sour. No wonder I've been raging. There used to be a time I couldn't contemplate going thirty days without release, but life with Matthew had a way of draining any desire and now here I am. I hadn't even missed it.

Until now.

I shake myself. The thing to remember here isn't how attracted I am to Aiden. The thing to remember is this whole situation is thanks to Matthew. Not only did my marriage destroy my finances and my confidence, but apparently it also tanked my libido. Kind of unsurprising I guess when you think about it.

Then again, *did* my marriage really tank my confidence? I mean, I did practically jump Aiden. Even before Matthew, I had never been that self-assured, but there's something about Aiden's desire for me that makes me feel...

Wanton.

Wonderful.

The best I've ever felt.

It's like I'm a new me, I think. *One that I like too.*

Impatient from waiting on me, Wookie whines and jams his cold, wet nose into my ear. I shove him away. "Oh, gross! Fine, we're going!"

I swing open the driver's door and he gallops over me, stomping on my stomach in his haste to the hit the parking lot. Air whooshes painfully out of me.

Guess that's one way to get my focus back, I think, rubbing the stinging skin. I shut the door and follow him up the stable aisle and into the tack room. "Stay," I tell him when we reach the spiral staircase's steps. Wookie whines, but parks his butt by a saddle stand, preparing to wait for me. "Good boy."

Upstairs, the apartment is surprisingly quiet, and when I open the door, I understand why. The kitchen is deserted and I can hear the faint sounds of cartoons playing from the living room. Not a good way to start their first day back at school.

"Brody? Bridget?" I call, unwinding my scarf and tossing it onto a chair. "Come help make breakfast!"

There's a beat of hesitation and the television flips off. The twins shuffle into the kitchen looking like they're about to be dragged to jail.

Considering they're starting classes today, I think, *I guess that's about appropriate.* I button on a bright smile. "Eggs? Toast? Cereal?"

"Cereal," Bridget mutters.

"Toast," Brody says.

"Great!"

They glare at me like this is the farthest we could possibly get from great but slide into their chairs at the table without argument, leaving me to dash around the kitchen.

And practically straight into Aiden as he walks in.

He steps back. I step back. My body lights up the same way it did the night before. *Keep your hands to yourself*, I think, but it's no good because my eyes are already dragging up and down him. He's wearing riding clothes—loose breeches and a thin sweater. It beautifully highlights the breadth of his shoulders and the flatness of his abs.

They were so hard last night, I think and mentally smack myself. In fact, I'd be kind of embarrassed for ogling him—if Aiden were doing the same thing to me. His gaze is locked on my breasts like he's remembering the feel of them, and when he jerks his eyes up, they're half-wild.

"Morning," I say, sounding professional.

"Morning," he responds, also sounding professional.

"Breakfast?" I ask, praying he'll stay and praying he won't.

Aiden swallows. "Uh..."

"Oh, please Aiden?" Bridget asks, fidgeting in her seat. "You never eat with us anymore."

She's not upset, but he winces like the observation hurt anyway and it makes my heart squeeze. He really does try to be everything he can for them. He nods. "Okay, love."

The twins grin and Aiden faces me. His gaze meets mine and he swallows again. "What can I help with?"

"Um..." My brain stalls out and then returns to me. "Toast? Brody wanted toast."

"I can do that." And he retreats to the other side of the kitchen, hovering over the toaster like it needs his constant presence. Getting distance between us is a nice thought, but in an apartment kitchen there's only so far either of us can go.

Concentrate on the twins, I think, but then I catch Bridget watching us with a suspicious look in her eyes. It makes my stomach wad up.

In the end, Aiden eats breakfast at the table with the twins, I drink coffee by the counter, and fifteen agonizing minutes later, he's out the door to start his day.

I catch myself staring after him.

"C'mon, you two," I say, stuffing my arms back into my jacket and feeling surly. *This isn't surly*, I realize. That's sexually frustrated.

And now I'm even more surly.

"Outside," I tell the twins. "My dog needs a walk before we leave for school, and you need exercise."

"What do you mean?" Brody peers up at me. "Are you putting us to work? We're dog-walkers now?"

"Yep, I'm offering you the opportunity to branch out from window cleaning." I wind my old, gray scarf around my neck, fluffing it until I don't feel like I'm being choked to death.

"Is it really that cold outside?" Brody asks, one brow arched so he looks like a tiny version of his uncle.

"Ha. Ha. Get your coat—and you both still have to clean your bathroom when you get home this afternoon. I haven't forgotten that you owe the Swear Jar."

"Joy," Bridget mutters, trailing into the kitchen. I'm pretty sure she's wearing the same sweatshirt from yesterday and I'm positive she hasn't brushed her hair. I try to think of a delicate way of pointing out that brushing one's hair is pretty much an everyday thing, and...

Yeah, I've got nothing. Anything I say will probably embarrass her, or irritate her, and success with the Swear Jar aside, I know I don't have the upper hand with these two.

Yet.

"Clean bathrooms are non-negotiable," I say, passing the twins their coats. "It's a life skill you'll need."

Bridget groans and Brody pats her arm. "Just go along with her," he whispers. "When I make it big as a superhero, we can have servants."

I glare at them. They look back with angelic expressions. "I heard that," I say.

"Heard what?" Bridget asks.

Heard the sound of my blood pressure rising, I think, but I don't press the matter. *Pick your battles*, I tell myself and motion for the kids to follow me. I pound down the spiral staircase, the twins clattering right behind.

Below us, Wookie's waiting by the bottom step, whole body wagging. As we spiral closer, he begins to pant and wiggle.

"Hey, buddy," I tell him, patting his head and urging him to the side so a groom can pass by. It's not even seven-thirty, but the tack room is already busy as people come through for equipment and supplies. Two grooms sit in a corner, cleaning saddles with some sort of fragrant citrus soap while the rest hustle by, faces intent. I don't blame them. Last I heard, Aiden rides ten to twelve horses a day—which is enough to keep anyone busy, but Jacks or Better also has broodmares, foals, and young horses to look after.

"C'mon, buddy," I say to my dog, trying to get him out of the way. Predictably Wookie doesn't 'c'mon.' He wiggles and prances in front of the twins, trying to tempt them into petting him.

"I like you too, buddy," Bridget says, sidling up to Wookie to give him a pet. He furiously wags his tail and wiggles closer, nearly knocking her down. I brace myself for an outburst, but she laughs and scratches him behind his ear.

She really does like animals, I think, mentally stowing that one away for later use. I open the tack room door and usher the kids into the stable aisle. *Look at me, getting on top of this already.*

Or something.

"So what are we really doing after school?" Brody asks me, picking at the skin around his thumbnail. He watches with interest as one of the grooms brings a horse through. "Another walk? Or something interesting?"

He sounds all kinds of innocent, but there's something calculating in the way he cuts his eyes in my direction.

Not good, I think. *I need to get ahead of these two. If I don't come up with something to occupy them, they* will*, and I won't like it.*

They look at me. I look at them, and as the twins smile, I suddenly know two things: positive reinforcement isn't the only thing that's going to work with them, and I'm going to need bribery.

CHAPTER 18 | Parker

"No way," Aiden says when I finally catch up with him. It's the first thing he's said to me in two days, and it's not even sexy.

But at the sound of his voice, my body heats anyway.

So freaking annoying, I think and force myself a step closer. Aiden's trying to eat a sandwich over the tack room sink, a quick lunch before his afternoon rides. This is also not sexy, but this close, I can see how I make his knuckles stand up white.

Good, I think, bitter satisfaction rolling through me. *Now we're both frustrated.*

"No way," he repeats and I scowl at him, ignoring the butterflies in my stomach. Even after riding four horses, he still looks incredibly sexy. I grew up around riders so I've never really had a thing for snug fitting breeches, boots, and laugh lines from too much sun, but on Aiden? It's pretty much perfect.

Pretty much ridiculous, I think, pinning my eyes to his even though it makes my mouth go dry. If I don't force myself to hold his gaze, my eyes will wander all over him. It's like our decision *not* to touch has made me want him even more.

"Aiden," I begin, and briefly, I'm pleased. I've actually made his name sound like it doesn't ripple through me. "You need an edge with these kids. Think of it as we're giving them some motivation."

He shakes his head, chews the rest of his sandwich bite and swallows. "Find another way. I'm not getting them riding lessons until they *earn* the riding lessons. It's a privilege."

Annoyance zings up my spine. While I do agree with him, I also think he needs to cut them some slack. "Then give them a taste of what they're earning." I cross my arms and lift my chin and ignore how even disagreeing with Aiden is somehow sexy to me. "It'll motivate them more."

102

"No way. You don't reward that kind of behavior. You...put it to work." Aiden blinks like he can't believe he just said that. Neither can I.

"*What?*" I demand.

He shakes his head. "Sorry. Something my mother said to me a couple days ago."

"Oh." I hesitate as questions like, *do you talk to her often?* and *She uses manual labor as punishment?* well to my surface. "She thinks you should put them to work? Like cleaning saddles or something?"

"No. She thinks I need leverage. She wants them to take riding lessons too."

I brighten. *Liking this woman already*, I think. "So she agrees with me."

"I didn't say that."

"But she does." I relax, uncrossing my arms and already thinking about the phone calls I'll need to make. Good riding instructors can be hard to find, and good ponies are even more difficult. I need to talk to Ellie.

"Okay, yeah," Aiden says. "She agrees with you, but Parks, riding is dangerous. The twins need to prove to me they can listen and follow instruction before I can put them on the back of some pony."

Drat. He does have a point—a pretty excellent one too. Listening isn't exactly a Bridget or Brody strong suit and riding can be quite dangerous when you consider it's basically strapping yourself to the top of a flight animal.

"You know what?" I ask at last. "You're right. I don't want the twins to get hurt, but I also don't think you're giving them enough credit. I think they'll rise to the occasion."

A vaguely alarmed look flits across his face. "That sounds like something my Mam would say."

I nod. "She must be a wise woman."

"The wisest."

I grin.

He grins.

This would be stupid if it didn't feel so good—actually, it's probably still stupid. We're adults and we can't even have a conversation about riding lessons without turning it into flirting.

I clear my throat and reach for my cell. "Well, good. We're in agreement then. Two against one."

Aiden leans into me. His chest brushes my shoulder and we both freeze. There is a groom cleaning equipment on the other side of the tack room, there are about three layers of clothing between his chest and my shoulder, and it's my *shoulder* for God's sake. It's the least sexy part of my anatomy.

And yet that one little touch pushes goosebumps across my skin.

"This is not a democracy," he whispers. I shiver.

And he notices.

His teeth touch his lower lip, like he's biting something back, and I suck in a breath. "Look at it this way," I manage, trying to sound professional and perky and probably failing because my whole body is suddenly too warm, "if they're at the barn, you can keep an eye on them."

A slow smile. It turns my insides liquid. "I thought that was why I had you."

"You can keep an eye on all of us." I lick my lips and Aiden's eyes drop to my mouth. He studies me like he can't look away and it takes everything in me not to grin. He's as hard up for this as I am. "Make sure I'm not helping turn them into pint-sized delinquents."

Oh. God. I can't believe I said that. It's pissy and sassy and almost definitely a result of my extremely sexually frustrated body. I thought I could put the brakes on my attraction.

Apparently I thought wrong.

I raise my brows, trying to look like the nanny who knows what she's doing and isn't getting wet from Aiden's focus. His gaze trails up and down my body and even though it was his idea to stay hands-off, I feel like he's taking me apart.

Undressing me, I think and feel my core clench.

"You said, I was going to handle everything, and guess what? This is everything. You're lucky I even asked you." I pause. "A month of riding lessons."

"A week."

"A *month*."

Those pale blue eyes go hot. "Two weeks."

I waffle. Part of me wants to hold my ground and force him to cave, but the rest of me knows I need to get away from this—away from *him*. We're at least three feet apart, but I feel Aiden *everywhere*.

"Fine," I say, making a show of shrugging like I don't care and my skin isn't prickling with want. "Two weeks. If you don't see any improvement in their behavior after two weeks of riding lessons, we cancel them."

"Fine."

"*Fine*."

Another slow, incendiary smile, and I'm not sure what to do with that. I made him come around to the idea, but Aiden's smiling at me like   *he's*   won.

CHAPTER 19 | Aiden

Arguing with Parker is almost as good as touching Parker, I think and then notice my balls are actually aching. Strike that. Nothing is better than touching Parker but arguing with her was...intriguing. Until now, she's been so sweet. Fighting for the twins though brought out a fiery side to her I didn't expect. Have to admit I was annoyed when she brought up the riding thing and didn't leave it when I told her to, but the way she didn't back down?

Christ, I've always had a weakness for women like that.

She's also right too. I'm so scared at the possibility of the twins getting hurt, I'm keeping them from opportunities to grow. Having my bullshite pointed out to me should be annoying, but for some reason, coming from Parker I like it. It's kind of...refreshing.

I watch her walk away, both hands tightening her already tight ponytail. She's almost shapeless in her enormous sweater and baggy jeans, but the way her hips sway is unmistakably woman, and I catch myself lingering. Christ, those hips. I want to slide my hands around them, grip her ass as I pull her down on top of me.

Ridiculous—and *dangerous*. Our little moment in the pantry was one thing, and the slightly more than a little moment out by her Bronco was, well...

I swallow, feeling my dick beginning to stir. That moment was fucking fantastic and I want a repeat. When she'd talked about me bending her over my desk, she'd visibly trembled. Ever so briefly, I'd thought she was scared, and the I realized she was trembling from *want*.

And more than our kiss, more than the feel of her body under my hands, it's her *want* that keeps me awake. The night we'd kissed, I'd gone back upstairs, made sure the twins were asleep, and then took the longest, coldest shower of my life—and it *still* didn't keep from jerking off twice to thoughts of Parker holding her thighs wide for me, or Parker bent over my desk, bare ass ready for me to kiss...or spank.

Two days later, you'd think I'd be doing better, but I'm not. Every time she's close, I go hard. Every time I *think* about her being close, I go hard. And as I jerked off *again* around three this morning, I was pretty positive I'd made a huge mistake letting her go.

Now in the light of day, I can safely say I did the right thing. I absolutely do not need a fling with the nanny—and even if Parker weren't the twins' nanny, she's best friends with my boss's girlfriend, for God's sake. There is no version of this game where I am not the asshole.

Think of the twins, I remind myself, tossing the rest of my sandwich into the trash. *Think of what losing her would do to them.*

Think of what losing the chance with her will do to you.

I swallow and my throat sticks. Forget it. She could not be more off the table, and if I work hard enough, I'll be too distracted—and exhausted—to keep this attraction up. Considering my work schedule, it won't even be that difficult. I'm already slammed. I have eleven sales horses in training, and at least five of them will be competing in the upcoming Winter Festival Show Series. It will be my first big competition since arriving in the States almost six months ago, and pressure's on to do well.

Although, I guess technically, pressure is always on because Caleb is all about winning. Then again, so am I. It's probably why we work so well together. But I can't kid myself into thinking he'll keep me around if I don't produce wins and sales. This is a business—and the best opportunity I've ever been offered. Being at Jacks or Better can lead to everything I want *and* provide for Bridget and Brody. I'm not going to let them grow up like I did, like their mother did. I'm going to do better for all of us.

The reminder coils tension at the base of my neck and I roll my head from side to side, hearing the joints pop. Honestly, it's fine—better than fine. I thrive on this shite. I'm really good at this shite. I'm just distracted.

"You ready?" John, our head groom, interrupts my obsessing. He's holding the reins to one of Jacks or Better's homebreds, a young stallion we're preparing for the jumpers.

"Definitely ready," I say, taking the reins. "Thanks."

"When should I have Cruiser ready? You want forty-five minutes with this one?"

Cruiser is another Jacks or Better homebred. An impeccably pedigreed stallion, Caleb and I are hopeful we'll eventually stand him for breeding. "Nah." I shake my head, tugging my riding gloves back on. "Let's make it an hour. I don't want to get in a hurry with this one. He's more anxious than I'd like."

"Got it." John disappears into the tack room, leaving me to get on with it. I lead the young stallion toward the lower riding arena. It's another great day for riding. Even though it's mid-January, the sun rides high in an impossibly blue sky. The fields are winter yellow, but the temps are almost pleasant. I love Ireland, but I don't miss the rain and clouds. Atlanta may not have the heat of Wellington, but it definitely has its own unique beauty.

I pause at the mounting block so I can adjust my stirrups and check the girth. The earlier tension in my neck is gone, and the anticipation of another afternoon doing what I love rolls through me.

Even so, I cast my eyes back toward the stable, wondering what Parker's doing now. The stable doorway is empty. No sign of her. It should be a relief, but it's not.

She's a distraction, I tell myself. *But you've had distractions before and you've always gotten them under control. She isn't any different.*

But   even   I   know   I'm   lying.

CHAPTER 20 | Parker

I walk away from Aiden with my knees trembling. Normally, that means I've been in some ugly fight—I *hate* conflict—but this time, it's pure lust. My head buzzes and my joints feel liquid. Even arguing with Aiden is somehow sexy, and I gotta admit that's weird for me.

It's because everything he does is sexy, I think, scowling. This is true and also deeply, *deeply* annoying. I stalk down the stable aisle, out into the sunshine, and speed-dial Ellie. She picks up on the second ring, and I say, "I need a riding instructor for the twins."

There's a pause. "And I need a million dollars."

"Not funny. I'm being serious."

She laughs. "So am I. Hang on a second." Before I can respond, she muffles the phone, saying something to someone on the other end. Like Aiden, Ellie has a huge string of horses to ride every day. I'm probably holding her up from schooling another one.

"Okay," she says. "I'm back. Tell me everything."

"Are you sure? Did I catch you at a bad time?"

"No, not at all. I'm waiting on a potential client, but she's already an hour late."

"Oh, gosh, I hope everything's fine."

"Totally." Her tone is breezy and light and I can picture her waving one hand in dismissal. "She's a trust fund baby. Being on time is for other people. So in all seriousness, why do you need a riding instructor for the twins? Does Aiden want them to ride? I thought Caleb told me he was dead set against it."

"Let's just say I persuaded him to think about it in different terms."

"Yeah? What're those?"

109

"The kind where we're offering incentives for them to behave."

"Bribery. I like it."

"Not entirely bribery. Just..." I pace in a small circle, trying to stay warm, but it's increasingly impossible. The wind's picking up and a chill is seeping under my clothes. I'd jump in the Bronco and run the heater, but I doubt Ellie would be able to hear me over the engine's rumble. "They need more in their lives. Think about what horses and riding gave us."

"Two concussions and a knee that gimps out on me when it rains?" She's joking, but I know she gets this. Of all people, she would understand the gift of horses and riding to her very core.

"*And* responsibility *and* empathy," I add.

"I know what you mean." She pauses. "I think it's amazing you got Aiden to come around on it. Thing is, it's been a minute since I've needed a little kids' instructor. I'll need to make some phone calls and see who's any good around here."

Relief floods through me. We'll make this work. "You know you're the best, right?"

"Just doing my part to make sure you don't take off to God knows where again."

I laugh. "Seattle is not 'God knows where.'"

"Well, it's definitely too far away. Look I gotta run. You're coming to Holly's for dinner tonight, right?"

"Definitely."

"Yay! Love ya!"

"Love you too!" We hang up and I take a minute to linger, reminding myself once again that I'm so lucky to have friends like Ellie and Holly. I'd been so embarrassed to come home and tell them what had happened with Matthew and I shouldn't have been. They were so understanding.

And, of course, now they're determined to put everything back together. They're determined to put *me* back together.

Is that actually possible though? I wonder, watching Aiden ride one of the young horses down to the arena for work. I met and married a man who was the love of my life and it turned into a nightmare. I'm never going to be the same.

And that's probably a good thing because look at what a disaster I am—no car, no savings, no future. The reminder threatens me with another shame spiral, and I hop into the Bronco, cranking the engine and turning the heaters on full-blast.

As I swing out of the parking lot, I catch one last glimpse of Aiden. His head lifts, his gaze following me as I drive past. Even at this distance, it feels like a caress.

Maybe you're not so different after all, I think and it hurls my stomach down around my feet. Hadn't I been head-over-heels for Matthew? Hadn't I felt the same butterflies? I can't let myself fall like that again. I *won't* let myself fall like that again.

But when it comes to Aiden, I don't think I can trust myself.

CHAPTER 21 | Parker

Aiden gets home early that night and takes the twins out for pizza so I can meet Ellie and Holly for dinner. It's not a far drive, maybe twenty minutes to Holly's house, but when I pull up, the winter dark is complete and the house lights are already on, backlighting the winter-bare trees.

In the spring and summer, Holly's cottage is surrounded by green leaves and bright pink azaleas. This time of year, it's pretty barren and makes the eye-poppingly yellow front door stand out even more. Ellie's Twelve Oaks truck is parked by the curb and I pull ahead, leaving the Bronco out of the way of anyone driving by.

"Hello?" I call, opening the front door.

"In here!" Holly calls. She sounds half-tipsy already and I grin. I drop my bag by the bench and jam my wool on top of the grinning warthog's head Holly got from God knows where and hung up as a hat rack. It's her mom's house, but Holly's lived here on and off for so long, she's made parts of it hers—saturated jewel-toned pillows, ridiculously fussy flower arrangements, ceilings painted in the softest grays and blues and pinks.

I like the updates. It feels like a fresh haircut on your oldest friend. The warthog? I dunno. I might be able to do without him—though his rakish grin is starting to grow on me.

I pad down the hallway and into the wide-windowed, open kitchen. Ellie's sitting on the counter, head thrown back in laughter, and Holly's gesturing at something with her wine glass.

"I want whatever you two are having," I tell them.

"Parker!" they chorus and I giggle. I can't help it. I can feel my exhaustion draining away and in its place is something begging to be silly.

"Oh my God, tell me we're eating soon," I say, hopping up on the counter next to Ellie. "Because it smells amazing."

It does too: cheesy and buttery and I keep taking deep breaths. Holly passes me a brimming wine glass. "Like ten more minutes?" she guesses.

I nod, taking the glass. "You look fantastic. All this for us?"

"Nope. For me." She flashes me a mischievous smile and brushes one hand down the front of her silk slip dress. It's cobalt blue, a total pop of color against the soft gray of her slouchy cardigan. The outfit would be totally feminine if she hadn't paired with her favorite biker boots. I could never pull something like that off, but Holly makes it look effortless.

"How are the kids?" she asks.

I take a sip of wine. "Wow, that's good."

Ellie snickers. "Cardboardeaux," she says, holding up a purple box of wine.

"Whatever," I tell her, smiling. "I like it. The kids are pretty great. Aiden's agreed to let them take riding lessons. Ellie's finding me an instructor."

"Nice." Holly leans one hip against the counter's edge and watches me. The kitchen light turns her blond hair into fiery gold. "That should be fun for you. It's been too long since you've been around horses."

"Yeah. Matthew didn't like them." I take another sip of wine—and then a bigger one because my disastrous marriage hits me all over again. I shake it off. The oven timer dings and we spend the next few minutes filling up our plates. I swipe an extra biscuit from the pan and follow Ellie to the kitchen table.

She drops into the closest seat, stabs her knife into the butter and then points it at me. "So. Thought anymore about Holly's idea?"

113

"The one about nannying won't be my job forever so I should jump Aiden now and thank both of you later?" I'm so proud of myself. There's no way either of them will be able to tell that even saying 'jump Aiden' makes me want to squirm.

He'd been just as sexually frustrated as I was today and I can't help but wonder if he'd take his hand to himself tonight. Would he go to the shower and pretend he was fucking me?

The idea leaves me breathless.

Holly laughs. "Y'all make me feel like the bad influence. I didn't say you should jump him, Parks. I said you should have some fun with him."

"I think you should too," Ellie adds, mouth half-full with green beans. "The night you took the job? I saw the way he looked at you."

My heart stutter-stops. *What?* I think and then mentally head slap myself. *It doesn't matter how he looks at you. You're only a tiny bit interested.*

I scowl. *Okay, you're way more than a tiny bit interested.*

"I've sworn off relationships," I tell them, helping myself to a wine glass and then the wine box. "And besides he has all the warning signs of being bad for me."

"How's that?"

"He says all the right things."

Ellie and Holly exchange a confused look. "Isn't that a good thing?" Holly asks at last. Her cardigan slips down one shoulder and she absently drags it back up.

"Matthew said all the right things too," I tell her.

"But Aiden isn't Matthew."

"*Matthew* wasn't Matthew until he was. I'm not going back to that." I shudder. I can't help it. Memories well to my surface and I push them back under. It doesn't matter though because now all I can

114

think about is how Matthew called Lell the love of his life. He said I'd never understood him the same way she did.

"Honey." Ellie's voice has turned soft. "You won't be going back."

"We don't know that," I tell her. The girls open their mouths and then close them. It's so in sync I almost laugh, but I can't. The whole thing is too sad. They know I'm right. They're trying to find a loophole to the whole "Parker can't be trusted to pick out guys," but there isn't one. God knows, I've searched.

Holly swirls her wine around and around in her glass, eyes on me. "So, you're going to...what? Never date again?"

"Pretty much. I'm swearing off men. I intend to have a quality relationship with my vibrator."

"You'd have to *have* a vibrator, Parks." Ellie gives me a knowing look. "And I'll bet you still haven't gotten around to buying one."

"True."

Holly shrugs. "I get the swearing off guys thing. We've all been there."

"No, you haven't." I shake my head, feeling suddenly so alone and so foolish and so *embarrassed*. I can't believe I fell for Matthew's lies. "Trust me. I'm not kidding around. I married a narcissist. I fell for him completely. I can't be trusted to pick anyone out again—especially when he seems too good to be true."

"I don't want you to be lonely," Ellie says, and it's so sweet and so gentle that I feel a bit wobbly. Thanks to Matthew, I almost lost my best friends.

"I'll never be lonely as long as I have you two," I tell them, clinking my wine glass against Ellie's and then Holly's. When I look down at my food, they exchange a quick glance, not something I can see, but something I can feel. I'm worrying them.

"Parker?" Holly asks. I lift my eyes to hers. Her expression is agonized, like she's been punched in the gut. "Why didn't you tell us what was going on?"

"I couldn't tell you. I didn't want you to hate him—and how stupid was that? I was ghosting on the two people I needed the most."

"Why'd you stay?" Ellie whispers.

"You know how many times I've asked myself that?" I try to laugh and it comes out all shaky. The girls wait for me. They aren't going to let this go.

They deserve answers, I think, shredding my biscuit into crumbs and gathering my courage. "Matthew was...Matthew was great. At first. We were so in love and I thought we were both doing everything we could to please each other. In the end, I realized I was doing everything to please him and he was...doing whatever and whoever he wanted. Honestly, I don't think I ever knew him."

"He took you away from us," Ellie says, tears making her eyes shine.

"Yeah. He did." And the shame of it makes my whole body burn. "I forgot what I was worth."

"I think you've still forgotten."

I try to swallow around the sudden thickness in my throat. I can't. I was gone for years. I left Holly and Ellie for Matthew, and they still see me like something amazing? Hot tears prick my eyes.

Under the table, Ellie nudges her foot into my knee. "What do you want to do next?"

I blush. "Dunno."

"Yes, you do. I can tell. Stop holding back."

My breath catches. Why is this so hard? *If you want things to feel different*, be *different*, I remind myself. And that means no more hiding. I lift my chin and meet Ellie's eyes. "I think I want to be an interior designer, but I'll have to go back to school for it, and that's pretty much out of the question."

Ellie whistles low. "How did I get such cool, artistic friends?"

"You're just lucky," Holly tells her.

"I am! I mean I can't even draw stick figures. I don't know where you guys get this stuff from." She flops back in her chair and plays with the ends of her dark braid. "So, the nannying thing really is just a phase. Barely counts as a job."

I grin. I know where this is going and suddenly it doesn't seem so bad. If I want to feel different, I need to be different. I didn't keep things with Matthew on my terms. With Aiden, I could.

Couldn't I?

And *that's* when I get the idea for a contract. A boss with benefits, sex with terms, orgasms with...

My brain fails me. It's caught up on Aiden and orgasms.

It's a good idea though. Maybe even a great idea. I just have to convince   him.

CHAPTER 22 | Aiden

I finish my rides a little after four, and as I'm turning out Praise, my last horse of the day, John greets me, looking like someone kicked his grandmother.

"The feed truck's not coming," he tells me. "We're out of the grain I use on the yearlings. Can you go pick some up? I need to wait for the farrier."

"No problem."

Surprise flits through the other man's eyes, but he nods. "Thanks."

I shrug, and the surprise appears again. John's one of Caleb's hires. He came to Jacks or Better after spending ten years at other top-notch farms. I thought we would hit the ground running, but it always feels like he's expecting me to pitch some sort of fit if asked to help out. I'd like to think it's gotten better over the six months I've been here, but so far no good.

"You need anything else?" I ask as we make our way up from the paddocks and into the stable.

"Nah, just the feed."

"Got it." I hang Praise's halter and lead outside his stall, and do a quick walk through, checking everything's ready for evening feed.

And possibly checking to see if Parker and the twins are around.

Okay, *definitely* checking to see if Parker and the twins are around. They aren't though and I swipe truck keys from the tack room, and head for the parking area out front. Caleb always keeps two work trucks for us to use, and I grab the closest: a late model Ford 4x4. We use it for errands or towing the two-horse trailer. It's perfect for picking up feed down at the local shop.

I pull out, and I'm about halfway down the farm lane before I spot the black Twelve Oaks truck powering toward me. It slows and Ellie pulls up next to me, rolling the truck window down. "Hey! I heard I'm finding an instructor for the kids."

Ellie's grin is huge. Guess Parker and Mam aren't the only ones who think the twins should be riding. "Yeah," I say. "We're going to try it."

"It'd be easier to have Parker teach them."

I pause. "She didn't tell me she rides."

Ellie's expression darkens. For an instant, I think she's disappointed, but then I realize she's incredibly sad. "She gave it up years ago— something about her husband didn't like horses or didn't like how she was risking herself? I don't exactly remember. She rode with my dad though. She was good."

I nod. Her husband sounds like a wanker, but she wouldn't be the first woman who's given up something she loved for some*one* she loved even more.

"Anyway," Ellie says, fingers drumming madly against the steering wheel, "I'm hoping now that she's home, she'll get back into it."

"Me too," I say and the response surprises both of us. Something secretive and amused enters Ellie's expression. She stares me down hard, like she's searching for cracks, but I shrug. "Bloody shame to give up something you love for someone who doesn't deserve it."

"Agreed."

"I'm off to the feed store," I tell her, lightening my foot on the brake so the truck begins to roll.

She eyes me. "I'll see you around, Aiden."

It sounds like a threat, and for a few seconds, I'm confused. *The hell did I do to her?* I think.

And then it hits me. Did Parker talk to Ellie about me? If she did, Ellie doesn't sound impressed. It bothers me—not because I'm so arrogant I need Parker gushing to everyone about me (although I'm not adverse to the idea), but because I know how important her friends are. If they don't approve of me, Parker will never stick around.

Which would be bad for the twins.

And for you, I think, waiting for that realization to bother me and...it doesn't. I might not be able to have Parker quite like I want her—my brain supplies quite a few positions I want Parker in and I shove them away—but I can still enjoy *her*.

Maybe we could go riding together, I think. It wouldn't be a big deal to borrow one of the older horses for her, but it could be a *huge* deal for Parker.

I catch myself smiling. Yeah, riding. Getting her back to something she loved and lost. Would be downright noble.

Even if I know it's just another opportunity for me to see her smile.

***

Even with the extra run to the feed store, I still make it back to the apartment before Parker and the twins. At first, I'm confused and then I check the calendar Parker created and pinned to our refrigerator and realize Bridget had math tutoring today.

They'll be starving by the time they get back, I think, opening our pantry and glancing over the contents. My brain tries to concentrate on making dinner, but my body can only think about how close I'd been to Parker in here, how I could've taken her against the shelves.

For a heartbeat, I'm convinced I can hear her breathing: fast, shallow, *needy*.

"Christ's sake, man," I mutter, swiping two tins of tomato puree from their bin. Clearly this whole keeping my distance from her isn't working. *Do I have time for a cold shower?* I wonder and then hear feet galloping up the spiral staircase. Bridget and Brody burst into the kitchen, calling for me.

"In here!" I sound a bit strangled and I hope they don't pick up on it. I swipe the onion powder canister as I leave the pantry and kick the door shut behind me. "Are you hungry?"

"Starved," Brody says, peeling off his jacket and dumping it on the floor. He gallops into the living room before I can tell him to pick it up.

"I'm starved too," Bridget says. She heaves her bookbag onto the kitchen table and starts taking out her homework.

I flip her an apple. "Give me thirty minutes, okay?"

She nods, but her attention has already turned to Parker, who's carrying in Brody's backpack and gym bag. She sets them down by Bridget.

"You want some dinner?" I ask her as she unwinds her scarf.

Parker shakes her head. "No, thank you. I wouldn't want to impose—plus, I'm having dinner at Caleb and Ellie's."

"Think of it as an appetizer then." I get down my biggest soup pot and put it on the counter. "Stay. You're not an imposition. We're having chicken tortilla soup."

Her smile hits me right in the gut. It's teasing and amused and sexy as hell all at the same time. "The Irish guy cooks Mexican?"

"I'm a man of many talents."

She opens her mouth and then snaps it shut. Something zings through her eyes and it makes her cheeks redden. I grin, dying to ask if she's remembering one of the many *other* things I'm so good at.

Like he's been shot from a cannon, Brody runs back into the kitchen. "Please, Parker? Please stay?" The kid's eyes are huge and he looks up at her like he's some Dickensian orphan and she's the sole thing standing between him and happiness. "Eat with us!"

Her face softens. "Okay."

Well, okay *then,* I think. She'll stay for them, but not for me. A lesser man would be offended. Instead, I see opportunity. I wonder what else Brody could convince Parker to do? Stay for a movie? A sleepover?

Yer a right bastard, Aiden Macken, a little voice inside my head tells me. The little voice sounds frighteningly like my mother.

"Aiden?" Bridget looks up from her homework, brows knitted in concentration.

"Yeah, babe?"

"How are babies made?"

I stumble, right myself, and try to pretend I tripped over my own feet, but the twins are too smart. They instantly picked up on my discomfort and now they're watching me with over-bright eyes.

"Well," I say, trying to decide how much I should tell a pair of five-year-olds. Hell, how much did I know when I was five? I think back and can't come up with much beyond what Frank and Sam told me at the time and I'm damn sure not repeating *that.*

"Well," I repeat. "The daddy and the mummy get together and they...work it out."

"'Work it out?'" Brody echoes. "Like a school project?"

Relief makes my knees sag. "Exactly!"

Bridget's nose wrinkles. "But what exactly does the daddy do?"

I hesitate. "He...reads the mummy the directions."

Her little mouth screws up as she considers this. "And then the mummy does the rest of the work?"

"Yes."

"Typical."

At the kitchen table, Parker snorts and ducks her head, shoulders shaking. I scowl. Like she could do better.

Actually, she could. She handles the twins way better than I do. They look at her like she's made of magic.

Our eyes meet over Brody and Bridget's heads and we share a small smile. It's nothing big, but my chest swells anyway. Like we're not just employer and nanny, not just two adults sharing a silent joke.

Like this is more.

Like   this   is   everything.

CHAPTER 23 | Aiden

The twins trade doing the dishes for some television before bed. At first, I think it's a pretty decent offer until I realize they want to watch some sort of forensic crime science program and *then* we have to fight about whether they should be allowed to watch something all about violence.

"Grandma said you and Uncle Frank used to beat each other up all the time," Brody says, scowling. "How's this different?"

"Because it is?" Honestly, I have no idea. It's just a gut feeling. Either my dad instincts are kicking in or it's self-preservation talking because the last thing the twins need to know is how to get away with murder. "How about a Disney movie?"

"How about Despicable Me?" Brody counters.

I pause. "Isn't that one about a bad guy and his minions?"

"Yes," the twins say in unison.

"It's fine, Aiden. Really." Parker's at the sink and her back's to us, but I can hear the smile in her voice and it rolls heat down my spine. "It's pretty funny."

Bridget and Brody don't even wait for my reply. They gallop into the living room, swatting at each other. Seconds later, the telly turns on. Parker dries her hands on a dish towel (and when did we get dish towels anyway?) and turns to me. "Don't worry so much," she says, a smile quirking up one corner of her mouth.

"I'm not worrying"

"You are. I can feel it. It's nice that you're worried—wonderful even. It shows how much you care."

Shows more how stressed I am, I think. "They *are* my niece and nephew," I remind her.

She shrugs. "Lots of people are family and don't really care about each other."

I pause, the words sinking through me. She said them so lightly, like the truth of it doesn't bother her, but it would have to. I haven't known Parker long, but I do know that. Know it unmistakably.

"Fine," I say at last. "You're right. I worry." Now I'm smiling too. We study each other, and even in the growing evening dimness, I can see a pink tinge climbing her cheeks. Christ, it's pretty. She licks her lips and it's like a blow to my gut.

"I guess you need to get going, right?" I glance at my watch. I've had enough dinners with Caleb and Ellie to know they eat pretty late. Part of it is work-related. The rest is just their habit.

"Yeah."

Neither of us moves.

"This is the hardest promise I've ever had to keep," she whispers.

I nearly burst out laughing. "Hardest, huh? I can safely say I have you beat there."

She giggles at the pun and slaps one hand across her mouth, eyes darting to the doorway.

"The telly's on," I say, joining her at the sink. I lean back against the counter's edge and feel myself relax. I take a deep breath and smell the fresh bread from our dinner. "We could set a bomb off and they wouldn't notice."

"You think so?"

"I know so."

She pauses. "Every time I go into that damn pantry, I think of you."

"Same."

"I'm never going to look at canned goods the same way."

"Nope." I'm nearly laughing again. It's funny and it's not. I shift from foot to foot, feeling my balls begin to ache. Definitely not funny.

Parker's attention swings to me. For a moment, there's nothing but silence between us and then, "What if we made a new promise?"

Blood rushes straight to my cock and I have to mentally shake myself. I clear my throat, clear it again. "I'm listening."

"What if we made a...contract?"

I have no idea what to say to that. I stare at her and Parker's pretty blush deepens. "I mean," she says, "clearly the whole avoiding each other thing isn't really working. We see each other all the time, right?"

"Right."

"And I don't know about you, but the more I tell myself I can't have you, the more I want you."

My throat closes up and my dick stands to attention, and for several seconds, I can't manage a damn thought.

Parker turns, pressing her hip into the cabinetry so she can face me and continuing on like she hasn't just given me a raging hard-on: "So I was thinking about how we could make this work and that's when I came up with a contract."

"And what would that look like?" My brain instantly supplies: Parker up against a wall, her legs around my hips as I pump into her. Parker on her hands and knees in my bed. Parker in my shower, all wet and glowing.

"Like appointments," she says, wrenching me back to the present. "The twins are the biggest priority so we schedule around them."

"Schedule...sex around them?" I sound like an imbecile and I can't help it. This whole conversation is surreal.

She gives me an encouraging smile. "Exactly. I don't know about you, but I could be ready to go whenever. We could schedule it after their bedtime or whatever."

Ready to go whenever. My brain stalls out again. I force in a breath and then one more. "Parks, there's still the whole employer versus employee thing. It's...gross."

It's also a lot more complicated than that, but I only have enough blood to run one head at a time and my dick is still hard.

Parker tilts her head back, considering me. "I like that you think about stuff like that, but you don't need to worry about it with me. I was looking for a job when I found this one, and let's be honest, this isn't going to lead to something more."

Discomfort worms through me and I push it away. I can't decide if it's discomfort from the truth—she's right, this isn't a long-term position—or the mention of how she'll eventually leave.

So not ready to think about that. Not that I probably could anyway. Parker's close now. I can smell her lemon soap and see how her usually tight ponytail has loosened. The tendrils brushing her cheeks look so soft. I want to push them back from her face.

"Anyway, no one can ever accuse me of sleeping with my boss to get ahead," Parker adds. "I mean, where am I going to go? I'm already senior management around here." Her smirk loosens the tightness in my gut. This is the strangest conversation I've ever had—and possibly the funniest, or it would be if I could manage to laugh around my blue balls.

"Let me get this straight," I say at last, profoundly grateful my voice doesn't crack. "It won't affect the twins because we'll schedule it around them."

"And because it'll just be for fun."

"Right. Fun..." My brain starts in again: Parker bent over the end of my bed. Parker sitting on my bathroom counter. Parker on her back, legs spread wide. Another rush of blood hits me and I nearly double over.

She hooks a strand of hair behind her ear. "And there's no worry about the power dynamic because we're both adults and the job is temporary and..." She trails off, her eyes dropping to my mouth and then my chest and then lower.

I should probably be embarrassed because I'm hard as hell, but Parker licks her lower lip and I go even harder. "And because we both want this," I say.

Her eyes fly up to mine. "Right."

The agreement is soft and breathy and I love it. I might be almost bent over from my blue balls, but Parker's not unaffected. I grin and offer her my hand. "Sounds like a deal. Shake on it?"

She trembles and takes my hand, pumping it once—and then drawing my hand to her lips. Holding my gaze, Parker gently kisses my knuckles, working around to my thumb and biting down ever so softly. A hiss escapes me and it makes her eyes go bright. Her lips part and she draws my thumb into the wet heat of her mouth.

And sucks.

It damn near puts me on my knees. She feels like bloody heaven, and the bold way she holds my gaze? It's perfect.

She's perfect.

I groan and I pull her to me. My thumb leaves her mouth with the faintest *pop* and I tilt her head back, meeting her lips with mine. She opens for me and I taste mint and heat and *Parker*.

My hands fall to her waist, pressing her into my hard-on. It feels amazing—until her palm covers me, rubbing me through the fabric of my jeans.

"Even better," I whisper against the corner of her mouth. I take a step toward her, eager to pin her against the cabinets, and she grips me, tugging me to her.

It makes my world spin around.

"You're so hard," she whispers. "It's going to feel so good."

I damn near punch through my zipper. *If she can still talk that clearly, I'm not doing my job well enough*, I think and skim my hands up her sides and across her breasts. She moans as I find her nipples through her shirt, arches into me as I play with her.

The volume on the telly rises. Some song comes on and the twins start singing along. Instantly, we break apart, both of us breathing hard.

I scrub one hand over my mouth. "Walk you out?"

"Absolutely not." Her eyes are shining and wide. She shakes her head hard. "I remember what happened last time."

I smirk. "And it wouldn't be on the schedule."

"Exactly," she says, but her voice is hoarse, ragged. "So. Tomorrow night? After they've fallen asleep?"

"Yeah. Grand."

She takes her things from the table and gives me a tiny wave before ducking out the door. For several moments, all I can do is stare at the now empty kitchen. I have just made a fucking appointment for fucking Parker.

How the hell am I going to last that long?

CHAPTER 24 | Parker

I am a bad ass, I think, fingers drumming against the Bronco's steering wheel as I watch for the twins to weave their way down the pick-up line at school. Coming up with that contract? Inspired. Going through with it? Will be the best thing I've ever done for myself. I'm sure of it.

Last night, I'd masturbated twice and it still wasn't enough to take my edge off. My skin feels too tight and my nipples are too sensitive and I'm counting the hours until Aiden's hands are all over me again—not good considering I need to be focused for this afternoon.

Libby Dale, the twins' new riding instructor, is coming to Jacks or Better for their first lesson and the kids are over the moon excited. Honestly, I'm excited too. I didn't realize how much I missed being around horses until I came home. It will be so much fun to share this with them.

The school pick-up line inches forward and I spot two little blond heads wandering through the crowd. Only a couple more minutes and we can get going.

Unfortunately, that's also a couple more minutes for my brain to circle back to Aiden. I touch my fingertips to my lips, remembering the feel of his mouth. I *love* the way he kisses me. It's demanding and teasing at the same time. My bones just melt.

I don't know that I'll be able to stay upright when he makes me come. I frown. Wait. Where *are* we going to have sex anyway? I hadn't thought to establish locations.

The Bronco's certainly big enough, but I'm pretty sure it breaks *lots* of best friend codes to have sex in Holly's car. There's the tack room at Jacks or Better, but what if someone walked in? There's—

From somewhere in the bottom of my purse, my cell rings. I fish around, pulling out two packs of tissues, a paperback, and a pair of Brody's socks before I find it.

"Hello?"

"Miss Lowery?"

"Yes."

"This is Libby Dale." The woman on the other end sounds thoroughly harassed and half-exhausted. "I have a scheduling conflict, and I'm waiting on the vet. I won't be able to make it to our lesson tomorrow."

I clutch the phone closer. "What do you mean you can't come?"

There's a pause and I feel heat rise all the way to my hairline. There's a pause because she's debating what to say. She thinks I sound like a madwoman. She's right too. I do.

I take a steadying breath, yanking on my ponytail with one hand. "I'm sorry. It's just the kids have really been looking forward to this and..."

And now I have to tell them they're not getting their lesson. I swallow.

"Look, Miss Lowery. I'm very sorry for the inconvenience, but life happens." Libby's tone is the perfect mix of regret and firmness, and even though it's directed at me, I like her even more for it. "I can't make it tomorrow and I'm so sorry, but I can definitely make it out next Monday though."

Days away. The downside of my master plan comes rushing at me full force: the twins have been wonderful for the past couple days and I wanted to reward them. Now I have no reward, but I do have two little kids who are trying to kick each other.

I watch them work their way toward me and plaster on a bright smile. *This is so going to bite you in the ass*, I tell myself. "Next Monday would be great. We're looking forward to it."

"Thanks." A sigh of relief barrels down the line. "Really appreciate your understanding. My barn help left for college and I'm afraid we're lost without her, and now the vet's had to reschedule. I'll send you a text Monday to confirm, okay?"

"Perfect," I say, and hang up, my bright smile draining. *Definitely going to be an ass bite*, I think. How am I going to make this work? Well, for starters, I can't.

Unless...unless I *give them their first lesson*. I mean, I could. When I was in high school, I worked off part of my board by teaching Mr. Lenox's beginner riders. We worked on learning how to walk, trot, and canter the ponies. This would be exactly the same thing.

Even easier because they've never ridden, I remind myself. Tomorrow's lesson would pretty much be all about staying on while the pony walked around, and yeah, I've been out of the horse industry ever since I got married, and I haven't taught since I was sixteen, but I can do this.

It actually sounds like fun too.

The idea uncurls behind my heart, like it's been waiting for me to notice it. It sounds like a *lot* of fun.

The Bronco's passenger door swings open and Brody's adorable, chubby-cheeked face appears. "Hi!" he says.

I grin. "Hi! Hop in!"

"You're in a good mood," he says, heaving himself up onto the seat. His sister scrambles after him and slams the door.

"I'm always in a good mood." Brody opens his mouth and I hold up one finger. "Except when you try to spit on Bridget, it really grosses me out."

"And it's rude," his sister adds.

I nod. "There's that as well."

Brody glares at both of us.

132

"Buckle up," I tell him, "or we're not moving."

Once the twins are settled, I check my mirrors and swing the Bronco into a gap in the traffic. "I have good news for y'all," I say, fully aware the twins aren't listening. I can't see what's going on, but it sounds like Bridget has Brody in a headlock. I keep hearing squeaking. "I had a conversation with your uncle about getting you riding lessons, but if you're not interested in listening I guess I shouldn't tell you."

Just as I'd hoped, silence descends. I glance in the rearview mirror, and sure enough, Bridget has her arm around Brody's neck. They've stopped struggling with each other and their eyes are narrowed to slits. "Did you say riding lessons?" Brody asks.

"I did."

Their little faces turn sharp with curiosity and they break apart, waiting for me to fill them in. The moment should feel triumphant—and it does—but it also feels a little like grabbing a lion by the tail.

I switch lanes and take the turn off for Jacks or Better. "I had a riding instructor lined up for tomorrow afternoon, but she had to reschedule so I'll do your first lessons and you can work with Miss Libby on Monday."

"You ride?" I can hear the frown in Bridget's voice. "We didn't know that."

I grin. "There's loads you don't know about me." *And maybe loads I don't know about myself*, I think. But I'm figuring it out. "So, what do you think? Do you want a lesson tomorrow?"

"Yes!" The reply is in unison. It makes my heart swing high and we spend the rest of the drive talking about the pony I've lined up. They're happy. I'm happy. I check the time on my phone's screen and my stomach squeezes.

Five and a half more hours.

***

133

But when Aiden meets us in the Jacks or Better parking lot, it makes me wish I had about five and half more minutes. He walks toward me with loose, graceful strides and I have to remind myself not to stare. It's hard though. I may be off relationships and this may only be a contractual thing, but the man is almost beautiful. His face is like something out of an Italian painting, but the way he moves is unmistakably male and predatory. It makes everything in me warm.

"Aiden!" Bridget shrieks. She hurls herself out of the Bronco and tackle hugs him. He hugs her back and then swings her into the air, her tiny feet arcing toward the sky.

"Bridget!"

"Parker's going to give us a riding lesson tomorrow!"

Aiden looks at me from over her head, eyes intent with curiosity. "Libby had to reschedule, but I didn't want them to miss out."

"You never told me you rode," he says, a tiny bit of reproach edging into his tone.

"Not enough worth bragging about." I smile, willing myself not to blush or stammer or do something stupid because he's suddenly too close. Way too close.

"Can we go look at the yearlings?" Brody asks, tugging at my sweater and pointing toward the young horses coming up to the fence line. They're all Jacks or Better homebreds, products of the breeding program Caleb wants to be known for.

"Only if you're very quiet and don't scare them," I say. "That means no fighting, no biting, and *no* kicking."

"Deal," Bridget says and races off, her brother in hot pursuit. They reach the fence and peer through the spaces between the boards. The yearlings peer back.

Aiden pushes both hands in his pockets, watching them. "So why *did* you give up riding?"

There's that reproachful tone again. I laugh. "You make it sound like I gave up eating meat or taking showers."

"I'd do either of those before giving up my horses."

"Well, you're you." I keep the retort light like I'm not having my personal summer here because Aiden is *still* too close. "Horses are pretty much your life."

They were pretty much yours too, a small voice in my head says, *but hey minor details, right?* I smile at Aiden and he gives me this expectant look and I realize he isn't going to let me sidestep this question. He wants an answer.

Why is this important to you? I wonder, and then immediately chalk it up to he's a Horse Person. Horse People never understand how Non-Horse People function. They say they do, but secretly, they're convinced we're all miserable without riding every day.

They might be a teensy bit right too.

"I gave it up for all the reasons everyone gives it up during college: not enough time and not enough money."

"You could've ridden after university."

I pause, trying to think of a response that won't make me look pathetic.

I got married fresh out of high school?

I thought giving up riding was temporary?

I thought giving up riding would make Matthew happy?

Nope. They're all pathetic. Some more than others, but still pathetic. I decide to go for brutal honesty: "My husband didn't like it. At the time, I thought he was afraid for me, but it was really about controlling me."

Aiden blinks, blinks again. His expression softens and embarrassment twists through me. I want to melt right into the ground and disappear.

"I know, right?" I force a grin like the whole thing is *hilarious*, but it only makes him frown.

"I'm sorry," he says at last. "I'm glad you figured that out."

"Took me long enough."

"But you still figured it out—that's the important part. My mam hasn't and it's been damn near forty years." An unpleasant prickle tiptoes up my spine. I want to say I'm sorry to hear that. I want to say I understand, but before I can open my mouth Aiden's turned to go.

"I'm glad you're in a better place," he says, voice low and rough. "And I haven't forgotten our appointment. I'll see you tonight. Don't wear   panties."

CHAPTER 25 | Parker

Almost time, I think as I help the twins into bed. They've showered, brushed their teeth, and finished all their homework, and usually by now, I'm falling over with exhaustion, but my body feels like it's flying high.

And every time I move, I remember I'm bare beneath my jeans. I'm wet already too. It will take next to nothing to bring me to come.

"Parker, can you get my dog?" Bridget asks as she snuggles deeper under her bright pink comforter. "I left it in the kitchen."

"Sure, honey." I pad back into the kitchen, find the dog on the table, and Aiden wolfing down a bit of dinner by the sink. He glances up at me and my toes curl into the tile.

"Hi," I whisper.

"Hi." His smile is damn near indecent. He looks at me like I'm perfect. "Sorry, I'm late for dinner. The vet ran late. Kids asleep?"

"Not yet but getting there."

He nods, takes one more bite of the casserole I made, and pushes away from the counter. "Let me take that in to her," he says, lifting the stuffed dog from my arms. "I need to say good night."

"Okay!" I sound like Minnie Mouse on helium again and we both laugh.

Aiden strokes a wisp of hair away from my cheek and leans close to whisper, "I told the grooms I'd do the night check and they should head home early."

My entire body clenches. That means privacy. If no one is coming around for night checks and Caleb is already up at the house, the whole farm is practically ours. "Good idea," I say coolly.

He smirks and I can't tell if it's because he knows it's a good idea or if it's because he knows I'm only pretending to be cool. "Meet you downstairs?" he asks.

I nod. He disappears down the hall to settle the kids and I press both hands to my stomach to settle me. I'm grinning like an idiot. I can't seem to stop.

Get it together, I think, grabbing my bag from the hook by the door and trotting down the spiral stairs. The tack room is dim, only one light is on over the desk and there's the faintest smell of fresh coffee from the afternoon brew the guys always do.

I drop my stuff at the desk and notice the framed pictures stacked on top. Aiden—maybe about fourteen—riding in Ireland. Aiden riding at Jacks or Better. Aiden holding one of Caleb's new stallions. In every picture, he's smiling that gorgeous smile and looks so happy it's breathtaking.

Upstairs, the apartment door *snicks* shut and Aiden comes down the steps. "Parks?"

"Hey."

He reaches the bottom, grinning at me, and my mouth goes dry. That gorgeous body, that easy smile, the way his eyes have gone electric blue, he's so sexy, so perfect—and now I'm nervous. Before, I'd loved the idea of scheduling sex with him, but now it feels...

Intense.

Aiden's gaze flicks up and down me, dragging heat across my skin. "Are you okay? If you've changed your mind..."

"God, no!" It escapes on a rush and I can feel my ears go nuclear. So much for smooth.

Aiden grins. "Good."

So why isn't he moving toward me? I wonder. He's still standing by the bottom step, waiting.

For me, I realize and it ripples through me. I love that. I take a step toward him and his eyes go even brighter. I take another and his breath shallows.

Almost toe-to-toe, I look up at him. "So, um, how does this work?"

He grins and it nearly knocks my knees out from under me. "I thought you had it all figured out, Parks: contracts, appointments, how you wanted me."

How you wanted me. It forks lightning across my skin. "I didn't figure out *everything*."

"It works like this," he says and kisses me.

It's exactly like it was before: I'm melting and he's demanding and I need more. I need all of him. I wrap both arms around his neck and his mouth nudges mine open. His hands pull me tight against his erection and I gasp.

So good, I think, and then his tongue finds me, setting a rhythm that leaves me breathless. Boneless.

I sag against him, delighting when his arms tighten. His hand slides between my legs and cups me. He sucks my lower lip and then releases it to whisper, "Are you bare for me?"

"Find out!"

He mutters a curse and yanks at my jeans' top button, freeing it and pushing my jeans to the floor. I step out of them and he pulls my sweatshirt over my head, freeing my bare breasts. After ditching my panties, I'd decided to lose the bra too.

Standing in front of him, completely naked for the first time, should be scary.

But it feels amazing.

He's still looking at me like I'm perfect and it...makes me feel perfect.

Aiden scrubs one hand over his mouth. "Christ," he mutters.

I grab his shoulders, dragging him to me and he comes so easily, *so* eagerly. He crowds my space but doesn't let our bodies touch. I can feel his heat and I want more. I squirm closer.

"Ah ah," he murmurs and his grin is wicked. He runs both hands over my breasts, squeezing and playing with my nipples until my head rolls back.

And then he moves on.

Skimming...skimming...skimming...his hands slide away from my sensitive breasts, down my sides, and gripping my ass. It turns my joints liquid. He grips me harder with one hand, the other slipping around to my front. He cups me again, rocking the heel of his palm into my clit and sending me up on my toes.

Colors spark behind my closed lids and I hear someone begging for more. It's me.

"I knew you'd be sensitive." It's half-groan, half-growl. He rocks me again then rubs the heel of his hand in an insistent circle. I gasp. Close. I'm so close.

Then he backs off.

His fingers continue exploring, sliding between my folds and feeling how wet I've gone. I grind against his hand as he dips his head for another kiss.

Up and down. Up and down. He strokes me lazily, like he has all the time in the world and it sends me out of my skin.

"I can't wait," he murmurs against the corner of my mouth. "You feel fucking fantastic."

I pull back an inch, panting. "I can't wait either. Now. *Please.*"

Aiden groans like I've punched him and I feel his erection twitch against my stomach. It gives me a wicked thrill. "Now," I repeat. *"Please."*

He responds by lifting me, wrapping my legs around his waist and pinning me against the wall. It grinds his hardness right over my clit and I hiss in a breath. He's still dressed and I'm naked and I would never have thought this would be so delicious, but it is.

"Wanted you like this," he mutters against my neck, one arm firmly holding me while his opposite hand explores. It plunges down between us, finding my clit and teasing me with soft strokes. I cry out, arching my breasts against his chest. It only drives me crazier.

My sensitive nipples brush his skin and his touch goes firmer against my clit, taking me right to the edge.

Almost there. Almost there. Almost—

"Come for me, Parks," he whispers and I do. He shatters me. I bite down hard on his shoulder, screams muffled against his shirt.

"Again," he breathes and strokes me harder. Once. Twice. He pushes me over again and I grind frantically against his hand, colors streaking behind my lids.

"Even better than I thought," he murmurs into my hair—or at least I think that's what he says. I lift my head and feel like the world has spun around. I'm almost dizzy from the pleasure. I'm definitely boneless. When Aiden slides me down his body, I have to cling to his shirt to stay upright. I press my forehead to his chest and feel his chuckle.

"Worn out already?" His hands are at his belt buckle, and as I watch, he pulls his shaft free from his pants. It makes my mouth water. Long, hard, and *thick*, it looks even better than it felt moments ago. Both my hands drop to it, circling him with my palms, and Aiden curses.

"Easy, love. I'm a hairsbreadth from coming."

"Then come." I stroke him from base to tip and his eyes roll back in his head.

"Christ, I love how demanding you are," he grates and fumbles with a condom wrapper. I snatch it away, tearing it open, and sliding the condom down his hard length. I cup his balls, teasing him as he teased me and he rewards me with a hard kiss.

Then lifts me again. My too sensitive nipples brush his chest and my too sensitive clit rubs along his shaft. Seconds ago, I was half-limp from my orgasms, but already I feel my body stirring.

Needing.

He fits himself to my entrance, sliding inside me, *stretching* me until I'm utterly and perfectly full. He mutters a string of creative curse words under his breath and lowers his forehead to mine.

"Okay?" he whispers.

I smile and clench myself around him, delighting in the feel and delighting in my power over him. His eyes roll back in his head again and there's another round of muttered expletives.

All from me, I think. *I do this to him.*

And the knowledge makes me wetter. "Please," I beg, grinding my hips into him.

His   eyes   spear   mine.   "Always."

CHAPTER 26 | Aiden

Parker's thighs tighten around me as I thrust into her, urging me on. Like I fucking needed it. She feels amazing: hot and slick, fitting me like a glove. I don't think I've ever been this hard and she takes me easily.

Greedily.

With each stroke, her core tightens around me. It's more than enough to make me come, but it's her expression that threatens to undo me *now*. Eyes wide and meeting mine, breathing fast and hard, she's the one pinned against the wall but she watches me like she owns my ass.

I fucking love it.

I also need to fucking slow down or I'm going to come before her. I grit my teeth, willing my body to stand down. Think of kittens. Think of puppies. Think of that time you walked in on Sam jerking off.

And that does it. For a second, I lose my attention entirely, but that's fine. I will makes sure she comes first if it kills me.

And it might, I think as Parker digs her heel into my back, once again urging me on.

"You feel perfect," she moans, fingers tightening on my shoulders. "I've needed this."

I almost laugh. *She's* needed this? "That so?"

The world's cockiest grin. "It is."

I tighten my grip on her, circling my hips and teasing her clit until that cocky grin dissolves on a gasp. Her head rolls back and her eyes slide shut. It exposes the beautiful column of her neck and I kiss my way up to her ear, nipping her earlobe before whispering, "Did you touch yourself while you thought of me?"

She nods vigorously. "So many times."

"Did you touch yourself here?" I brush my thumb between us, teasing her clit with the lightest tap. She shudders against me.

"Yes!"

My cock twitches hard, straining to come, and I slow my pace even more. I want to draw this out. I brush her clit again, lighter this time. "Are you sure?"

"God, yes!"

Her eyes open, gaze meeting mine, and she grins. She's loving this.

And so am I.

Her grin goes naughty. "Maybe I should show you some time." My cock goes even harder and she pulls me closer, whispers pouring into my ear. "I could sit on your desk. Play with myself while you watched. Would you like that?"

"Fuck, yes." And admitting it nearly makes me come. Parker on my desk with her legs spread wide for me? I could watch that every night and not get tired of it. "Do you like being watched?"

"I would like it with you."

Another wave of pleasure hits me and I have to fight down my orgasm. Before might have been sexy teasing, but *that* was pure honesty. She would like it with me.

I'd damn sure love it with her.

"Could you come like that?" I ask, voice gone so hoarse I almost don't recognize myself.

"For you?" Her pretty brown eyes go wide. "Like that? God, yes!"

I groan. *Have to get her to come*, I think, bouncing her higher. The faster, firmer strokes make her mouth bend into a perfect O. She might've been driving me on with her teasing, but I'm in control again and she melts for me.

"Aiden! Yes! Yes, please!" There's a panic in her pleading that nearly drags me under. She pulls me to her and I shove her tight against the wall, sliding my hand between us. My thumb finds her swollen clit.

"Yesyesyesyes!" Her head rolls back and her spine arches under my arm, brushing her breasts into my chest. I rub her once and she shudders. I rub her again and she comes.

It's a hot, wet rush as she arches against me, core clenching harder and harder as I thrust. It sends me flying over my own edge and I have to bite down my shout as my own orgasm bends me in half.

For several heartbeats, there's only our ragged breathing and the faint hum of the tack room's fridge. My arms are starting to ache and I'm holding Parker so close I can feel every breath she takes, but I don't want to let her go.

"So worth it," she mutters, cheek against my shoulder.

I'd laugh, but I suddenly don't have the energy. My brain's gone tingly, like someone's filled my skull with ginger ale. I ease out, sliding Parker carefully down until her feet reach the floor. For a few seconds, she leans her forehead against my chest and catches her breath. I know the feeling. It's like she damn near shattered me.

And yet I want her again.

"See?" She peeks up and gives me a shaky laugh. "Fun."

"It was."

But I'd be lying if I didn't think it was something more—and I'd be blind if I didn't see in her eyes that she agreed. She slips away from me, already searching for her discarded clothes. In my haste, I left them all over the place.

"You should listen to me more often," she says, turning away and bending over to grab her jeans and treating me to a life-changing view of her bare ass.

"Tomorrow?" she asks, slipping her sweatshirt over her head. She glances around at me, dark brown eyes gone almost sleepy. "Same time, same place?"

"Any time. Any place." It's way more fervent than I want, but a smile quirks one corner of her mouth. She likes that.

And I really like that she likes that.

Christ, she *does* own my ass.

***

Hours later—after checking on the twins, finishing my paperwork, refilling water buckets for three horses, and checking on the twins again—I slide into bed. I'm bloody exhausted, but my mind won't quiet. It bounces from Parker to the upcoming Masters Cup to tomorrow's chore list and I'm almost grateful when my cell vibrates with an incoming call.

I check the screen and sigh. My mam. No doubt she wants an update on the twins. I thumb the answer button, already grinning. "Mam, this is an almost downright reasonable hour. Do you want to wait until I'm asleep and call back?"

"The cheek of you, I swear. I wanted to hear how you were doing. Is that such a bad thing?"

"Not at all. Tell me how you're doing first though." I lean back against my headboard and study the patch of night sky visible through my window. It's midnight here and the stars are full. They'd be setting in Ireland right now. Dawn would be coming, but Mam chats away like she's been up for hours. We cover the twins, Praise, the Masters Cup, Caleb's choice in stallions for the upcoming breeding season, and finally, her trip to Atlanta.

"I'm looking forward to it," I tell her.

There's a pause. "Are you really?"

"Mam, you know I love seeing you."

"But not your father."

My free hand tightens into a fist and I force myself to relax. "You know how I feel about him," I say at last.

There's another pause, longer this time, and I can feel her worry seeping through the phone connection. We've been having this conversation—or variations of it—since I was fourteen or fifteen and we never come out in agreement. I want her to leave him. She won't. I say he's a right bastard. She agrees.

But she still won't leave him. She's still hoping against hope he'll change. I'm past believing in any of that, but if I want her to be in my life, I have to accept him.

"And the new nanny?" Mam asks suddenly. "How is the dear thing getting on?"

Heat climbs the back of my neck. For a few seconds, I feel like I'm fifteen and she's busted me with a choir girl. I clear my throat. "She's grand. Better than grand, not only do the twins really like her, they behave for her. She even unpacked the apartment."

"Aiden, you've been living in the States for months now and you still hadn't unpacked?"

A mistake to admit, but I'm in too far to deny it now. "Ach, well, I took out the important things."

"Like the family photos I sent you with?"

I blink. Actually, I have no idea where those are. She'd put together a mix of old farm pictures and newer family portraits and crammed them into a box for me. I know I brought them when I moved. I had meant to put them up, but work was busy and the twins were struggling.

Ask Parker if she's seen them, I think, and then realize my silence has stretched on for too long and Mam knows I haven't done anything with the family photos.

"Men," she says and I can hear the eye-roll in her voice. "Now. Back to Praise, do you feel ready for such a competition?"

I turn the question over and over in my mind. Honestly, I've been asking myself the same thing for months. It's a huge and prestigious competition, the first time I'll represent Jacks or Better on an international stage.

My stomach squeezes and I ignore it. "Ready as I'll ever be."

"That doesn't precisely reassure me."

I smile. To anyone else, this might seem especially prying or doubtful of her, but it isn't. She's worried.

Makes two of us, I think, studying the far wall of my bedroom. Bridget's sleeping on just the other side. To keep us all going I need wins—good ones—and I need it to start with the Masters Cup.

"Let's put it this way, Mam," I say at last. "I can't afford to lose."

CHAPTER 27 | Parker

It's been sixteen hours and I *still* can't stop thinking about Aiden—specifically, the hardness of his abs, the tight muscles across his shoulders.

His perfect dick.

I didn't know there was such a thing as a perfect dick, but Aiden's is and I can't stop thinking about it, and maybe because I tell myself to stop thinking about it, I start thinking about how he always made sure I came first, how he looked at me like I was amazing.

How I *felt* amazing when I was with him.

Don't go there, I tell myself. It gets me closer to liking him. I mean, I like Aiden. Of course, I do. But noticing how he treats me differently—better—makes me start *like* liking him.

And I'm not getting into that.

The twins and I wheel into Jacks or Better's parking lot after school, and they practically levitate out of the Bronco, punching and kicking each other as they go. "Hey!" I call after them. "Slow down!"

To my immense relief, they do. They even wait for me by the huge stable doors, shifting from foot to foot in anticipation. I shoulder my bag and follow them down the aisle. Thanks to one of the amazing farm grooms, there's a pony already waiting for us in the closest wash rack. He looks half-asleep and doesn't even budge when the twins rush up to him.

"Shouldn't there be another pony?" Bridget asks, looking around. "There's only one."

"I know." I set my stuff down and glance over one of the grooming kits left out for us to use. There are plenty of brushes to go around—which is good because I know where this conversation is headed. "You'll have to share."

"But I don't like sharing with Bridget," Brody says. The twins both nod, looking at me like I should've known this.

I put both hands on my hips. "Well, you do if you want to go riding."

They think this over while I get the tiny pony saddle and bridle from the tack room. By the time I'm back, any aggravation over having to share seems to be gone. The twins stand shoulder to shoulder, surveying Al Capony.

"He really is beautiful," Bridget whispers, face slack with reverence.

"He is," Brody agrees.

I take a closer look, trying to see Al Capony through their eyes...and failing. A deep seal brown now dusted with *loads* of white hairs, Al Capony probably *was* beautiful back in the day, but now he's a wizened old man with the 'been there, done that' expression of a pony who once killed a tiger in his youth and now has nothing left to prove.

Which is fantastic because I don't want him proving anything to the twins. I want him to put up with their new rider flailings and naughty kid ideas and not come up with any of his own naughty ideas.

"Okay," I say, taking the grooming kit off its shelf and passing it to the kids. "Before we can ride, we have to clean him up. Deal?"

"Deal," the twins say, and we get to work. Fifteen minutes later, Al Capony is asleep, but much cleaner. Bridget got the tangles out of his bushy mane and tail, and Brody brushed the mud off his hindquarters. I taught them how to get dirt out of his tiny hooves with a hoof pick and showed them how the saddle and bridle go on.

"Well, look at Al Capony," John, the head groom, says. He sets two saddles down on the wash racks' stands and takes a minute to admire the twins' work. "Nice job, guys. You look ready to ride."

"I hope so," I say, and point to the riding helmet and gloves waiting. "Bridget, you're first since Brody ate your snack yesterday."

Bridget punches the air in triumph while her brother glares at her. She crams the helmet onto her head and carefully pulls on the riding gloves. The fingers are a bit long, but they'll do.

"Ready," she tells me.

"Great!"

John elbows me. "You teaching them?"

"Yeah. For today."

He nods like this is no big deal, and I mean, it isn't—or it shouldn't be—but my heart is going about a hundred miles an hour, and we make it all the way out to the practice arena before I realize *why* I'm so cranked:

I'm excited.

Brody opens the arena gate for Bridget. She leads Al Capony through, and I lock it behind us.

Okay, I think, taking a deep breath. The smells of damp sand and horse rise over me. It feels like coming home, and for the next hour, there's nothing in my world except for Al and the twins.

"Good job," I tell Brody after we've practiced his steering—a bit wild, but already showing improvement. "You were such a good listener today."

He smiles, but looks away, like he doesn't want me to see how pleased he is. Bridget hangs over the top rail of the riding arena, clearly desperate for another go. "Can you hold Al while Brody dismounts?"

She nods, and I grin as she not only helps her brother get down, but she doesn't kick him or punch him in the process. *That's progress*, I think.

"Nicely done," a voice says behind me.

I turn, and realize we're being watched by a youngish guy—maybe in his thirties—wearing khakis and a polo.

"Hi, I'm Brandon Lane," he says, extending a hand.

"Parker Lowery." We shake as confusions makes his mouth knot up.

"Parker? Sorry. I thought you were Libby. She asked me to meet her here to watch the lesson. I'm thinking about enrolling my daughter." He pats his pockets, finding his phone and checking the screen. "Am I in the wrong place? I have Jacks or Better Farms written down in my calendar."

"No, you're right. Well, sort of. She had to cancel. Something came up."

"Oh." He glances up at me, frowning.

"Sorry."

"Don't be." His blue eyes wrinkle as he smiles at me. "If she'd remembered, we might not have met."

Brody makes a gagging sound and his sister swats him. *So much for not hitting*, I think. "Knock it off, you two."

Brandon gives me another smile—a knowing one. He's definitely a dad and he's definitely attractive.

So why is my raging libido completely standing down? I wonder. I glance past him, up toward the stables and spot Aiden at the top of the hill, watching us. Butterflies wheel through my stomach and I have to swallow hard.

There's my raging libido, I think, ducking my gaze. Apparently, it's still there, it just doesn't feel anything for Brandon Lane. Shame too because Brandon is *way* more appropriate for me than Aiden ever will be. He's a safer choice. For some reason I can tell that instinctually. I would never lose myself over Brandon.

The idea drags my attention back to Aiden. He's still standing on the hilltop, watching the twins. Except...no, he isn't.

He's watching me, I realize, and it scatters goosebumps across my skin. *Hold it together, Parker. You have four more hours.*

CHAPTER 28 | Aiden

The twins should've started their first riding lesson over an hour ago and I'm still stuck in a staff meeting. Crazy as it sounds, I usually enjoy these things. It's an opportunity to catch up with the guys and find out what's working—and not working—with our schedules and job duties. But today I can't settle. I still have Praise to ride and invoices to sign off on and probably two or three more things I'm forgetting.

And now you've missed the twins' first riding lesson, I think, trying not to frown. I know they're in good hands. I asked around about Libby Dale and she's supposed to be a genius with children. She runs some sort of therapeutic riding center on the weekends and teaches riding lessons on the side. Her schedule's as jammed-packed as mine and we were lucky she even took on the twins. No doubt Ellie called in favors to make it happen.

And the only reason she would do that is because Parker asked on your behalf, I think. I'm leaning in the tack room doorway, staring at Caleb and looking for all the world like I'm listening, but I can't get past that thought. The things she's done for us...I can't pay them back. The apartment actually feels like a home. Brody's stopped swearing. Bridget's stopped trying to kill him. They seem happier too—and that makes me happier.

I glance at the clock above Caleb's head, realizing it's only a few more hours until our scheduled fuck. *Maybe there* are *ways I can pay her back*, I think and try not to smile.

"Okay then," Caleb says, finishing his coffee in one long pull. He's leaning against the tack room desk, still wearing the business suit from his morning flight. "I guess all that's covered then."

Everyone begins to stand, shuffling around for more coffee or heading back outside. Caleb catches my arm as I pass. "So we're good, right?" he asks. There are dark shadows under his eyes. "The twins are settled with Parker so you're covered for Masters Cup?"

153

The Longines Masters Cup is the final competition in the Atlanta Winter Series. It's prestigious as all hell with a million-dollar payout to the winner. I've been looking forward to it for months. Praise will be my ride and I'm excited to see how he'll fare. I nod. "Definitely covered."

"Fantastic." Tension leaks out of Caleb's shoulders, and it's like a kick to the stomach. If he thinks I would miss a competition like the Masters Cup then he definitely thinks my focus is for shite.

Not that I can blame him, I guess.

I'll have to do better, I tell myself, and it should leave me energized, but instead I feel even more exhausted.

You're not handling things for shite, a little voice inside my head says.

It's right too. I've missed the twins' first lesson, I rushed through the young horses' training this morning because I had so many other rides I needed to do in the afternoon, and I still haven't gotten to my share of the farm's paperwork. I'm drowning.

And even admitting it to myself is embarrassing as hell.

I want more from myself than this. I *need* more from myself than this. I need it for the twins. Too much depends on me.

Praise is waiting for me in the wash racks, our youngest groom, Danny, standing with him. "He's ready to go, Aid," Danny says, patting the big gray's neck. Praise lifts his head as if to agree and it makes me smile.

At twenty-five, I've probably ridden hundreds of horses by now, and while I enjoy almost all of them, only a few feel special. Praise is one of them. He enjoys his job. You can actually feel his joy come through when we're out jumping.

"C'mon, old man," I tell him, pulling on my helmet and taking his reins from Danny. "Thanks for the help."

"No problem."

Everyone's eager to get on to their afternoon assignments, but Caleb is still talking to John and two of the other grooms and I can tell the guys feel like they should stick around. Caleb makes them nervous. His intensity comes across as anal-retentive perfectionism. And, yeah, I guess some of it is. He wants his program run right, but the rest of it is drive and...him. Ellie helps mellow him out.

"You should come up for dinner," he tells me before leaving with John, and predictably, there's a moment of weird silence among the staff now that the boss has left.

I turn to Praise as one of the guys mutters something about Caleb learning to unclench and everyone laughs—well, everyone except for me. I'm not any better. I want this championship as much as Caleb does.

More, I realize with a sick twist to my stomach. Jacks or Better—and Caleb by extension—have plenty of championships to its name. I don't. I need this. Winning means getting my name out. It means being *seen*. It's how you get sponsors, owners, and horses, and I need it more than Caleb ever will.

Praise snorts, bringing me back to the present moment. "Sorry, bud," I tell him, one hand resting against his sleek, black neck as I lead him out of the stable and into the winter sunshine. Briefly, I'm blinded and then my surroundings return: the yellowed grass of the pastures, the black board fencing, and Parker down in the riding arena with Al Capony, and the twins.

And some other bloke.

I adjust Praise's girth, watching them from the corner of my eye. Wearing khaki pants and a button-down, the guy isn't one of ours. I don't know what the hell he's doing here—and why's he watching Parker like...that. As Praise paws the gravel, desperate to get going, I watch Parker and Khaki Pants exchange a laugh.

And just like that I go from fine to annoyed—deeply annoyed.

What the fuck are they doing?

Why the fuck do you care? I ask myself, trying to logic away the rush of feelings. *She's not doing anything wrong.* Our contract spells out fucking. It didn't spell out friends.

Or potential boyfriends.

Christ. What if he *is* a potential boyfriend?

I yank down my stirrup with way more force than necessary, and Praise flattens his ears at me, the horsey-equivalent of giving me the finger. "Sorry, old man," I tell him, but my attention is only half-focused.

It's none of my business, but I watch another minute of them. Khaki Pants grins and pants at her like he's a human Golden Retriever, and Parker doesn't tighten her ponytail even once. She's relaxed with him.

Unlike with me.

Jealous, I realize. *You're fucking jealous.*

"Aiden?" John calls from behind me. I turn, and he starts toward me, slinging a halter and lead rope over one shoulder. This time of day, he's probably heading out to catch the young horses, bringing them in to eat dinner. "Everything okay?"

"Fine." And for the next six hours, I work hard enough to pretend it actually is.

***

I open the apartment door and silence washes over me. Too much silence actually. I kick off my work boots and check the time on my phone. Fuck. It's almost ten. I completely lost track of time.

I pad into the kitchen, and Parker has a pot of something waiting on the stovetop. I check under the steamy lid, and find taco meat, and there are soft tortillas warming in the oven. My stomach growls. The twins and I both love this dinner, and for some reason, I'm annoyed all over again.

I toss my cell onto the counter so I can check my emails while I eat and start to grab a plate from the boxes on the floor before I remember the boxes aren't there anymore. The plates have been put away. It takes me a second or two to find them though. I open one cabinet door, and then a second.

Finally, I think, opening a third and finding a stack of mismatched dishes waiting for me. I really should've been here for the unpacking. I have no idea where everything is. Of course, taking time to unpack would've taken time away from the stable and the horses so I know I made the right decision.

"Hey."

Parker. It's one stupid little greeting, but it ripples up my spine. She walks into the kitchen, carrying an armload of dirty laundry and heading for the washing machine and dryer tucked by the apartment door. "Hungry?"

I don't answer—not that she seems to notice. She glides past, and I catch that perfume of hers again. My head fills with something sweet and lemony, and just as fast, it's gone.

"I tried to keep the kids up," she continues, having to lift her voice a little so I can hear her, "but they were so tired." She reappears, arms empty and hands already tightening her ponytail. "I went ahead and sent them to bed. I hope that's okay."

"It's fine."

Parker's gaze swings toward me, and sticks. Two words and she can already tell I'm tense. Clearly my bluffing is for shite. I was going to just pretend this never happened and stick to our scheduled fucking, but now I don't want to let it go. If she wants to be with Khaki Pants, I need to know.

No matter how much that might fucking kill me.

"Parker?"

She turns to me, head tilted so the end of her ponytail falls over her shoulder. "Yeah?"

"A   word,   please."

CHAPTER 29 | Parker

Definitely pissed, I think, anxiety winding the base of my spine tight and then tighter. I catch myself mentally flailing around for whatever I've done and I come up with...nothing.

Stop it, I tell myself. *You haven't done anything. If he's mad about sending the twins to bed before he got home, he should've been home hours ago.*

Sadly though my anxiety doesn't respond to orders, and the pit in my stomach grows as Aiden disappears down the hallway.

"I'll be right back," he says. "Want to check on the twins."

I nod, leaning one hip against the counter. *Bzzz. Bzzz. Bzzz.* His cell practically spins around next to me as emails come through.

I frown. Wonder how much more he'll have to work tonight before bed? Judging from how his phone is lighting up, probably a while. Sounds tough to me, but this goes together with the horse life: long hours, laser focus, and, oh, long hours.

And I'm tired enough. I drag myself to the sink, checking to see if the kids put their dishes away (they did), and spend a minute puttering around until I hear the faint scuff of feet against the linoleum. I glance up as Aiden returns.

He puts himself directly opposite of me, and braces his back against the countertop, arms crossed, glaring at me. "Who was that guy today? The one down by the arena with you."

I stare at him. "What?"

"The guy today. The one who watched the lesson."

It comes to me in a rush: Brandon was an outsider. Aiden's probably worried about security. "Oh," I say, breath releasing in a whoosh. "That was Brandon...something. I didn't catch his name. He's interested in his daughter taking lessons with Libby. She had to cancel, but she must've forgotten to call him. He decided to stay and watch the kids go anyway. His daughter would be sharing lessons with them. I think he wanted to see how they handled themselves."

The corner of Aiden's mouth twists like he can't believe what he's hearing. "Sweet, the only thing he was interested in handling was you."

I feel my mouth open and then close and then open. Nothing comes out though. Did I really just hear him say—

"Ellie told me you're more than capable of leading beginner lessons, but you still need to focus."

"I *was* focused."

"On—what was his name? Brandon? Sure you were." He pauses, bare forearms tightening as he glances away and then back to me. "Al's a great pony, but accidents can still happen, and my kids deserve your full attention."

"Wait. Let me get this straight, *now* they're your kids?" It shoots out of me so fast, for a second, my brain can't catch up. I don't usually say stuff like that. Correction: I *never* say stuff like that.

Fury turns Aiden's eyes bright. "Come again?" he asks softly.

Oh, God, I think, everything in me screaming to run for the hills. I hold my ground, but only barely. He isn't Matthew, I remind myself. *Yeah, you just said something horrible, but the worst that can happen is you'll get fired.*

Oh, shit, I really hope I don't get fired.

I lift my chin. "You told me you needed me to 'handle things' because you didn't have time. Well, I'm handling them—and how *dare* you imply I was flirting with that guy!"

Aiden's laugh is deadly cold. "You really don't know how he was looking at you, do you?"

First cold, and now condescending. What an asshole! I gape at him. I don't know what to do. I don't know what to say—until suddenly I do. "Nothing was going on between Brandon and me. If you saw something, you're inventing it." I pause, the truth of what I'm about to say weighing so heavily I almost can't summon enough courage. "No one looks at me like that."

His eyes meet mine. "I do."

My breath strangles.

"In fact," he continues, "I look at you like that all the time and you know it." That nasty smirk of his spreads into a deadly smile. "And furthermore, I know you look at me the same way."

It's true. It's so true that I catch myself already nodding even though I don't want to admit it.

"Fine," I grate through clenched teeth. "I like looking at you. What of it? We have...a thing."

"We do," he says softly.

"Doesn't mean anything."

"Nope."

"Because it can't," I add. "That's why we have the contract."

"Right."

"Exactly." I'm nodding like a bobble head and growing wetter by the second because with every word between us, Aiden's coming closer—so close, I have to look up at him to meet his gaze.

You could touch him, I think, my fingers already curling. Even through his sweater, I can tell the lines of his chest are hard, lean.

Perfect.

"See?" Aiden whispers, and I shiver. "You're doing it again: looking at me like you want me to kiss you."

"Maybe I do."

Something in his expression flickers and hardens. He doesn't move though. He's waiting.

For you, I realize, my stomach swooping down around my feet, and then—

"So kiss me," I say, and his lips part in surprise. I swallow, heart thumping in my toes now because I know what I'm about to say is going to push us off a cliff: "Because I'm wondering if it's worth it now that I know you're the possessive, jealous type."

Aiden bends to me, hands cupping my cheeks, fingertips reaching my hairline. For a second, he holds me and then his mouth fits to mine. Warmth bolts through me. Heat. One hand strokes my face while the other slides down my neck, holding me. It's perfect. It's light. It's teasing.

It's not enough.

Touch him, I think, but my hands are already sliding up his chest and he hisses against the corner of my mouth.

He pulls back an inch, and I can hear smugness in his voice when he says, "Worth it?"

"Maybe."

His dark laugh curls around me as his hand wraps tight in my hair, tugging me back, *opening* me, for a firmer kiss. I give in, and he rewards me with a small, delighted moan. His lips part mine. His grip pulls me to him, demanding I give.

Everything about him demands I give, and the realization washes over me in fresh heat.

He pulls away, hands already at my T-shirt. "Worth it now?"

"Still not sure," I pant, helping him with clumsy fingers. We yank it over my head and I don't even have time to think about how I'm wearing the ugliest sports bra *ever* before he lifts me, wrapping my legs around his waist so I can feel his hard length. "Means you're going to have to prove it to me."

Aiden's fingers tighten, biting into my skin through my jeans. "Then I better do everything I've been wanting to."

He moves his hips once, hitting that sensitive place between my legs and making me gasp. This is going to be good. It's going to be *so* good. He rubs me again and I moan.

"I like that," he murmurs, and I can hear a wicked smile in his voice. "Do it again."

Another delicious rub. This one as firm and demanding as his order. My head falls back as I moan. I'm unraveling.

Aiden steps back and I reel, opening my eyes to stare at him in confusion. "What's"—I swallow—"Is something wrong?"

"God, no. I'm just trying to decide where to start." His fingertips tug the bottom of my T-shirt. "Take it off."

I reach for him and he steps away again. "Ah ah. Take it off."

My face goes hot, but I do it. What is this? Another game? I can't figure it out. Then his hands are on me, squeezing and pinching and I can't think at all.

"Please," I manage, swaying.

And he flips me around, bends me over the kitchen table until I'm pinned, exposed, *his*.

He runs his hand down my spine and across my ass, finding the tender spot where cheek meets thigh. "I've been thinking about this for ages." He squeezes me, both hands spreading me now. I whimper.

"Thinking about what?" I whisper.

His laugh is low and dark. "I think you know."

I do.

His thumbs fan across the tender skin of my ass. "I think you just want me to tell you."

I do. Heat leaps up my face at the realization, but I do. I want to hear how he's wanted me. I want to be...wanted.

He wraps his hands around the backs of my thighs and I hiss. "Tell me," he says.

"Tell you what?"

That low laugh again and now a stinging slap across my ass. I jerk, but it's no good, I'm pinned against the table edge and it makes me go wetter. He pushes me forward another inch and my toes brush the cold floor. I can't move. I love it.

And Aiden leans closer.

His chest presses into my back, pinning me further. "Is this what you want? Because I can stop—"

"Don't you dare."

His erection twitches against me, brushing my entrance with his hardness. He loves this as much as I do. "Tell me." His whisper is molten and I shiver. "Tell me you want to hear how I've been fantasizing about you."

"Have you?"

"Every damn day."

I lick my lips. "Fantasizing about what?"

"You're   soon   to   see."

164

CHAPTER 30 | Parker

His hands skim down my shoulders and across my arms, flattening me. He reaches my fingers and curls them around the table edge, squeezing them firmly. The order is clear: I'm to stay like this.

Why? I think. *Why when I could touch him? When I could turn over, and*—the realization hits me in a rush: he wants me like this so he can do what he wants. He already can. I'm on my tip-toes, bent over, pinned. My ass still stings from the open-handed slap and I want...more.

Aiden straightens, and there's a whisper of fabric hitting the floor, the clink of his belt buckle opening.

He's undressing, I think, pussy clenching. I'm desperate to look, but it's so sexy waiting, listening, *anticipating*.

Then...nothing. I tremble. He's so still. What is he thinking? What is he *doing?* I lift my head, start to look around and—

"Ah, ah. This is for me." His Irish accent is thicker now, harder. His fingers go between my legs, sliding between my wet folds. "I could look at you like this all damn day, do you know that? Waiting on me with your perfect ass in the air, getting wetter and wetter as I play with you."

It's true, of course, but hearing him say it makes me grow even wetter—and way more frantic. I need this release. I need it *now.*

"Please?" I try to move my hips against him, increase the pressure, but I can't get purchase. My toes slip. My arms are too far ahead to push me back. A frustrated noise escapes me and he continues to play. Up and down. Up and down. One knuckle finds my clit, rubbing, rubbing, rubbing. I moan.

"I love how you melt for me," he says and takes away the touch, moving on to tease my entrance. "You give so sweetly."

I growl. "I'm not going to be sweet if you keep playing with me like this."

"Aren't you?" He pushes in one finger and I gasp. He pushes in another and I squirm, delighted by the sudden fullness. He strokes me once, twice, again. "Because I think this is exactly what you need."

"I *need* an orgasm," I grate—or rather, I *try* to grate. The more he plays with me, the harder and harder it's getting to hold onto my frustration. I'm going boneless, relaxing into him.

"Oh, you'll be getting your orgasm." He twitches his hand, sparking pleasure through me and reminding me who's driving. "But right now, you need this."

"I don't—" I do. *He's right*, I think, and the realization rolls through me like honey. I lean my cheek against the cool table top and feel my tension fall away. There's nothing left but Aiden stroking me. Aiden making me wet. Aiden setting our pace. He nudges my legs further apart and I let him take them wide.

"Christ, yes," he whispers, fingers retreating. I whimper and his thumb pushes in, his wet fingers finding my clit and beginning a new kind of play. I arch my back and his free hand slides under me. He cups one breast and then the other, his fingertips going to the peaks and twisting them lightly. I cry out, growing wetter and warmer in a single rush.

"I love how sensitive you are." Another pluck. His thumb rubs over and over the peak and I squirm helplessly. "Would you like my mouth on them?"

I whimper.

"Good." The smile is back in his voice and it is *wicked*. "Because I want my mouth on them too. I'll be enjoying that later as well."

"Enjoy it now," I moan.

"No. I'm enjoying this."

"Aiden?" I peek around my shoulder, and to my surprise, he lets me. In the half-light, his face is shaped with shadows. "Why are you doing this?"

"Because it's the only time I ever see you soft, and I know it's *because* of me." His grin could not be smugger. "It's *only* for me."

And then his fingertips find my clit and pinch.

It sends me flying over the edge. I'm biting down my scream and arching my back, eyes wide from shock and then because I can't look away from him. He's watching me.

"Again," he whispers, and his fingers rub me twice as his thumb arches forward, tapping a hidden place inside me that sends me screaming into pieces.

"Mmmm," he breathes, pulling me off the table. My back curves into his chest and he settles us both in the closest chair: my back to his chest, my legs draped on the outside of his. It leaves me open, exposed.

He runs both hands down my body, tugging my knees wider apart. I shiver. I've never felt so exposed, so open. His shaft pushes up between us, the scorching heat of it caressing my overly sensitive clit. Every time it brushes me, Aiden hisses in a breath.

"Christ, I don't think I've ever been this hard," he mutters, pulling on a condom one-handed. "Are you ready?"

For about two seconds, I'm completely confused. Ready for what? And then it hits me, he's going to take me like *this*: when I'm soaked and exposed and under his control. I'm no longer pinned to the table, but sitting on his lap like this? My feet still don't touch the floor. He'll have to lift me. He'll have to control us.

Me.

"Parks?" he whispers, lifting his hips so his shaft skims across my clit again. It's a promise of what's to come. I only have to say I'm ready. "Are you okay?"

167

"Don't you *dare* stop."

A small noise of approval, and he lifts me, his head prodding my entrance. "Yes, what?"

I grin. I'm boneless, weightless. I have never meant it more when I say, "Yes, *please.*"

He pulls me down onto his length and I gasp, feeling as if I melt around it. He pumps me once, holds tight, and curses. "You are fucking *perfect.*"

Heat floods all of me. I squeeze my eyes shut, aware all over again of how exposed I am, how he can see everything, how he's touched everything.

And how wildly I responded.

I was wrong, I think. *This is more than simple attraction and it's* way *more than a reemerging libido. It's Aiden. How am I ever going to look at him again and know I—*

A shallow pump and Aiden's hands on my breasts. He tweaks both my nipples as he kisses my neck. "Stay with me."

A small moan escapes me again, and his grip tightens. His hands close down over me and his knees spread mine wider. "Stay with me, or I'll bend you over the table again."

I gasp, eyes flying open and meeting his. He doesn't look away. He holds my gaze until I know into my very bones, this is a one-time warning. He'll take away this perfect fullness. He'll tease me until I burn alive.

"Stay with me," he whispers, "and I'll do this for you." Another pump and my pussy clenches around him, spiraling pleasure and warmth through me. His fingers and thumb were amazing, but *this*...this is incomparable.

My head falls back, and his low laugh curls around me. "That's right. Just enjoy." He lifts me and settles me on his cock again, lifts me and settles me. The rhythm is perfect.

Then slowly and suddenly it isn't.

"More," I moan and feel his fingers spasm at my hips. He bounces me harder and I gasp, new waves of pleasure cresting over me, building and building. "Yesyesyes, like that."

"Again," he whispers and grips my ass, pumping me up and down as one hand slides around to find my clit again. I jerk. It's too sensitive. I can't.

"Come for me, Parks."

I squirm. Shake my head. He grabs my hair, wrapping it around his fist and pulling me backward until I'm arched over him, impaled and trembling and *needing*.

The hand at my clit thumbs me once. Twice. "Come for me, Parker. Come for me *now*."

And I do. Aiden pushes me over the cliff again until I'm smothering scream after scream against his forearm, until all that's left is his name   on   my   lips.

CHAPTER 31 | Aiden

She's barely coming down before I'm pushing her for another climax, pushing her to give everything to me. She squirms against my chest, pussy clutching my shaft as wave after wave washes over her.

Give it to me, I think, pumping her harder, opening her for me so she'll go even wetter. She gasps. Moans.

"Never going to get tired of hearing that," I manage, fingers flexing against her hips. "Never."

And Parker must like hearing me say it because she begins to flex against me, taking me how *she* wants me. She thrusts her hips back and a hiss escapes me. She grinds down and I'm done. I come in a blinding rush, pleasure bowing me into the chair back.

"You're perfect," I bite out. "Beautiful, so beautiful."

And she is.

She's always been, I realize and the idea pulls me out of my glow. Everything distills. Carefully, I shift underneath her, withdrawing, but keeping her close. It slows our breathing, brings her back to me.

She's amazing. Just fucking amazing. Responsive, sensitive, *flexible*—I'm exhausted as hell, but my dick threatens to stand up straight again when I think about how I bent her back to me and rode her until she came again—Parker is straight out of every fantasy I've ever had.

She's *better* than any fantasy I've ever had. The chemistry is insane. I've never felt so good before.

I really haven't, I think with a start. *Love at first sight*, a little voice in my head breathes. *You're well and truly fucked, my man.*

In more ways than one.

"Are you okay?" she whispers at last. She's trembling and I run my hands up and down her arms, feeling goosebumps chase my palms.

"I'm fucking fantastic." The absolute truth, but she glances over her shoulder, studying me like she's searching for the lie.

I grin. "Parks?" I stroke her hips and feel my dick stir. "You okay?"

Now she's grinning. She gives me a tiny, shaky laugh. "Yeah, it was fun."

"Only fun?" Want punches through my exhaustion. I can do better than 'fun.' "Is that a challenge?"

For half a heartbeat I'm convinced I went too far. Parker isn't the kind of woman who's going to stick around for more. She said this was a contract thing—an attraction only thing—and I believe her. Women like her know their mind.

Which is why it's fucking fantastic all over again when she peeks up at me with the world's most calculating, challenging, *sexy* expression, and says, "Definitely a challenge. Try again."

***

Over an hour later, we're lying in bed and my Fucking Parker High still hasn't worn off. I feel good—really good—and that sneaky realization is circling back to me. When's the last time I felt this relaxed? This content?

I don't actually remember, and that...bothers me. I'm living the dream. I don't have any reason to be unsatisfied. If I'm tired, it's because I work long hours. If I hurt, it's because riding is tough on your soul and tougher on your body. But this is still my dream.

Isn't it?

My stomach turns over, and I scowl. Whatever. It's nothing to worry about. So I'm tired. So's everyone. I mean, hell, when's the last time *Parker's* been this relaxed?

I take a moment to look over her again—breathing softly and dead to the world—and it's enough to make me smug. Okay, fine, yeah, I'm completely smug.

Lying next to me, she almost looks like a different woman. Her dark hair is loose from its ponytail, and it's longer and softer than I would have expected. Her face isn't pinched with tension, and her lower lip, usually always being chewed, is soft and full.

She's bloody perfect. I knew our chemistry was killer, but I had no idea how adventurous she'd be, and my attention returns to that soft and full mouth of hers. Would she wrap it around my dick? Suck me until I see stars? Considering the electricity between us, it wouldn't take long and the temptation is almost enough for me to wake her up, but I don't.

I'd like to think it's because my Mam raised me to be a gentleman, but it really isn't. I need some time to think this through, and settling in next to Parker's warm, naked body seems the best way to do it too.

I tuck one arm behind my head and watch moonlight crawl across my ceiling. The way I see it, there is roughly a shite-ton of moving parts to a Being with Parker Thing. There's the twins to consider, the whole boss versus nanny bit, Caleb's whole "you do not sleep with staff" stance.

Hell, there's also *my* "you do not sleep with staff" stance, and, there's probably a lot more—make that *loads* more, but suddenly I can't think of a thing because Parker's stirred and she's pressed herself closer to me, and now I want her all over again.

Get a grip, I think, shaking my head and going back to studying my ceiling. The mere fact that I'm trying to figure this out is new for me. It means I want a repeat.

No, be honest, I tell myself. I want more than a repeat. I want this thing between us on loop for the foreseeable future. It feels too good to stop.

Parker stirs again, and a wedge of moonlight falls across her face, casting deep shadows underneath her eyes. She's definitely exhausted. Hell, I should be too, but my adrenaline is pumping too hard. She sighs, and I pull her closer.

I want this, I think, slipping lower into bed so I can feel her whole body against me. *I want* her.

***

I wake up around six-thirty, just as light is beginning to edge the horizon, and a warm, boneless Parker is still asleep next to me. I roll onto my back and the shift of my weight slides her closer to me, her perfect ass tucked into my side.

I'm pretty sure she didn't mean to fall asleep last night—not in the contract stipulations—and I'm curious what she's going to say when she wakes.

And what exactly are you going to say? I wonder. Around midnight, I'd been half-ready to propose. By three this morning, I was scared shitless. Now? Now, I'm not entirely sure what I'm going to say, but I know I want to see where this thing between us goes.

Parker sighs in her sleep, rubbing her feet together under the covers. She's surfacing and I expect some sort of delicate eyelid flutter or soft feminine gasp, but Parker jerks hard and sits up like someone's just launched her from a cannon.

"Whattimeisit?" she hisses, hovering about half a foot off my bed. She's wild-eyed, and wild-haired, looking everywhere but at me.

"Chill." I run one hand up and down her bare arm. "It's early. The kids aren't up, and even if they are, I can distract them and you can slip out."

She throws me a filthy look and hops up, treating me to a mind-scrambling view of her bare ass. I'd had my hands all over it last night and I want a repeat. I reach for her and she dances out of reach, pretending like she didn't notice.

I lean back, debating my next move. I wasn't lying. It *is* early. We have plenty of time, but she's rushing around like she can't get away from me fast enough.

A lesser man's ego would sting from that.

Then again, a lesser man wouldn't have made her come that hard and that many times. Maybe I should remind her.

"Come back to bed," I tell her, not bothering to hide that I'm admiring her half-naked body. "I'll make it worth your while."

No answer. Her hair swings forward in a loose, dark curtain, hiding her face from me, and I have the sneaking suspicion she's doing it on purpose. Is she embarrassed?

"Parks," I say. "Are you alright?"

She nods. It's clearly a lie, but I let it go, watching her continue to dress. Morning light has turned my bedroom pale gray and paler pink. It makes her skin look delicate and the shadows under her eyes more pronounced.

Fuck it, I think. *I'm going for it.* I tuck both arms behind my head and watch for her reaction as I say, "Next time, we should go out."

She stops dead, *finally* looking at me. "What?"

"Our next appointment, we should go out."

"Like a *date?*"

"Well, when you put it like that." I grin—and falter. My heart does a weird dip thing, like I've lost something and I don't know how it happened. "Wait. Why would it be a problem to go on a date with me? Let's play this out, see where it could go."

She pauses, nibbling her lower lip before asking, "Why do you want to date me?"

"Because."

"Because of this?" She gestures to the bed, and I can't help it, I stare at her like she's being deliberately obtuse. She *is* being deliberately obtuse.

Isn't she?

"Yes," I say slowly.

She shrugs one shoulder, and sighs. "At least you're honest. So you think we should be together because we had sex?"

"I didn't say 'be together.' I said 'date'—and that was more than sex, Parks. We have chemistry. We *like* each other. We owe it to ourselves to see where this goes."

"It's not going anywhere." She tugs her T-shirt over her head and her bare tits bounce. My mouth goes dry. "I've sworn off men."

I raise one brow, waiting for her to think that one through.

"Fine." She blows a strand of dark hair out of her eyes. "I've sworn off relationships."

"Then don't call it a relationship." Have to be honest, I'm a little at a loss here. She likes me. I like her. Isn't this how it works? "You can call it...having pizza."

"No."

"Why not?"

"Because that would be ridiculous." She yanks her hair back into its ponytail and starts searching for her jeans.

"What's ridiculous about feeling more relaxed?" Relief hits me as her hands slow. I've got something here. She's listening and not fleeing, and if this is the angle I need to take, I'm all in. "Seriously?" I press, easing out from under the covers and edging a little closer to her. "You needed that, and so did I. What's wrong with us helping each other out?"

"You make it sound like some sort of favor, like I'm giving you a ride."

I grin.

She scowls. "Very funny, and I'm not interested."

"Why *not?*" I try to bite back my irritation, but it leaks into my voice anyway. Of all the freaking arguments to have. She enjoyed last night. She'd come onto me. "Is this because of the contract? Why the hell are you denying us?"

"You want honesty?" She glances up from untangling her shirt, that cocky look in her eyes again, the one she uses whenever she's about to say something she knows I'm not going to like.

"Yeah. Honesty."

"I liked it too much."

"Come again?"

Her lips quirk.

"I'm not being funny," I say, chest tightening. "That makes zero sense."

"I liked it too much," she repeats. "It's a bad sign."

I take a deep breath and slowly, *slowly* let it out. "I still don't get what you're on about."

"You don't need to understand."

"I think I do. I think you owe me that. At least."

Bingo. Her spine stiffens. My comment hit home, and when she looks up from tying her trainers, I can tell she's weighing several responses. Finally, she takes a deep breath, her expression softening into something usually reserved for the twins when they're clueless.

"It's not your fault, Aiden. I don't trust myself. I've had these feelings before, and I married the guy."

I pull up straight, stomach down around my feet. "Whoa. No one said anything about marriage."

"Unclutch your pearls." Her eye-roll is even better than Bridget's. "I'm not angling to marry you. I'm saying, I've had this kind of attraction before and it didn't end well. I may be a slow learner, but I do learn and I'm not making the same mistake twice."

I pause. "You think I'm in the same league as your narcissist ex?"

She gives me the saddest smile. "I know you are."

CHAPTER 32 | Parker

"I'll be back later for the twins," I tell Aiden, keeping my eyes on my sneakers so I don't have to look at him. "Give me an hour. Tops."

No response, but I don't look back. I leave him in bed, closing the door softly behind me and hurrying down the hallway. Downstairs, the tack room is dim and empty, but two grooms are already in the stable aisle, dumping the morning feed into the horses' buckets and I *know* they saw me. Ugh. The walk of shame.

Or maybe not. After all, I'm the nanny. One of the kids could've been sick.

And it's not like you're dressed for sport sex, I think, noticing a stain on the sleeve of my sweatshirt. When had I gotten that? It looks like...*Oh*, I realize, frowning. *That's from Brody's dinner.* How very charming.

Why on *earth* did Aiden want me?

My face is about fifty shades of red right now. Images of being bent over his table and straddling his lap war with the knowledge my hair is sticking out in every which direction and my clothing is stained.

I hop into the Bronco, and fumble with the keys. I've been out in the winter cold for barely five minutes and my hands are already icy. Or maybe it's because I was so honest with Aiden. I don't know what I was thinking there. Then again, that increasingly seems to be the way I operate around him. I've never jumped a guy like that.

I've never *been* jumped like that.

Now that I can think straight—or straighter—saying he's just like Matthew is a bit of a stretch—a lot of a stretch actually. I wasn't fair. They couldn't be more different. Matthew looked down on everyone, and for some crazy reason, it made them—*me*, I remind myself—compete harder for his approval. Aiden gives out approval

178

like it's nothing. He always has an easy smile for everyone. He's so assured.

But my reaction to both men is the same. I want Aiden. I don't want to want him, but I do. I could get infatuated with this guy, not see what he really is until it's too late. Better to take a safer choice. Someone I can see straight with.

Someone I don't care enough about to be hurt by?

Exactly, I think, reversing the Bronco out of its parking spot. I slide it into drive, rumbling away from the stable yard. The morning is clear and cold, and my breath rises in soft puffs. I rub my eyes, expecting to feel exhaustion tugging at me and it...isn't. Shockingly, I slept really well last night.

"All that exertion," I mutter, and then feel my face go bright red when I flash back to said 'exertion.' It doesn't feel clinical and detached. It still feels naughty and wanton.

I feel naughty and wanton.

"Oh my God, get a grip," I whisper, turning up the heater as high as it will go. Semi-warm air blasts the cab, nearly deafening me. I'm glad. It drowns out my thoughts. Too bad it can't stop me from feeling my nipples—they're the tiniest bit sore and *entirely* too sensitive. Thinking about Aiden makes them ache.

I grit my teeth and swing the Bronco around the last bend and power up the Reeses' driveway. The house sits, white and dark windowed, on the hilltop and I'm so relieved, I'm giddy.

And then I see Ellie coming out the front door with her coffee in hand.

She watches me park the Bronco next to the family vehicles, leaning her shoulder against one of the massive white pillars. Even from here, I can see she's grinning.

"Good morning, sunshine," she says as I scrape up the walk toward her. She's entirely too perky for this time of morning, but then again, she's also Ellie so she has inhuman amounts of energy. "You're up bright and early."

"The twins," I say, shaking my head like they've been up to something. "What can you do?"

It shouldn't be possible, but Ellie's grin widens. "The twins, huh? Bridget or Brody give you that stubble burn?"

My hand flies to my mouth, feeling around for any chapped skin. Ellie laughs so hard she nearly spills her coffee. "Relax. No stubble burn, but we need to work on your poker face."

I groan. "Does anyone else know I was gone last night?"

"Nah. Caleb got in late, and the Colonel went to bed early." She sits down on the wraparound porch's top step and pats the bricks next to her. "Sit with me?"

"In the *cold?*"

That grin turns wicked. "Unless you want to go inside where Mary can hear you tell me all about how good Aiden was?"

"Good point." I sit down next to her, the cold bricks biting through my jeans. I link my arm through Ellie's and steal her coffee mug, taking a huge gulp before saying, "How do you know it's Aiden? I could've been somewhere else."

"Oh, please. Now spill before I have to go." She snuggles closer, her puffy jacket sleeve squishing between us. "Did you get a babysitter and go out, or what?"

"We're not dating."

"Having fun?"

I pause. Yeah. That'll work. "Okay. We *were* having fun, but now we're not. We're over—technically, we weren't even together enough to be over, but now we're really, really over."

She searches my face for a moment. "I don't understand. He's a good guy. I'd be over the moon if you two hooked up."

"He isn't good for me."

Ellie's eyes flash. "What did he do?"

"Nothing!" I tighten my grip on her arm, pulling us closer. Some of this is for warmth, the rest of it is to keep Ellie from flying off the handle. She's super loyal, and also sort of, kind of prone to defending her loved ones to death. She ambushed her brother-in-law once to make sure he was going to be loyal to her sister. Granted, there'd been alcohol involved, but Ellie will do anything for those she loves.

"It wasn't his fault," I say, resting my chin on her arm and staring out the farm stretching out below us. I'm usually so on the go I forget to notice how beautiful Jacks or Better is, but it looks especially perfect this morning. The fields are frosted white from last night's hard freeze, and the rising sun dips the world in syrupy gold light. "It's my deal. My problem."

"I don't understand. Why is it a problem to date Aiden?"

"Because he's pretty much amazing." I lift my head to look at Ellie and wish I hadn't. She's staring at me with an expression remarkably similar to Aiden's. "He makes me lose sight of myself," I explain. "I've done that—I *married* that. I'm not getting involved with someone who makes me feel like that ever again. I can't be trusted to see straight."

Ellie's face softens. "Aren't you being a little hard on yourself?"

"No." I laugh. It's a short, hard noise, and once I would've been surprised the sound belongs to me. Not anymore. "You don't know what it was like, El. I spent five years with Matthew—eight if you count high school. He had me so twisted up, and you know how that happened?"

She shakes her head.

"It happened because I was infatuated with him. He used that. I let him use that."

"Aiden isn't Matthew."

I clamp my lips together, refusing to have this argument again. I know he isn't Matthew, but the feelings I have for him are *exactly* the same as I had for Matthew. I don't trust myself. Ellie nudges my side, prompting me for some sort of response, and I'm suddenly so tired I know I can't give it to her. I can't play along. I can't lie. All I have left is honesty and it isn't what anyone wants to hear.

God knows I didn't want to hear it for years and years.

"I need someone I can see straight with," I tell her, repeating precisely what I'd thought earlier. Out loud, it sounds...different. Not quite right.

Judging from Ellie's horrified expression, she agrees. "Are you really saying you'd rather have someone boring? Someone you aren't exactly into?"

I pause, thinking this over. "Yes. Definitely."

"That's nuts."

"It's *safe*."

Ellie grits her teeth hard enough to make the muscles in her jaw jump. She looks away, down toward the stables, and takes several deep breaths. "I freaking hate Matthew, you know that? He's made you doubt everything you are."

I open my mouth and close it. She's right. That's what narcissists do. Making you doubt yourself is how they keep control over you. I should feel very grown-up and well-adjusted for now knowing this, but instead it just makes me want to curl into a ball.

"I want someone safe, someone who's going to make me happy."

"You really think this is the way to do it?"

"Definitely." Except I feel like I'm lying and I'm *not*...right?

CHAPTER 33 | Parker

Even with my little chat with Ellie, I still make it back to Aiden's inside of an hour. Showered and in fresh clothes, I hoof it up the tack room stairs and into the kitchen in time for pancakes. Aiden slides me a full plate without a word and eats his over the sink.

Regret nearly sucks away my breath. I wasn't fair to him. *I* might be a disaster, but he's always been lovely, has always made me feel like I'm more than I am. I push bits of pancake around on my plate and think how I should say that to him.

But I can't figure out how without making this worse.

Can it get worse? I wonder, hearing the twins finishing up in the bathroom and knowing I have roughly one more minute to make this right. I open my mouth, close it, open it again, and—

Bam! One of the twins slams the bathroom door hard enough to shake the whole apartment and the both gallop down the hallway and into the kitchen.

Too late, I think and I'm ashamed of how much I'm relieved.

"Pancakes!" Bridget shrieks.

"Parker!" Brody yells and they plow into me for a hug. I spend the next few minutes getting them settled with breakfast and when I finally look up, the oven clock has inched toward eight and Aiden is still goofing around with Bridget.

"Why did the pony go to the doctor?" he asks her.

"Why?"

"Because he was a little hoarse."

The twins howl with laughter. I grin, thinking about reminding him he has clients arriving just after eight and deciding against it. I'm supposed to be taking care of the twins, not taking care of him as well. Part of me wants to though. I'm not sure I like how easily I fell into that role. We work like a team.

"I'll see you later," Aiden says.

I glance up, fully expecting a pissy look or a cold expression, but he's *smiling* at me. I don't get it. After our argument, he should be mad. Matthew was a big fan of silent treatment. What's Aiden's angle?

Maybe he doesn't have one, I think, and suddenly realize the silence between us has stretched on for too long and Aiden isn't just amused. He's holding down *laughter*. He knows I don't know which end is up, but he isn't using it against me.

"Yeah." I clear my throat. "See you later."

"Don't forget our seven o'clock."

My body heats in a rush and Aiden smirks like he knows.

So we're still doing this, I think, relieved. Nothing's changed. We're back to where we were. Back to where I want to be: *under* Aiden, not *with* Aiden. My skin goes even hotter.

"I won't forget," I manage at last.

"Good." He hugs the twins good-bye, nods at me, and walks out the door without a single glance back.

I'm glad. I'm pretty sure lust is written all over my face. I check the clock again. Ugh, eleven hours and counting. At this rate, I'm never going to make it. I need a serious distraction.

"Guys?" I ask, still staring at the door because I can't seem to drag my eyes from it. "Get your stuff. We need to run some errands."

***

Of course, in order to run errands, one actually has to *have* errands and I don't. Not really. I mean there is the whole 'go pick up a vibrator' thing, but that's definitely not something you bring a pair of six-year-olds to, and there's also the whole 'find an apartment' thing, but I'm not sure Bridget and Brody are ready to be introduced to possible landlords.

So that leaves dropping off one of Ellie's bridles to be repaired at the shop, I think. It would be a nice thing to do since she's keeping Wookie for me today so I could focus on the twins. I remember she brought the bridle back to the house. I bet I could find it. A little drive through Atlanta traffic would be fabulous for distracting me.

After we clean up from breakfast, I pack the twins into the Bronco and drive them around to the Reese's place.

"God's teeth," Brody mutters, staring through the windshield as we draw closer.

I grin. I probably said something along those lines too when Ellie brought me home. I'd known the Reeses were wealthy, but I had no way of knowing they were *this* wealthy.

The family mansion is massive—not only in the sheer square footage, but the scale. Sixteen-foot ceilings sweep above us, enormous windows dominate many of the walls. Though much of the furniture is antique, a lot of the artwork is modern, lending an eclectic feel to the spaces. I never met Mrs. Reese, but I wish I had. Woman had fabulous taste.

"You live here?" Bridget whispers.

"I do. I'm a guest so we have to be very polite and very careful while we're here, okay? No touching."

Wide-eyed, the twins nod. *Of all the things to intimidate them*, I think. *Who would've thought it would be a huge house?*

But whatever. I'll take it. I park the Bronco in the back and hold the passenger door open while they climb out. "You've been living here for months and you've never been to the Reeses' before?"

The twins exchange a glance. "Aiden worries too much," Brody says at last. He's trying for innocent looking, but at this point, I know something happened.

"Uh huh," I say and motion for them to follow me inside. Mary's nowhere in sight and the kitchen is quiet as we hurry through. It takes a couple minutes of searching, but I eventually find Ellie's broken bridle hanging up in the mud room.

"What are you going to do with it?" Bridget asks as I sling it over one shoulder.

"Take it to the repair shop and then..." I check my wallet for cash and realize I don't have any. I left a twenty in my room though. "And then I'll take you two for ice cream, if you're good."

"We'll be good," Brody says quickly. His sister nods.

"Awesome. I need to get some money from upstairs." I hesitate, trying to decide if I should leave them down here or take them with me. I nearly laugh. Leave them here? What am I thinking? "Follow me, don't touch anything, and be quiet, okay?"

They shrug and we all troop upstairs to my room. It's at the end of the hall, a sun-drenched bedroom lined with hand-painted wallpaper and crown moulding wider than my thighs.

"Pretty," Bridget whispers, inspecting the flower pattern that climbs the wall.

"One second," I tell them, pawning through the vanity. "I know I put a twenty around here somewhere."

One of the bags I used for moving is still in the bottom drawer, and when I lift it, a picture frame falls out and slams into my foot. I wince, rubbing my toes with one hand and picking up the frame with the other. Matthew and I smile from behind the cracked glass.

My fingers tighten. I thought I'd gotten rid of all of our pictures together, but this one must've made it through somehow.

"Who's that?" Brody demands.

"Her, stupid." Bridget shoves him and he stiff-arms her away.

"Don't call your brother stupid," I say, and I sound like I'm about ten feet underground. I'm muffled, far away.

Not far enough, I think, sinking down on my bed. I know I shouldn't give myself even a few seconds to process this. I should throw it out *now*, but I'm unable to get myself to move. This was from our honeymoon. Two weeks in Thailand, after getting married fresh out of high school. I should've been deliriously happy, but our relationship had already started to shift.

"I know it's *her*," Brody says. "I want to know who the bloke is."

"That's—" I clear my throat. "That's Matthew, my ex-husband."

"Oh," the twins say.

I peer closer at the picture, remembering how warm the sand had been under my bare feet, how perfect his arm felt around my waist. You can't tell he would make me cry that night. You can't tell he would be disgusted with me. You *definitely* can't tell I would spend the next five years trying to make him happy and failing at every turn.

I almost don't recognize this girl. Back then, I was confident. I was sure in my decisions and didn't second guess myself. Now, I feel like I can't be trusted to pick out the right breakfast cereal let alone another man.

Aiden isn't Matthew, I remind myself. But *Matthew* wasn't Matthew when we first met. He changed—and he changed so slowly and carefully, the man I divorced was nothing like the man I married. I didn't see it coming until it was too late.

"C'mon," I tell the twins, grabbing the bridle, the cash, and my bag and taking everything downstairs. I toss the cracked picture frame into the kitchen trash, tie the plastic garbage bag shut, and then haul it outside to the bin. A bit dramatic? Yes, but I would've felt its presence—*his* presence—for the rest of my day and I'm ready to be done with that.

I slam down the bin's lid and take a deep, slightly stinky breath of garbage. "Kids?" I call. There's no answer, but I don't need one. I can feel them watching me and what I'm about to do? It's happening. Even if I have to drag them along kicking and screaming and terrorizing innocent bystanders. "Hop in the car. We have a change of plans."

Because I'm starting over, and I'm starting today.

CHAPTER 34 | Parker

A few hours later, I pull into a salon parking lot with a pair of very quiet twins riding in the backseat. They'd been excellent today—no complaints as we sat in traffic and no bad behavior at the saddle shop—but I know I'm about to push it with them.

"What're we doing here?" Brody asks around a mouthful of muffin. As a preemptive strike against his inevitable hunger, I'd bought them Starbucks instead of ice cream. Now they're nursing small hot chocolates and huge blueberry muffins. He leans over the front bench seat and peers up at the salon's sign. "Kaya Salon? It doesn't sound like somewhere we should go."

"Yeah?" I ask. "Why's that?"

"Too fancy."

Kid has a point, I think. Even through the darkened windows, I can tell the place is swankier than any salon I've used before. The walls are done up in soft grays, the styling stations are all in dark wood, and there's a hand-carved table dominating the main floorspace. It's dotted with tiny and no doubt expensive bottles of hair stuff.

"A friend of mine recommended it," I tell them and we all get out. The 'friend' was Holly. I'd texted her as we'd left the Reeses, asking where I should go for a haircut and she'd sworn by Kaya Salon.

What brought this on? she'd asked when I'd texted back my thanks. I'd sat in the Bronco's front seat for a full minute thinking about it. What *did* bring this on? Leftover anger from Matthew? Or new confusion about Aiden?

Aiden. Even his name ripples through me.

I'm bringing it on, I'd texted back. Time for a change.

Hells, yah, she'd replied. Send me pics when you're done. Also, sent you a care package to the house. Have fun at haircut.

I hold my phone close and steer the twins toward the salon's front doors. Have fun indeed. This is risky stuff. The place is filled with shiny things to grab, fragile things to break, and strangers who could be accosted. It's like taking Bridget and Brody straight into temptation.

But I want my hair cut that bad.

Or maybe it's because I'm scared I'll chicken out. Probably that. I've had long hair my whole life. I don't know what I look like without my slicked-back ponytail or a haze of hair hanging across my eyes.

But I'm about to find out.

I open the salon's glass door, usher the twins inside, and park them on the closest couch. After that, it's the usual shampoo, cut, and blow out. Although technically there's a lot more cutting and a lot less to blow out after the stylist is done.

"You ready?" he asks, turning the chair around before I can answer.

The face looking back at me in the mirror is me and not me. The shaggy pixie cut somehow makes my eyes look bigger and my cheekbones look sharper than they ever have. I like it—a lot—but it's a lot to get used to. I don't look anything like me.

That's a good thing, I tell myself, touching the fringe of bangs again and meeting Bridget's eyes in the mirror.

"You look *really* different," she says.

"I feel really different." I pause as the stylist pulls off the protective gown. "Do you like it?"

"Why would you care?"

I focus on grabbing my wallet from my purse and keep my voice light. "Because I care what you think."

Bridget pauses. Whether this is because she's annoyed or thinking this over or thinking something else entirely, I don't know. "I like it," she says at last. "It's very...chick."

"I think you mean chic."

"No, I mean chick. I read it." She nods toward the magazines fanned out on a dark wood coffee table. "In one of those magazines. It's chick."

Pick your battles, I tell myself, holding down a laugh.

Brody heaves a long-suffering sigh and slouches lower on the waiting area's couch, legs kicking. "Can we go already? I'm bored."

"Definitely. Let me finish paying."

"I'm hungry," he adds.

"You're always hungry," Bridget and I say in unison. I stuff my hand into my bag, rooting around until I find a granola bar. I toss it to him and sign the credit card slip. "Let's go."

Brody mumbles something that sounds like "thank Christ" and follows Bridget and me outside. I load the twins back in the Bronco and then take a quick selfie for Holly. I text it to her, adding: Look! I'm bald!

Two seconds later, she sends me back a dozen kissing emojis and I laugh.

"Are you coming to dinner tonight?" Brody takes a ferocious bite of granola bar. "Aiden's promised to make stir-fry. Usually, that just means he burns stuff and we order pizza."

"Don't forget our seven o'clock." The memory of Aiden's reminder makes my whole body clench. The kids might be having pizza, but I doubt I'll be able to manage a bite. I'm too keyed-up already.

"Yeah," I say at last, buckling my seatbelt before steering us out of the parking lot. "I can stay for dinner, but I have to leave to meet Ellie later, okay?"

191

"Okay." The twins sit back, pleased, and we spend the rest of the drive talking about school and Al Capony and how excited they are their grandparents are coming for a visit next week. Honestly, even with the traffic, I enjoy the trip. More and more, the twins feel like fun, little kids who have occasional bouts of being holy terrors rather than holy terrors who were rarely fun, little kids.

"Why do you keep scratching your neck?" Brody asks me as we turn down the Jacks or Better drive.

"I have hair bits down my shirt." I glance in the rearview mirror, debating my options: stay uncomfortable for the rest of the evening or risk having the twins wait for me while I shower. "Can you guys be good while I shower and change? It won't take long."

They nod.

"Promise?"

They nod again.

I take a deep breath, hope my luck with them is going to hold, and drive past the stable and up to the house. It's almost luminous in the early evening light. Around back, Ellie and Caleb's cars are still gone, but it looks like Mary's here.

We pile out of the Bronco and head inside. The kitchen smells like warm bread and Brody's stomach growls. "I'm wasting away here," he tells me.

"I can tell. You two sit there. Do not move. Mary?" I call, going to the fridge and grabbing the kids a couple of apples. "Here. Eat these and do not move."

"You already said that," Bridget says.

"Because I mean it."

They do identical shrugs and I know I need to hurry.

"Parker? Is that you?" The pantry door swings open and Mary emerges with arms full of leafy produce. She blows a wisp of white hair out of her face and spots the twins. Her eyes go wide. "Oh. You brought...friends."

"Very well-behaved friends," I assure her. "*Very* well-behaved."

Another shrug from the twins. "Where's Wookie?" Bridget asks.

"With Ellie. She was nice enough to take him to work today so I could concentrate on you two." I glance at Mary. "I need a shower. I promise to be quick and they promise to be good."

"Okay." She isn't looking at me. She's watching the twins like they might bite. "A package arrived for you today. I left it in the foyer."

I didn't order anything, I think—and then remember Holly's text. Care package. I grin. Knowing Holly, this is going to be good. Depending on her mood, the box could have anything from ridiculous penis lollipops to books on finding yourself to a roll of caution tape.

I know it sounds bizarre, but the first two years I was away, we mailed it back and forth among the three of us. It was a gag gift, totally stupid to outsiders and totally hilarious to us. The idea we might be starting it up again makes me stupid giddy. I'm so lucky to have my friends back. I won't screw it up again.

"Thanks," I say. "Do you mind watching them while I clean up?"

"We'll be fine," Mary says, sounding like she actually believes it. Her attention switches to me. "Your hair looks lovely, by the way."

"See?" Bridget says around a bite of apple. "Chick."

I dash down the hallway, spotting a brown cardboard box sitting on the antique table by the front door. It's way bigger than something that would hold caution tape. In fact, I can barely get my arms around it.

"What did you send me?" I mutter, lugging it upstairs. I drop it on my bed and slice open the packing tape with a pair of nail scissors. The faintest scent of Holly's perfume—something clean and delicious—wafts up. She's been wearing that scent since high school and it makes me smile.

I push the tissue paper aside and find a stack of fabric inside—no, not fabric. She sent me *clothes*. Soft oversized sweaters with plunging necklines, filmy camis embroidered with lace, perfectly worn skinny jeans, a pair of thigh high silk stockings, and gorgeous satin panties with sexy, see-through backsides and bow-tie finishes.

I trail my fingers through the curling ribbon. *I'd look like a present*, I realize, and my thoughts instantly fly to Aiden and how it would feel to wear these for him.

There's a Post-It note stuck to the top of one sweater:

All my love, H

Tears prick my eyes. I would never have bought any of this for myself, and she knows it. She should also know I'm not really bold enough to wear this stuff. The panties alone are way too hot for someone like me.

Holly's always been fearless when it comes to getting dressed. I've seen her pair vintage satin smoking jackets with battered jeans and ballet flats, thigh high boots and silky slip dresses. It's stuff I would never come up with and yet she looks effortless and perfect.

Can I be that brave? I wonder, holding up a v-neck sweater soft as rabbit fur. I think it's designed to be worn drapey and off the shoulder. Definitely outside my comfort zone. Pathetic that it would actually take some bravery for me to wear it. Was I always like this?

I hold the sweater up to my chest and look at myself in the mirror. I guess the better question would be: Who do I want to be now?

CHAPTER 35 | Aiden

The prospective buyer's been riding Pele for the better part of an hour, and from the looks of it, she's enjoyed every minute. Normally, I would get slightly concerned with buyers over-riding one of my sales horses, but Pele, God love him, has always enjoyed work. Mostly American thoroughbred with just enough Irish Sporthorse thrown in his background to give him the world's goofiest personality, Pele enjoys attention—any kind of attention. Whether that's jumping around an arena full of huge fences, or tearing up the water troughs in his paddock, he likes his humans close, and in my experience, he doesn't care if we're cross or not because he's sunny enough for everyone.

Which happens to be part of the reason I think he'll be an excellent fit for the young woman looking to purchase him. He's unflappable and has the personality of a golden retriever.

The young woman canters down another line of jumps and Pele makes short work of them. Three strides to the vertical. Six strides to the spread. A nice turn to the wall. They're looking more and more like a good fit, but when his rider completely bungles the last set and Pele hops over anyway, I know they're a *great* fit. A lesser horse would've dumped her.

"Such a good boy!" the rider gushes, patting his neck like he just jumped her around the Olympics rather than the training arena. Pele's ears go floppy and his eyes soften under the praise.

"He *is* a good boy," the trainer says, expression a little annoyed like she's told her rider a thousand times not to choke her approach and is going to have to tell her again. "And he's a firm seventy-five?"

"Worth every penny," I say, and Pele is—he's amazing—but I'm still always slightly shocked I sell at this level now. At my parents' farm, we were lucky to sell horses for eight to ten thousand. At Jacks or Better those prices won't even get you in the door.

You've come a long way, baby, I think, my attention wandering to up to the stable. The evening sun is settling over the rooftop and the temps are dropping fast. John hustles past, leading Praise in for dinner.

My gaze trails to the apartment windows. They're dark. Wherever Parker took the twins today, they're still gone. I glance at my phone's screen, checking the time. She still has over an hour before our appointment.

If she even shows up, I think, my insides settling. It had taken everything in me to leave her this morning. I'd wanted to stay. I'd wanted to argue it out, but somehow, I also knew it would be a mistake to push her. I needed to act like we were back on our original sex-by-contract terms.

But we're not. I want her in my life.

And she doesn't want to be, I think as Pele and the client canter by again. To be sure, it's a problem only...is it? We both enjoy fucking. We both want more. I'm sure of it.

Yes, Parker says she only wants me for *more* sex, but I can get her past that. And I've always liked a challenge.

I get the feeling someone's standing under the stable overhang, watching us, and after a moment, the shadows move. Someone steps forward, and I *think* it's Parker. The hair doesn't look right, but we're at a distance.

I lift my hand, wave, and she waves back. There's a flash of white as she grins at me. It makes my heart thump hard. Are we talking again? She's been avoiding me ever since we fucked.

Correction: ever since we argued, I remind myself. Asking Parker for a date is what really started this whole thing. I don't know what I was thinking. I should've stuck to fucking her. After all, it's what we're good—really good—at.

I pause, the reminder simultaneously threatening to give me a hard on (not a good look in breeches) and also giving me an idea. If

Parker's a commitment-phobe, there's no reason we can't still be together.

I just can't *call it* being together.

"Thanks again for your time," the trainer tells me, reaching for my hand. "I'll be in touch soon."

We shake and she strokes her fingertips against the inside of my wrist, a subtle suggestion of what we could 'soon' be doing.

I smile and pretend I didn't notice. "You're a good man, Pele," I tell the gelding as we lead him up to the stable. John hustles out to meet us and whisks Pele away, leaving me to walk the potential clients to their car.

"Let me know if you have any other questions," I tell them. We do another round of hand-shakes, they're off, and I'm suddenly...tired.

"Aiden! Aiden!" Bridget's shriek carries straight across the courtyard. "Look what we helped Parker do!"

Uh oh, I think, turning in time to see the twins and Parker headed toward me.

Parker who now has super short hair.

Super short, *sexy* hair.

For a second, I have visions of Park's hair getting cut because the twins spit chewing gum into it. "What do you mean 'helped?'" I manage at last.

Parker grins like she knows what I'm thinking. "They went with me to the salon. I had to run errands so we made a day out of it."

"Oh." I can't take my eyes off her. Her hair's shaggy and choppy and I want to run my hands through it.

"What do you think?" Bridget asks me. She's hanging off my right arm and I can barely feel it.

What do I think? "It's a...surprise." Color creeps into Parker's cheeks and I realize how that must've sounded. "I mean I like it. Really. I just didn't expect it."

"I didn't either," she says, shrugging one shoulder. She turns her attention to the twins. "Do you still want to say hello to Al?"

They nod vigorously. "Can we show him to Gram and Grandad next week?" Brody asks me, eyes wide and hopeful.

"I think you'd have a hard time not showing him to your Gram and Grandad."

Parker smiles and glances down at her phone screen, checking the time. "If you want to say hello to Al, you'll have to hurry. I don't want you late for dinner."

"I'm never late for dinner," Brody tells her, but he rushes into the barn just the same. Bridget looks from Parker to me and back again.

Damn, I think, trying to keep my face suitably blank. *She suspects something.*

"Bridget!" Brody yells.

"Coming!" She dashes off after him and they disappear into the stable. Means I have roughly two seconds before one of us needs to follow them.

"You joining us for dinner?" I ask, already moving after them.

"Definitely. I wouldn't miss our seven o'clock."

My entire body goes hot, but the whole thing sounds so innocent. Even if someone were eavesdropping on us, it seems like an everyday exchange.

"I'm meeting Ellie afterward though." She bites her lower lip in a way that makes me want to kiss it. "After she gets done at Twelve Oaks."

I nod. "Then it'll have to be fast."

And just like that I know *exactly* what I'm going to do to her.

***

It's the longest fucking dinner of my life. Not only did I manage to burn the stir-fry, but then the pizza guy was late and the twins didn't want to go to sleep. It should've been frustrating—and it sort of was—but I kept finding myself more amused.

Mostly because Parker made it amusing.

She had the pizza place on the phone before I even realized the stir-fry was inedible, talked the twins into an extra book if they got in bed, and when I finally follow her downstairs to the tack room, I realize my earlier exhaustion is gone. I feel energized.

Because of her.

Parker hops up on the desk, watching me as I double-check that the tack room's door is locked. She tugs at the ends of her hair like she can't quite believe how short it is.

"What made you cut it?" I ask. I'd liked her hair long, but the longer I look at it now, the more I like it. The shaggy bangs somehow make her eyes look even more doe-eyed, and the choppy layers seem effortless—a lot like Parker herself. Pretty without having to try.

She shrugs, the edge of her sweater spilling off one shoulder. "It was time for a change."

"New clothes too."

"I did." She pauses. "Do you like them?"

Like them? I can't wait to take them off. The jumper looks so damn soft and touchable. Every time she moves, the shoulder slips down a little more, exposing equally soft and touchable skin. She's wearing some kind of lacey tank top underneath and it skims across her cleavage, begging me to trace the edges with my fingertips.

My tongue, I think, my dick stirring. *Christ, get a hold of yourself.*

199

I glance up in time to catch Parker catching me staring. Her eyes drop to my mouth, and ever so quickly, she licks her lower lip. Blood thumps hard into my dick.

"Is this the part where you want me because I've changed?" she asks, spreading her legs for me and filling my head with a dull roar. For the first time ever, she's wearing a skirt—a flimsy bit of silk that had skimmed demurely just above her knees all through dinner—and she hikes it all the way up her thighs. "Is it better for you because I look different now?" she asks.

I make my way slowly—carefully—toward her, turning the question over and over again and still not getting it. "Not getting what you mean, love."

"You know...like in romantic comedies." Her words are picking up pace, revealing her nerves. I'm standing between her open legs now and she pulls her skirt even higher.

Christ, yes, I think, and step closer.

She licks her lips again. "The girl changes, like she takes off her glasses or loses a bunch of weight or gets a makeover or whatever, and suddenly the guy is all over her."

The pin finally drops and I grin. "Ah. Right. Romantic comedies."

"Exactly."

"Only..." I lean into her so my whisper pours into her ear. She shivers. "Only you're forgetting one thing, Parks. We fucked well before you cut your hair and got new clothes and *I'm* the one who wanted to do it again."

And again.

And again.

She swallows. "True."

"If you forgot, then it's definitely time for a repeat."

"Definitely." It's barely beyond a breath. Her eyes are pinned to my mouth and I can feel my grin widen.

"How should I begin?" I touch my fingertips to the sweater's plunging neckline, gauging her reaction. Her breathing hitches, but she doesn't move away. I begin to explore, dipping my fingers lower...and lower.

"Because if I had to guess," I continue, caressing the tops of her breasts with my knuckles, "I think you'd quite enjoy me teasing you through that scrap of silk under there."

Parks moans, arching into me and turning me instantly and *achingly* hard. "Are you wearing a bra?" I whisper. "Or are you already bare for me?"

She sucks in a breath. "Maybe you should find out."

CHAPTER 36 | Aiden

"Maybe you should find out," she whispers and my dick threatens to punch through my zipper. I skim my hand down her throat...past her collarbone...and cup her breast, finding her nipple through the jumper—Christ, she *is* bare for me.

It's just a silk tank under her jumper. I could pull his up and have my mouth on her in *seconds*. I feel the tiny bud harden under my touch and my air escapes me in a whoosh. I need her. Now.

But I force myself to wait. I roll her nipple between my fingertips, teasing her in the way that I know always drives her wild. "You had a lot of reasons we shouldn't be together this morning. Maybe I should show why that's such a bad idea?"

Her eyes lift to mine, daring me. "Maybe you should."

Another wave of blood rushes to my dick. Christ, I love that look. Love it.

Can't resist it.

I drop into the desk chair and pull her on top of me, making sure she's tight against my cock. I want her to *feel* what she's doing to me.

"God, yes!" she breathes and her mouth finds mine, pushing me open as she bends me back. Her hands are suddenly everywhere: along my jaw, in my hair, at my shoulders. "I love how hard you are!"

It should be impossible, but that makes me go even harder. I rub her along my length, delighting in how it turns her breathing ragged. Her kiss goes frantic, desperate. She digs her nails into me and I cup her ass, grinding her along my dick until I feel like I'm going to explode. The heat between her legs scorches me.

So fucking perfect, I think, my eyes nearly rolling back into my head. She grabs my face, sucking my tongue and rubbing herself against me. I'm supposed to be in control, but she's riding me, taking what she wants.

I fucking love it.

I want to give her everything.

I stand up, lifting Parks with me. She breaks our kiss on a laugh. "What're you doing?"

I lean forward, carefully placing her on top of the desk. She drags her soft palms down my chest, and when she reaches my belt, gives me a hard tug. "No. Lean back," I order, yanking her panties down.

She does, smirking. "What's with you and this desk?"

"I think it's more like *you* and this desk." I shove her skirt up around her hips and she hooks her leg around me, dragging me close.

"You like me like this," she whispers.

"You like it too." And Christ does she ever. Her core is already wet for me, needing me. She pulls me in tight and I feel her wetness brush my shaft and nearly come on the spot.

"Now," she begs.

"No."

Her eyes open wide in disbelief. "No?"

"No." I pull her hands down her soft stomach and splay her fingers along the insides of her thighs, closing my hands around hers to tighten her grip. "Spread yourself for me."

She gasps, hesitates.

"Shocked?" I ask, rubbing my thumbs across her tender skin. She feels absolutely amazing.

She grins, the prettiest pink climbing her cheeks. "A little shocked."

"You shouldn't be. You just said you knew I like you like this." I push her thighs apart with her own hands, push until she's perfectly exposed and I can do anything. I blow a warm breath across her clit, watch her core clench. "And Parks?"

Another tiny gasp. Her breath is coming fast, but even as I watch, she's going wetter and wetter. We both love this play. I squeeze her thighs gently, bringing her back. "Parks, answer me."

"Yes?"

"I don't just *like* you like this. I *love* you like this." I slide my hands higher, watching how her mouth rounds into an O, how chill bumps climb her skin. She moans. "Do you want it?"

"Yes!" She whimpers, the hold on her thighs beginning to wobble. It would be so easy to take control, to pull her apart exactly like I want her, but I force myself to wait. It's the sexiest thing I've ever seen to watch her hold herself open for me, to want me as desperately as I want her.

Another moan. Her hold on her thighs loosens even more. "I want it so much, Aiden!"

"Ah ah. Then open them." I nudge her legs apart again, and this time, I take them as far as they can go. I love her like this. Open and needing? It's perfect. "And *keep* them open for me."

The order makes her arch off the desk, eyes sliding shut. *She loves being taken like this*, I think and the realization makes my dick throb. I slide my hands under her ass, gripping her hard as I set on her in a frenzy: licking, sucking. She thrusts against my mouth, demanding more and I pull back. She whimpers and I give her more.

I give her everything.

I lick her, stroke her. I slide my thumb into her entrance and drag it upward to swirl it around her clit, using her wetness to pleasure her.

"Oh, God!" Her heels slam into the desk's edge. Her grip falters again, one hand going to my head.

She wants to guide you, I realize. It makes me smile.

It also makes me pull back. I twirl circles around her clit until her hips lift to my mouth, until she strains against me. I lighten my touch even more, scattering kisses along the heated skin. "You didn't really think I'd give it to you that quickly, did you?"

"Bastard," she mutters, head thrashing from side to side. "Please!"

Her pretty pink flush has spread down her throat and over her chest. She's hot to the touch. Burning.

Frenzied.

Which is perfect because so am I.

"Calling me names won't make me give you what you want," I tell her, taking a leisurely lick up one side of her clit and then down. "But begging? Begging might."

Parks turns her face away, that pretty pink climbing into a fiery red, and I know I've gone too far and then... "Ohmy*God*, please! I need this!"

I kiss the inside of her thigh and set in again, licking gentle circles around and around her clit while easing one finger inside her...then two fingers. She goes even slicker for me, riding my fingers and my mouth. This is for her, but I can't help but enjoy it too. The way she moves. The way she *moans*.

She spreads her thighs even wider. "AidenAidenAidenAiden!"

I pull back a bit, blow across her swollen clit. "What is it, love? Do you need something?"

It's meant to tease. I'm already grinning when I look up at her, but she's watching me with wide eyes.

Worried eyes?

My hands tighten around her ass. "Parks?"

"I need," she whispers, sounding dazed and faraway. "I need...I need..." It's begging born of what I'm doing to her, but the way she's staring at me feels like something more. It tiptoes up my spine as the air between us changes into something charged.

"You need me?"

We both suck in a breath. The question escapes me before I even knew it existed, like it had been living under my skin all this time. I could play it off like dirty talk, but we both know it isn't and we've both gone still. Her muscles stand up rigid beneath my hands and I mentally curse myself.

"Give it to me," I order and suck her clit into my mouth. She arches, heels scrabbling at my spine.

Resisting, I think and pull back, giving her a leisurely lick. If we had more time, I'd enjoy working out her tension, but right now, she needs this and I need to make her understand she needs this.

We need it, it's an unwelcome thought, but true. Parker might've been able to walk away from me this morning, but I haven't been able to stop thinking about her. If I want her to stay, I need to make this something she can't live without. I need to make *me* something she can't live without.

I need to make her need me like I need her, I think, and for a moment, I'm spinning. I'm lost because I've fallen for a woman who can't—won't—fall for me.

I run my hand up her stomach, finding one nipple and then the other, playing with her. She inhales sharply at my first twist, squirms into my mouth at the second.

"Please," she whispers as I stroke her with both fingers. I twirl my tongue around her clit again, lick it once. Her hips jump.

"Come for me." I lick her, suck her. She's so close, but she isn't coming. She's on the edge, but I can't push her off.

Still in her head, I realize, and for a second, I don't know what to do.

"Parks?" I scoop my fingers toward me, and she shudders, enjoying how I stroke that secret place in her, but not giving in to it. "Parks, look at me."

Heavy-lidded and slow moving, she does. She looks at me and I know   exactly   what   to   do.   "Watch   me."

CHAPTER 37 | Parker

My eyes flick to his and hold. "Watch me," he says and I do—I *can't* look away—and Aiden's head drops. Holding my gaze, he licks me once, twice, and then pinches my clit lightly between his fingertips.

It sends me flying over the edge.

My mouth opens on a scream and finds his forearm instead. He presses the taut muscles into me, silencing me, and I bite down, screaming and screaming, as he takes me again and again. My pussy grabs his fingers frantically, and he pumps me, licks me, taps his thumb against my clit and spirals me into a million pieces all over again.

I've barely crested one release before he's pushing me for another, riding me mercilessly until I don't even feel like I'm my own anymore.

I feel like I'm his, I think as he finally lets me come down, kissing my burning skin softly, tenderly. I suck in a ragged breath and open my eyes. He grins at me, and I have to say, he could not look any smugger.

Or more gorgeous.

"That was fun," he murmurs, and without looking away from me, sucks my wetness from his thumb. "Seems you have a thing for my desk as well."

My body clenches even as heat pricks my cheeks. His control over me is unbelievable. Every time we fool around, I feel lost. Well, not lost. More like...

I feel like I'm his, I think again and maybe it's the sex glow, but my stomach doesn't knot at the idea.

Gotta be the sex glow, I tell myself. My body has never felt this good. No one has ever made me feel this good. I roll my hips enjoying how all my muscles feel loose and thoroughly used and we haven't even fucked yet.

Not that Aiden seems to be in a hurry to get there. In spite of a raging hard-on, he's lounging in the desk chair like he could wait around all day.

I swallow thickly, dragging my eyes from his hard-on. "You aren't...?"

"This was for you. Come down and enjoy."

I open my mouth to respond and headlights arc behind the tack room's curtains. We both stiffen. Did someone just pull up?

Aiden puts one hand on my bare knee and squeezes. "Stay put. I'll check it out."

He walks outside, taking care to close the door firmly behind him and leaving me to catch my breath. I slide off the desk and take a second to rearrange my clothes. Sweater no longer bunched above my breasts? Check. Skirt no longer shoved to my waist? Also check.

I find my panties on the floor and wiggle into them, catching a glimpse of myself in the mirror above the sink. My eyes go wide.

Good Lord, even with rearranged clothes, I still look like I just rolled out of bed and my drapey sweater reveals a hint of the stubble burn across the top of my cleavage. I tug at it until everything disappears, but I can still feel how my skin tingles, how my nipples are tender in the best way. I love how he sucks them, twists them.

"We fucked well before you cut your hair and got new clothes," he'd reminded me. My face goes hot. Dirty talk aside, the truth of it threatens to put me on my ass. We did...*fuck* before I changed my look.

My face goes hotter, and I tell myself to stop acting like some sort of pearl-clutching grandma. The point is, he wanted me even before any of this, before I changed. The woman in the mirror is way more polished than I've ever been, but he wanted me even when I was wearing my ponytails too tight and had buried myself in baggy clothes.

The chemistry is still there too—maybe even better after I dared him to take me. The way it lit Aiden up, *God*. The memory of the heat in his eyes makes my insides squeeze. Holding my thighs apart for him like that? Sexiest thing I've ever done with a guy.

I wonder what else we could do? I think, going trembly at the thought. I'm satisfied and yet still hungry for him. How is that even possible? It's like I feel *great* and I'm still greedy for more.

You need him, I realize and it takes me back to the moments before, when I'd almost said 'I need you' while he was licking me. I need you. I need Aiden.

And it was like he'd known.

The tack room door opens with a whisper and Aiden appears again. In the lamplight, his golden hair is even brighter. "It's fine. Just Ellie and Caleb driving past. They're headed for the house. Means we have what? Thirty minutes before Ellie comes looking for you?"

"Twenty, but I'm not done with you." I grab his face with both hands and pull him down to me. His cheeks are rough with stubble beneath my palms. "I want you."

It isn't 'I need you,' but it's the closest thing I have at the moment and I hope Aiden knows it. He's gone still beneath my hands. For a moment, it's only silence between us and then I realize the silence is really a question.

And I need to answer it.

"I *need* you to fuck me, *finish* me." I pause, the words echoing and echoing in my head. *He loves it when you beg*, I think and it makes me smile. "Please?"

And just like that, he's on me. His mouth falls on mine and his hands grab my ass, gathering me to him. My skirt hikes up and cool air brushes my hot skin. I never should've put my panties back on. I want him. Now. Immediately. This very freaking instant.

But Aiden goes slowly, carefully. His hands skim up my sides, over my breasts, and cup my face. He kisses me lazily with deliberate strokes of his tongue that make my toes curl and my panties dampen. He's taking his time and I don't need it.

I nip his lower lip and tug his hips into my stomach, delighting in his hardness. "I'm ready," I whisper against the corner of his mouth.

"Are you sure?"

I take his hand and slide it between my thighs. Seconds ago, I'd regretted not staying bare for him, but now I'm grateful I didn't. I want him to feel what he does to me. I want him to *know*.

"I'm soaked," I whisper. "Feel how wet you make me."

His eyes go lighter as his fingers pull the damp silk aside. His eyes are hot and all over me. Watching me closely, he arches his thumb across my slick folds, teasing me. I gasp and cling to his shirt, riding his thumb and biting down a moan. "Please?"

He doesn't respond, keeps stroking my sensitive clit with this thumb until I feel like I'm going to come. "Aiden, please," I pant. "I need it. I need *him*."

It's exactly the right thing to say. His thumb withdraws as his free hand pulls my panties away. My skirt gets shoved around my hips and he lifts me onto the desk. I wiggle to pull my top down as he slides on a condom. My breasts pop free, nipples already tight and ready for his mouth. They're aching. I'm aching.

He thrusts into me, and he's harder and *thicker* than he has ever been before.

I gasp. "So good!"

One hand grabs my ass, grinding me close, while the other goes to my hair, tugging me back until my nipples are in his face, in his *mouth*. He sucks me hard.

Sucks me perfectly.

"Aiden! Oh my God!" It's heat and friction and bliss. Then he releases my breast with the softest *pop* of his mouth. I thrash. Before I can protest though he strokes me with his dick, fucking me hard and fast and exactly like I need. I hold on, dissolving in his arms, until he rubs his hips against my clit.

And I'm lost. I'm coming again. My pussy clenches around him. I come and I come, wave after wave. I shudder against his chest finally—*finally*—coming down to realize...he's still rock hard.

I suck in a shuddery breath. "Aiden?"

Keeping his eyes on mine, he moves, a hard thrust against my tender core. I jerk, already feeling another wave of pleasure mounting, and he tightens his hold. "Always want you," he grates, giving me another deliberately hard and delicious stroke. "You feel so damn good."

I do. He's making my joints go liquid, my body feel boneless. Every thrust takes me higher, promising a release even more power than before. My head lolls back, my whole body relaxing into the pleasure he's giving me.

"You're fucking perfect, Parks."

And it pushes me over once more, but not before I think: *I'm not perfect, but together we might be.*

CHAPTER 38 | Parker

After we come down, I don't give myself any time to linger against him. I can't. It's not just the whole 'I promised Ellie we would hang out tonight'—well, not entirely. It's Aiden and me. This thing between us is way more than it was ever supposed to be. I need more of it. I need more of...him.

I need a bit of space.

I kiss Aiden until we're both breathless and go straight home, parking by Ellie's truck and sliding out of the Bronco still feeling totally and deliciously boneless. The lit-up windows cast huge wedges of golden light across the cobblestones and through the open curtains, I can see Ellie feeding Wookie something from her dinner plate.

"Oh my God," she says as I let myself into the kitchen. "He's *always* hungry. What do you feed this dog?"

"Children from the looks of it," Caleb says as he slips past. He drops a quick kiss on Ellie's head before turning toward the study. Jacks or Better does a lot of work with European buyers and sellers and Caleb often does conference calls before bed. Ellie grabs him and spins him around for another kiss. A proper one.

"That's better," she says after releasing him.

He grins, his whole face relaxing. She's still wearing riding clothes and her hair's tucked into a baseball cap, but looking at her, his eyes go bright.

I want that, I think and then immediately realize Aiden looks at me the same way. Remembering it makes me shiver.

"You two are sickeningly cute, you know that?" I ask, taking a seat on one of the breakfast bar stools.

Ellie watches Caleb disappear down the hallway and gives the tiniest, most contented sigh. "Yes, we are," she says and pulls me in for a one-armed hug, nearly dropping her dinner plate as Wookie shoves himself between us. "I didn't expect you back so soon. You want dinner? Mary's made roasted chicken. It's amazing. Seriously."

For about two seconds, I think about telling Ellie that my sex glow has killed my appetite and then come to my freaking senses. Besides, asking me if I want dinner isn't really asking. She's already fixing me a plate.

"Thanks for keeping him today," I say, scratching Wookie's back as he does his happy dance and stomps all over my feet. "I really appreciate it. He wouldn't have enjoyed being stuck in the car all day."

"No problem. I love having him around. He's hilarious." Ellie looks me up and down, eyes sparkling. "Holly's right. The clothes look awesome on you."

"You knew what she was sending?"

"I could guess. It's Holly. There was bound to be some sort of off-the-shoulder sweater and silky skirt." She gives me a big smile. "Do you like them?"

"Love them."

Her smile goes even bigger. "I can't wait for you to see her new ball gown designs. We should make her send pictures. She showed me a few sketches before she left. Here. Eat."

I take the offered plate and we both dig in. I take a huge bite of roasted chicken and buttery goodness dissolves in my mouth. "Yep, you're right," I say around my second mouthful. "The chicken is totally amazing."

"I know, right? We're so lucky to have Mary. I'm still a disaster in the kitchen and Caleb is big on takeout. We wouldn't starve, but we wouldn't have this." Ellie examines a forkful of roasted chicken with something very close to reverence before shoving it into her mouth.

214

"You could always learn to cook."

"Boring." She pivots on her stool to face me. "How're the terrible twosome? Mary said they came here and *behaved*. I said you'd replaced them with pod children. Mary said she would believe it."

I laugh. "Nah, not really. We've kind of reached...I don't know, an accord? I think they've been struggling. Their mom taking off and Aiden working all the time and now living in a strange new country? I think it was a lot to process."

"Yeah, true." Ellie takes another bite of dinner and chews for a moment before saying, "I'm still impressed Aiden took those kids on."

"He's a really good guy."

I realize my mistake about a nanosecond after I say it. Ellie's grin goes straight to delighted. "Oh, he *is*, is he? Because I seem to remember someone doing a walk-of-shame while saying he was the worst idea ever?"

I hesitate. Usually, this is the place where I would come up with some lame excuse, but...I don't want to do that anymore. If I can be honest with myself about wanting Aiden, I can be honest with Ellie.

Right?

Right. I clear my throat. "Actually...he's better than any guy I've ever met. We, uh, have a thing. In fact...I think I'm falling for him."

And saying it out loud like that makes me realize how much it's true. It's so true.

Then I realize Ellie's eyes are bugging ridiculously and the moment's over. I laugh so hard I choke and have to pound water before continuing. "You don't have to look so shocked!"

"I'm not! I mean, I *am*, but it's in a good way!" She flings both arms around me in a fierce hug. "I'm *so* happy for you!"

I start laughing again. "It's not like we're getting married! Calm down!"

She shrugs, settling back on her stool to eat like everything's cool, but her eyes are still gleaming.

"Seriously. Stop it with that look. You'll be getting married way before I go down that road again." I push some of the buttered carrots around on my plate suddenly realizing I never needed space. I needed someone to talk to. "How'd you know Caleb was The One?"

Ellie tilts her head, considering. "He's always trying to make me happy—not just flattering me or something. He makes a huge effort to make sure I have what I need to be me."

I nearly drop my fork. She makes it sound so simple, and it isn't, is it? I try to think back over my marriage with Matthew, probing and pushing for any memories where he tried to give me what I needed and I can't find anything.

Instead, I remember all the times he told me I needed to sacrifice for the good of our marriage. I needed to be a team player. I needed to think of others.

But he never thought of me and I didn't realize until it was too late.

"I'm so glad you have Caleb," I tell her. "You deserve all the happiness in the world."

Ellie covers my hand with hers and squeezes. "How can you say that about me, but not believe it about yourself?"

A slap would've shocked me less. Honestly? I'd never thought about it like that, and when I look at Ellie, I know she knows. "You made a mistake, Parks—and who could blame you? In the beginning, we thought Matthew was everything you needed. We didn't know enough to see the signs, but sometimes...sometimes our worst mistakes can lead us in the best directions. You're rebuilding a good life. A *great* life. Even if Aiden turns out to be a loser and we have to hit him with Holly's car"—I squeak and Ellie pats my hand like she's kidding. But we both know she's at least half-serious—"You'll *never* fall for a guy like Matthew ever again. We all screw up. I wish you would quit punishing yourself."

"Is it that easy?" I mean for the question to sound light, but it doesn't. It sounds like I shoved it off a cliff, like it's going to be the toughest thing ever...which of course for me, it will be.

In order to move forward with Aiden, I have to forgive myself and I'm not quite sure how to do that yet.

Ellie leans close, bumping her shoulder into mine. Under the kitchen lights, her eyes are shining and huge. "It's that easy and that hard."

***

She's right of course, and I can't stop thinking about it as Wookie and I drag upstairs to go to bed. I flip on my bedroom's lights and catch a glimpse of myself in the vanity mirror: short hair, stylish clothes, a shine still in my eyes. I look nothing like the woman who married Matthew.

So why do I still feel like her?

Wookie heaves himself onto my bed and collapses into a boneless pile of fluff. I ruffle his fuzzy head and he leans into my hand. "Tired, buddy? Ellie wear you out?"

Wookie gives me a weak tail wag before his eyes clamp shut. Definitely worn out. I smile, peeling off my sweater and silk cami and slipping on an oversized T-shirt. I flip off the light and crawl into bed, wondering what Aiden's doing.

Then wondering what I'm doing because I like him. A lot.

Maybe more than a lot.

Maybe even more than maybe.

Definitely more than maybe, I think. I'm *falling* for Aiden Macken. The way he lights me up? Those butterflies and sparks? They aren't *I want you* butterflies and sparks—well, not entirely—they're *I'm falling for you* butterflies and sparks.

And if I want this to work between us, I need to make peace with the choices I made before him. Yes, I did meet and marry the love of my life—the way my life was before. Before I knew who I was. Before I knew what I wanted.

Yes, I'm never going to be the same. Matthew broke parts of me I'll never get back, but I've made new parts of me too and *those* are the pieces of me I want to share with Aiden.

Of course, sharing anything *with him at this point would be progress*, I think, scowling up at the darkened ceiling. This evening, I'd nearly told him I needed him and even though I'd chickened out. It was like he felt it anyway.

Like he'd known.

Because he needs you too, I realize, and it's as if I've been dropped from a great height: Aiden needs me too. He might have power over me—he *does* have power over me—but I have power over him as well. The way he wants me. The way I bend him to me. I might beg, but he always gives. Always.

I blink and blink, feeling as if the world has shifted on me. Maybe it has. I'd told Ellie I wanted someone safe, but suddenly I realize that isn't what I meant at all: I want someone I can *be* safe with.

And that someone is Aiden.

Now I just need to find the courage to tell him

.

CHAPTER 39 | Parker

The next morning, Aiden has a breakfast meeting with Caleb so I hustle the twins off to school on my own and it's pretty much mass chaos. Well, maybe not mass chaos. More like...controlled chaos. Yes, Brody couldn't find his backpack and we had to tear his bedroom apart, but Bridget did brush her hair and they *both* brushed their teeth so...win?

It's a win, I tell myself as I wave good-bye to them before turning the Bronco back toward the farm. I want to talk to Aiden before he starts riding, to tell him everything I thought about last night before I forget the right words.

Or chicken out entirely.

I stomp on the gas. I'm not chickening out. This is worth being brave for.

But it doesn't mean I'm not a little shaky when I park next to Aiden's truck and walk into the stable. It's still early, but most of the horses are already turned out and the grooms are cleaning the stalls. I hurry down the aisle and spot Aiden near the wash racks, saddling up Praise for his morning workout.

"Hey," I say softly—probably too softly but Aiden hears me anyway. He turns around with a smile that makes *me* smile. I can't help it.

"Morning. Didn't expect to see you so early."

"Uh, surprise?"

One of the grooms hurries past, side-eyeing us, and Aiden notices. He nods for me to step out of the aisle and closer to Praise, closer to him. "Did you need something?" he asks quietly. It makes that gorgeous accent turn rough.

"I wanted to talk. Do you have a minute?"

219

His hands slow as he tightens the stallion's girth. He's thinking something, but I don't know what. "I need to hack out Praise and Lila. Want to come?"

My heart double-thumps at the thought of riding with him. "Yes!"

"Good." His gaze switches to me and holds. Briefly, I feel as if he's pulling me apart. "I'll be right back."

***

An hour later and I'm still giddy I said yes. I can already tell this is going to be one of my favorite Coming Home moments. For one, you can't beat the scenery. Jacks or Better Stables is probably one of the most beautiful properties on the south side of Atlanta—maybe even all of Atlanta.

Set on thousands and thousands of acres along the Chattahoochee river, the farm specializes in showjumpers—breeding them, training them, selling them. Ellie worked here for years before she was hired away by Adele Mar, a billionaire heiress who also shares a passion for showjumpers.

Looking at the place now, I know why it must've killed Ellie to leave. If you face south, you'll see the silvery ribbon of the river. If you face north, you'll see miles and miles of forest pressing toward the sky with dark branches.

During the summer, sticking to the paths through the woods would your best bet for staying cool, but since it's winter, we keep to the pastures, enjoying the sunshine on our faces even as the cold wind nudges under our clothes. I shift around in Lila's saddle, arranging my coat even closer.

"Cold?" Aiden asks, smirking.

"So observant." I settle again, and the mare's ears flick forward, concentrating on the scenery around us rather than the person flopping around on her back. Originally purchased by Mrs. Reese when she was just a four-year-old, Lila has been a successful broodmare for the farm—and is apparently a brilliant babysitter for me. So far none of my flailing seems to faze her in the least. "I don't know how you manage in just a sweater," I grumble.

Not that I'm complaining. The thin burgundy wool shows off his shoulders and chest beautifully. With his tall boots and charcoal-colored breeches, Aiden looks like he fell out of a Ralph Lauren ad.

Until he flashes me another borderline indecent smirk, and all my insides tighten.

"You doing okay up there?" he asks.

"She could dump me right now and I would limp back home grinning."

That smirk turns into a very pleased smile. He holds Praise back for a couple strides so Lila and I can walk around a frozen patch of ground and then catches back up. The stallion is light on his feet beneath Aiden, eager for a run. He prances closer to Lila and she wrinkles her nose at him.

"I didn't realize how much I missed riding," I say, marveling at how my chest feels incredibly light and open, like I'd been holding my breath for years and finally released it. "Bummed my position isn't what it used to be though. My muscles are already tired. It's embarrassing."

"You can always practice your posting on me."

"Clever," I say, rolling my eyes like my body isn't completely cheering this idea on. "Maybe later you can make perverted comments about the whip I'm carrying."

Aiden laughs so hard Praise startles forward, and in one smooth movement, he brings him back. He pats the stallion, murmuring encouragement under his breath. "I can't imagine giving up riding," he says, relaxing again. "I'm sorry you felt like you had to do it."

"It made Matthew happy—or I thought it did."

He squints into the winter sunshine for a beat before glancing back at me. "To be expected. You probably married a narcissist."

I pause, feeling like someone's sucked all the air from my lungs. For a moment, all I can feel is Lila's swaying strides beneath me. "What do you know about that?"

"Pretty sure my da's one. The way he's run my mam's life...it explains a lot."

I nod. Funny how being involved with a narcissist *can* explain so much, but it's so *hard* to explain it to other people, people who have never experienced them at least. "I'm sorry, Aiden. That's...well, it's a living hell. I'm sorry for your mom."

"Me too. He loves to say 'family is destiny,' and at this point, I believe him: she won't leave him. You have to understand, she's Irish, and though the Church isn't what it used to be, when she was growing up, it was all powerful and 'death do you part' was ingrained in her. It *is* her destiny."

Bitterness leaks into his voice, and it's nothing like I've ever heard from him—or expected—and suddenly I realize I'm not talking to Aiden Macken, the superstar rider. I'm talking to Aiden Macken, the person.

The path through the field widens and I urge Lila forward, matching her strides to Praise's. "I'm sorry," I repeat, not sure if it's the right thing *to* say, but it's the truth. "Are you very close to her?"

"Fairly. We're not as close as we could be—fought too much over him—but she trusted me with the twins, and we talk a good deal."

I nod. More Aiden Macken, the person, and the hard stuff too, not just favorite colors and movies. *If he can be this brave so can I*, I think and take a deep, *deep* breath before saying, "It's incredibly hard to leave a narcissist—especially after you've been with him for so long. Matthew...shaped my world view. I'm ashamed I stayed for as long as I did, that I bought as much of his bullshit as I did."

Aiden jerks around to look at me, and Praise dances beneath him, feeling the weight shift, or the emotion shift, or both. Our relaxing ride just turned into something way more.

"But you got out," he says at last.

"Only after I gave him everything—seriously, everything. Things I'd paid for. Things I'd loved. And then I ran. I'm a total coward, which coincidentally, is also what he tells everyone I am."

"Of course, he does, and it doesn't make you a coward. It takes tremendous amounts of bravery to start over."

The path narrows again and Aiden drops Praise back so we can pass. I turn my face into the sunshine. Tremendous amounts of bravery? I'm not sure. Yeah, okay, I was brave for getting out, but it isn't like I'm over *everything*. Not yet. Leaving my marriage and stuff behind wasn't the end. It was the beginning. I'm still figuring out who I really am after years of being with Matthew.

But I'm getting there. In fact, being with Aiden and Ellie and Holly make me feel more like myself than I have in years.

Maybe you should pay attention to that, I think.

"Earth to Parker?" Aiden's still a few strides behind us, and even though I can't see his face, I can hear the grin in his voice. "Is this really what you wanted to talk about?"

The path opens up once more and I pull Lila to a halt, turning in my saddle as Praise and Aiden join us. "Pretty much," I tell him. "I want to talk about everything with you. Everything is just so...easy with you—including me, now that I think about it."

"Are you saying you want to be with me?" he breathes, his pale eyes going dark. "On a date? In public?"

"That's exactly what I'm saying, but I'm still holding you to our contract."

He grins. "Get down now. It's seven o'clock somewhere."

CHAPTER 40 | Parker

Is this what happily ever after feels like? I wonder as I drive the twins back to Jacks or Better. The idea is kind of scary even if it feels...right. I turn down the winding drive and amend the question: *Is this what happily for right now feels like?* I think it over, searching myself for any signs of panic and not finding...anything.

Well, anything except a bunch of stupid smiles because now I'm thinking about Aiden again and grinning like an idiot. It's been a week since we decided to go public—and by 'public' I mean we told the twins we were dating.

"Good," Bridget had said, digging back into her pancakes like it wasn't a big deal. Honestly? I'd expected more of a reaction.

Even Brody had been remarkably Zen about the whole thing. He'd shrugged and said, "Just don't kiss in front of me."

"Wasn't planning on it," I tell him.

"Excellent." He held out his empty plate. "What's a man gotta do to get more pancakes?"

"I'll get them," Aiden had said, grinning at me while taking Brody's plate. From start to finish, I think it took us ten minutes. It really couldn't have been any easier.

Let's hope his parents are the same, I think, parking the Bronco next to Aiden's truck. I'd picked the twins up from school and they were wired for sound, bouncing around in the back seat.

"There they are!" Bridget squeals and hurls herself out of the Bronco, Brody coming in hot behind her. They run toward the practice arena where two slight figures in dark jackets are watching Aiden ride Praise. They turn as the twins dash toward them and the older woman—Aiden's mom—nearly gets flattened when Brody tackle hugs her.

Even knowing what I know about the Macken family dynamic, it's still a beautiful moment and I hesitate before following them down there. I'm not family and they haven't seen their grandchildren or son in months. I can't imagine they would want the intrusion, but Aiden spots me right away. He slows Praise to a walk and waves, grinning.

It makes me grin. *We are so ridiculous*, I think, winding my way down to the arena. It's another gorgeous winter day—all silvery sunshine and robin's egg blue skies. Aiden's only in a long-sleeved T-shirt, but his parents are as bundled up as I am and I decide immediately that I like them.

"Mam, Da," he says as I draw closer, "this is Parker. She's been holding all of us together."

"Lovely to meet you," his mom says, offering me a delicate hand to shake. She has Aiden's blue eyes and her palm's warmer than I expected. The skin is tougher too. She's definitely known hard work in her life.

"Pleasure to meet you as well," I say, trying not to blush as both the older Mackens look me up and down.

"I just need a few more minutes to finish and then I can put him away. We'll do dinner out. I know just the place. You're coming, right, Parks?" It's a question, but Aiden says it more like a statement and my face goes so red it tingles.

"Sounds great," I manage at last.

"Gram, come meet Al," Bridget says, dragging her grandmother away by the arm. "He's the most beautiful pony ever."

Mrs. Macken cuts her eyes to Mr. Macken who shrugs and turns his attention back to Aiden and Praise. The air between them is charged—and familiar. Prickles climb across my skin as I remember how much can be said between two people without using a word.

To her credit though Mrs. Macken does leave. She walks up the stable with the twins bouncing along next to her and their enthusiasm makes me grin all over again. Interesting how they wanted her, not him. Telling too. Kids and animals always know assholes when they see them.

I turn back to Aiden and Praise, watching Mr. Macken from the corner of my eye, and for a moment, I have the strangest sense of déjà vu. The whole moment is *so* familiar. Then I realize I haven't done this before at all. I've watched Aiden watch horses like his dad watches horses.

This is what Aiden will look like in forty years, I realize. Looking at Mr. Macken is like looking at older Aiden. "Family is destiny," Aiden had said during our ride. It was supposed to something his dad liked to say, and right now, it seems true.

"I'm very glad you decided to come visit," I tell Mr. Macken.

"Of course, Aiden doesn't appreciate everything I've done for 'im, but I've always been there. Always."

Cold slithers down my spine. It's Mr. Macken talking, Mr. Macken standing in front of me, but it's Matthew in my head right now. How many times had I heard him say such things about me?

He glances at me, and for a horrified beat, I think he wants me to agree with him, but he continues on, "I could've had something like this, but I was always taken advantage of. Seems to be how it works now. You help people and they forget you got them where they are. Shame."

Always the victim, aren't you? I think, stringing up a tight smile.

Thankfully, Aiden finishes up and rides toward us. This time, his grin isn't for me, but for Praise. "He looks good, doesn't he?"

"Fantastic," I say and it's the absolute truth. The Masters Cup is only a few days away, on Sunday night, and Praise looks ready to go.

And to win. I watch Aiden hop down, admiring how beautifully and easily he moves. Winning would mean the world to him. It would kick-start the career he's been dreaming about.

226

Mr. Macken's eyes narrow. "If it's all the same to you, Parker, we need to speak with Aiden privately this evening. You won't be joining us."

"Anything you need to say to me you can say to Parks." Aiden's tone is light, but his eyes have gone shark flat and all the hair on the back of my neck rises.

"That so?" His father sucks his teeth for a beat. "Fine. Have it your way. When we leave after the Cup, we're taking the twins with us."

***

In the end, Mr. Macken was right: I didn't go to dinner with them. This was mostly because they didn't actually *go* to dinner. They argued instead. Mrs. Macken took the twins up to the apartment and Mr. Macken and Aiden followed.

As much as I wanted to...I didn't. Heart in my throat, tears pricking the corners of my eyes, I waited by the Bronco. I know I should drive back to Ellie and Caleb's. I know I should mind my own business. I should at *least* get out of the cold. I can't bring myself to do any of these. I need to know what's happening with the twins.

And apparently that means I don't mind sitting in the Bronco, looking up at the apartment like some sort of stalker. Shadows flick back and forth against the bright windows. Is Aiden pacing? Is his dad lecturing him? It's probably not his mom moving around. She looked like she'd given up fighting a long time away ago.

A shadow passes through the stable doors and scrapes to a stop. Aiden. I hop out and join him under the overhang.

"You must be freezing," he murmurs, closing his warm hands over mine. He pulls me to him and snuggle into his chest, listening to his heartbeat. It unwinds me.

"I wanted to see you," I tell him. "I didn't want to intrude, but...what happens now?"

"They go home with my parents."

My hands...my face...my *everything* goes cold. I yank back a step from Aiden and then one more. "You can't...I don't...*what?* They've made such progress. They have a life *here* now."

In the moonlight, his eyes are dark hollows, and when he tilts his head to consider me, it dips his whole face into shadows. "It's what's best for them."

"You've got to be kidding. Going home with that...*asshole* is what's best for them?"

"That asshole is also their grandfather." There should be a note of warning in Aiden's tone. I did just call his father an 'asshole,' but there's no warning or irritation, just bleak acceptance.

Which I suddenly realize *I* can't accept.

"Aiden, you know that would be terrible for them. You know what he's like. You lived with him."

He shrugs. "I survived."

"That's all you want for them? Survival?" I try to swallow and can't. My throat's funneled shut. "And what about Bridget? Do you really think this won't affect her? Watching her grandmother bow down to him and being expected to do the same?"

His body goes live-wire tight. I've hit a nerve and I'm glad. I'm *so* glad because I'm not just standing up for the life the twins have made here. I'm standing up for the way they'll look at their relationships in the future. I'm standing up for them the way I wish someone had stood up for me.

I exhale hard, my breath rising in a pale cloud. "I *know* what that kind of life looks like, feels like. I nearly lost myself."

"It's not the same thing. They need stability and a proper home and—and I can't give them that, can I? My career's just starting out. I work too much. I worry too much. I don't know what I'm doing."

"But you love them and you always put them first." A cloud rushes across the moon, spreading even more shadows, and I'm so glad. I don't want him to see I'm close to crying. "If you let your father take them, you're giving in. You're making his 'family is destiny' thing true. You have to stop them."

"It's already done."

It nearly cracks me in half. Briefly, I think my knees will give out. "Then undo it."

I pause. He pauses. I don't think he knows what to say to me and he's *always* known. "You said you understood what I'd gone through. You said you'd been there and you pitied your mom for what she's *currently* going through. Stop this. Don't let it happen to them."

"It's *done*, Parker."

I inhale hard, feeling like something inside me just pitched over.

And shattered.

"Then so are we, Aiden. I can't stand by and watch you let this happen."

CHAPTER 41 | Aiden

Even after Parker's taillights dissolve into dark, I can't bring myself to go back inside. Our argument is on repeat in my head, but it's her expression—eyes shining with tears—more than anything that I can't shake.

Every time I close my eyes, I see her behind my lids. Every time I take a breath, I realize she took part of me with her. There's no going back from this. She won't be able to look at me the same way after knowing I let the twins go.

I won't be able to look at me the same way either. The right thing is hard. That's what makes it the right thing.

I do one last barn check before heading back upstairs. Most of the horses are dozing in their stalls. Praise is actually lying down, breathing so deeply and sleeping so soundly, it makes me smile. I'm glad he's resting. We'll haul to the show grounds tomorrow. It'll give him plenty of time to settle before the Sunday competition.

Unsurprisingly, Lila is up and she checks my hands for treats when I reach for her. "Hey, big girl," I whisper, sticking my head into her stall to check her water buckets. Since she's such a good drinker, they're only half full and I take a moment to top them off before going upstairs.

The apartment is dim and quiet—unlike when I left it—and the silence leaves way too much room for thoughts. I kick off my boots by the door, rub one hand through my hair, and suppress a groan.

What an utter shite show, I think. I don't even know where to begin—and that pretty much proves my earlier point: I don't know what I'm doing. I'm out of my league here and I've known it for a while.

I pad through the kitchen and down the hallway to check on the twins. Brody's door is slightly cracked and I hover outside, listening to him snore softly. He'd been remarkably silent all through my argument with Da. I hadn't noticed at the time, but remembering it now tugs something deep in my chest.

There's the softest rustling to my left and I realize Bridget's up. Light edges the bottom of her door and I crack it open, peering in. First thing I see is the enormous picture of Al hanging over Bridget's bed. Second thing is the blindingly pink comforter Bridget picked out. That deep thing in my chest twists hard. This is all thanks to Parker. She's not here, but she's still all around me. She hung that picture and she found the all-pink bedding set and in the middle of it all is Bridget, bundled up and reading.

"Hey, love." I open the door a little wider and lean against the door frame. "What are you doing up?"

She smiles at me, looking so much like my sister it nearly punches me in half. "Can't sleep."

"How come?"

Her mouth clamps into a thin line and she shrugs, looking down at her book. Her eyes don't move though and I know she's only pretending to read.

"Are you worried then?" I ask.

"No."

The back of my skull prickles. She's lying. "Want to talk?"

Bridget's whole face lights up and it's another blow. I'm going to miss that. She scoots over, and pats the bed next to her, all twelve or so inches—even so, I wedge myself in next to her, and she cuddles into my side. It kind of leaves me stunned. Bridget's a force of nature, but right now she feels like a little kid, which, I mean, she *is,* but usually I don't see her like that. Usually, she acts like a teenager who's about to take over the world. There's something worryingly fragile about her now.

She leans her head against my shoulder and I brush her fringe of blond hair away from her face. "Tell me how your lessons are going?"

"Oh!" She grins and flops into me, wedging her stuffed dog between us. "They're so much fun! Al is the best pony ever!"

And for the next few minutes, she goes excitedly on, burrowing even closer and telling me all about how Miss Libby is working on their leg position and it's really hard to find her rhythm in the trot. The comment makes me think back to how I learned to ride. There had been a lot of falling off. The ponies we had weren't nearly as sporting about the situation as Al.

"Parks said she'd help me with my position though," Bridget finishes, weaving her stuffed dog's tail around and around her fingers.

I smile, rubbing my chin against her head. Oddly, I can feel myself relaxing, and I can't tell if it's because we're talking horses, Parker, or if it's because I'm hanging out with Bridget. Maybe all three. I feel like I can finally breathe, like I've been holding my breath all this time.

"You really like Parker, don't you?" I ask.

"Of course!" She glances up at me and Regular Bridget has returned. She's looking at me like I'm a moron. "Parker's really good at listening, and I should know."

I laugh, and nearly fall off her bed. "Because you're such a good listener?"

"Of course, I am, but also because no one listens to kids. Grown-ups are good at telling us what to do, but they don't listen to us."

She's right, I realize. I'm guilty of that. How many times have I told Bridget to go do this or go do that, and I haven't even met her eyes? *Gotta do better*, I tell myself.

Not that it will matter, the little voice in my head reminds me. *She'll be gone soon.*

232

And Da will talk to her like that all the time, I realize. Bridget and I are already close, but I pull her closer anyway. It's his way—like silent treatments and explosive screaming and always *always* being right are also his way.

"Aiden?" she asks after a moment.

"Yeah, love?"

She concentrates on her dog...the edge of the sheets...the collar of my shirt, and then says, "Don't hurt Parks, okay?"

Cold surges over me. "What do you mean?"

"You know." She squirms, focusing on her dog again so she doesn't have to look at me. Honestly, I'm glad because I don't know what she would see right now. My horror that she's worried about that? Or the knowledge that I've *already* hurt Parker? "She doesn't know what you're like."

"What am I like?" I barely manage.

"That you belong to everyone else." Finally, she looks up, giving me a luminous smile of understanding. One I *damn* sure know I don't deserve. "You're really busy and important and Caleb needs you. She might not understand that like we do so you have to be careful."

I swallow past the thickness in my throat—or try to swallow past the thickness in my throat. It doesn't really work, and my blood's thumping in my ears now. Is that what Bridget and Brody think?

Of course it is, I realize with horror. *It's what you've taught them.*

"I'm sorry. I'm sorry I haven't been around much since we've gotten here, by going home with Gram and Grandad you'll have more attention."

Her smile falters. "No, no, you've been around lots since we've gotten here, but you weren't around before, when we lived with Ma and then with Gram."

I pause, turning this over. I'd been out working during most of that, living on different farms and riding for different owners. "I didn't realize you'd been missing me back then."

The skin knots between her brows. "I guess we didn't. Not really. But now we know you. Now there will be a hole in me that used to be you. Now I have to go back without you."

I take a steadying breath. "'Back' is home, love."

"Not anymore." She fidgets, pulling at the dog's tail again. "So don't hurt Parks. I want to see her when we come back to visit."

"I won't," I say and it's the hardest lie I've ever told.

"Good!" The luminous smile is back, and Bridget rolls onto her pillow, clutching her dog tight. "I don't want her to leave like Mama left. I'm sick of people leaving. Our family's really good at it, and I wish we weren't."

I smooth her hair away from her face again. "Me too, honey." And I don't even realize the full truth of it until I've said it. "Bridge?"

"Uh huh?"

"I won't leave you."

She wavers, something far too close to disbelief living in her eyes. "I won't leave you," I repeat.

"Does that mean I can stay?" she whispers.

"Do you *want* to stay?"

She nods. "So does Brody. We...we don't like Grandad. I know we're supposed to, but...he makes Gram cry and I don't..." She trails off again, shrugging her shoulders. I get it. She doesn't yet know the words to describe the situation. I had to learn them too.

So did Parker.

And just like that our argument comes rushing back in stereo: *You said you understood what I'd gone through. You said you'd been there.*

"Undo it," she'd said and I didn't think I could. I didn't think I *should*, but Parker was right and I was wrong. I have to fix this. All of it.

But before I can make it up to Parker, I'll have to fix the situation with my niece and nephew. I'll have to do the right thing by them and yeah, it'll be hard. It's the only part of this I've gotten right.

I hug Bridget for a long moment. "I won't leave you, Bridge, and you're   not   leaving   me."

CHAPTER 42 | Aiden

I've been sitting outside Caleb's house for the better part of twenty minutes, trying to decide how I'm going to make things up with Parker. I'm pretty sure this is also part of a romantic comedy, but the irony isn't nearly as amusing as I'd like. It's been two days, seven hours, and thirteen minutes since we fought.

And when she opens the back door and steps outside, I can feel every single agonizing second written on my skin.

She's looking down at the car keys in her hand and pulling her bag close against the non-existent winter wind and I'm going to startle the hell out of her when I say her name. She doesn't even realize I'm here.

Fuck me, this isn't a romantic comedy, I think, sliding out of my truck. *I've gone stalker.*

She glances up and freezes, knuckles standing up white as she clutches her keys harder. She's wearing one of those super-soft jumpers again and a pair of practically painted-on jeans. Her hair's tousled and sexy and she looks so different from the Parks I met over a month ago.

But the way those eyes of hers spear mine, it's exactly the same.

"Parks." I sound half-strangled. Hell, I *am* half-strangled.

She hesitates and then comes to me, one hand lifting to tighten a ponytail that isn't there anymore. She drops it limply at her side. "Aiden."

"Can we talk?"

She winces like I've struck her and it knocks the air from my lungs. Is that how she used to look at Matthew? Has it come to this?

She gives herself a tiny shake. "Of course." Her voice is stamped through with professionalism. "Do you want to come inside? Mary's here, but..."

"Could we go upstairs for a moment? Your room?"

"I don't—"

"We need to talk and I'd rather not say everything in front of my boss's housekeeper."

A hesitation and then she nods, a fringe of dark hair falling across her eyes. "Yes. Okay."

But she doesn't sound okay at all and I notice how her hands shake as she lets us back inside. Mary's at the stove and waves distractedly as we walk through the kitchen.

"Soufflé," Parker whispers, like this is an explanation that should make sense to me.

Only in America, I think, shaking my head and following her down the hallway and toward the stairs. This far inside, the house is over-stuffed with silence and good taste.

"In here," Parker says, opening one door and leading me into her bedroom.

Doesn't fit her, I think immediately. The flowered wallpaper and thick crown moulding are tasteful as hell and somehow too heavy for her. She needs something with more windows. More light.

With me.

Parker crosses both arms over her chest. "Aid—"

"Me first." I hold up one hand. "I'll get it wrong if I wait any longer. I told you once the twins needed something steady in their lives, and it's still true. But they also need more than steady. They need you. We all do."

She sucks in a breath and holds it.

"I need *you*, Parks, and I've given my dad up to have you. To have you and the twins," I add quietly. Parker's held breath whooshes loose and she takes a step toward me. Deliberately, I step back. I need to say this. "I've been told my whole life family is destiny, and after we fought, I realized it wasn't true—and then I realized it *was* because you're my family. You're my destiny and I could be yours...if you want me."

She's backed me into the door. My shoulders hit the dark-stained wood as her chilled hands touch my chest. "Wanting you has never been a problem."

And then she pulls my head down to kiss me. I half-expected it to be wild, lost. I half-expected for us to fall on each other, but we don't. Her mouth moves over mine like a promise.

She feels perfect, I think. Because she is perfect. She's perfection I want to drink until I drown.

We break apart, stare at each other until I find my words again: "Am I forgiven then?"

A teary smile. "Should I kiss you again to prove it?"

"I like that idea."

"You would." But she's already tugging me toward her bed, fingers working my belt buckle loose. My dick roars to attention and I drag her hand from me.

"As much as I want to, love, we still need to talk."

Parker nods, sitting down on her bed and pulling me down next to her. She takes my hand in both of hers. "Where's your dad?"

"Gone." I glance down at my phone screen, checking the time. "Probably getting ready to board right now."

"And your mom?"

"She's staying." Her eyes widen and I nod. "I think losing Anna and me was bad enough, but losing the twins was the last straw. When I said I was keeping them, she chose us."

"She chose herself too."

I brighten. Parks is right. She did. I hope Mam will remember that over the next few months. Staying was best for her, but figuring out where to go from here? That will be the hard part. "She did," I say at last. "Never too late to change, I guess."

"Do you think you'll ever reconcile?" she whispers.

I consider it for a beat, thinking over a childhood of working for him and watching him and watching others react to him. He can only maintain his illusions for so long. The truth of him always surges to the surface and everyone takes off. "Do *you* think he'll ever change?" I counter.

She shakes her head.

"There's your answer." I suck in a slow, deep breath. "If I were a betting man, I'd say he'll get sick within the next ten years, and he'll be sick enough that it will scare him into trying to be the man he could've been all along. *Then*, he'll call me. He'll want to reconcile."

"Will you?"

I frown. As my American friends would say, 'that's the million-dollar question' and I don't know the answer. I do know the thought of having to make the decision winds my chest so tight I can't breathe. I know I'll want to do right by him. Even if he hasn't been the dad I wanted and needed, I can be a better man to him than he was to me.

I force in another deep breath. "I honestly don't know what I'll do— and maybe I'm wrong. Maybe it won't go down like that at all. Maybe it'll be something completely unforeseen and I'll have to make a decision I never thought I'd have to make." I pause, the magnitude settling on me with thousand-pound weights. "Will you be with me when I do?"

Her cold fingers thread into mine and tighten. "Of course. It's the one of the few things you can count on."

"And the others?" I mean it teasingly, but her whole face brightens. She squeezes my hand again.

"That you're an amazing rider with an equally amazing future ahead of you and that I love you." She brightens even more, her smile turning playful. "Oh, and Bridget will someday rule the world so we better stay on her good side or she'll banish us to Siberia or something."

I laugh, leaning down for a light kiss and then it turns into something more...and more. Her tongue finds my lower lip, tracing so *so* softly as her hands cling to my chest, dragging me closer. It's sexy as hell and something more. She feels like I can finally relax.

Like I'm home, I think, pulling her onto my lap so I can rub my hardness against her. Parker gasps, mouth opening wider and inviting me in deeper. She grinds into me, bursting stars behind my eyelids before pulling back to cup my face.

"Life is sticky," she whispers.

I grin. "That it is. Much simpler in romantic movies where the girl gets a makeover and the guys suddenly sees what he's been missing."

Pink climbs her cheeks. "Yeah, okay. That might've been a little unfair of me. I was feeling insecure."

"I don't want you to ever feel insecure with me again." I cup her face with my hand and she leans into me so sweetly. "I can't promise I won't mess up. I can't promise I won't make mistakes, but I can promise I will do my best to make them right by you."

She nods. "Me too. I can't promise I won't overthink things and get in my head, but I promise to try to do better."

"Ach," I chide, flipping her under me. Her legs open wide, inviting me closer. "I'm not worried about any of that." I rub against her, enjoying her moan. "I know how to handle *that*."

She grins, hands at my belt buckle again. It pops loose and I hiss in a breath. "I can't believe I broke up with you."

"I can't believe you did either." I grind against her once, twice. It makes my name ride her gasp. "Do you need a reminder of why that's such an incredibly bad idea?"

"Yes!"

I laugh and she joins me, pulling me so close everything else disappears around us. It's only her and only me, and for the first time since she left, I feel like I can breathe fully.

"I love you," I say. This close, my words are too loud, but they feel just right. "I love you for you."

She smiles. "And I love you for you. Now kiss me."

"Gladly," I tell her, and then I do.

THE END

Click here to leave a review

Want To See Where It All Began?

Get the compete Deeper than Love Series, Collection 1 (Books 2 – 5) or check out Emma Ashe's other titles at: **emmaashe.com/books**

...

Read on for a description of Deeper Than Desire, Book 1 (FREE - Prequel) in the Deeper Than Love Series

...

Libby

Four years ago, I gave away my heart. And I've never gotten over it. Finn was my best friend, and for one weekend, my lover.

He said I was his everything—and then he walked out. Totally ghosted and I have no idea why.

Now he's back and old feelings won't stay in the past. We can't keep our hands off each other—and I can't keep my heart from wanting him.

Finn

Four years ago, I was forced to walk away from the only woman I've ever loved. My father caught her father embezzling millions from their company.

To save Libby and her family the shame of prosecution, I had to give my dad what he wanted: Libby. I had to give her up. I had to walk away. For four years, I did just that. I tried to move on.

But seeing her again? I know I can't continue like this. I have to win her back.

Even if it costs me everything.

Enjoyed the Teaser?

...

Get the full version for FREE from your favorite book sellers:
emmaashe.com/deeper/deeper-than-desire

LEAVE A REVIEW

Thanks so much for reading! There are a lot of books out there to choose from, I appreciate you trying mine. Even if you completely hated it (really, really hoping you didn't!), I'm a big believer in the importance of reviews. If you could take a moment to **leave a review** to let everyone know what you think, it would be so appreciated. Not only does it help other readers, but it also helps me become a better writer.

All the love,

Emma

ABOUT THE AUTHOR

Hi! I'm Emma and I hate writing about myself in the third person. I write fairly steamy contemporary romance. I'm having fun with these, and I hope you enjoy them too.

...

Deeper Than Love Series

Deeper Than Desire, Book 1 (Prequel - FREE)

Deeper Than Destiny, Book 2

Deeper Than Lies, Book 3

Deeper Than Secrets, Book 4

Deeper Than Temptation, Book 5

...

Deeper Than Love Volume 1, Books 2-3

Deeper Than Love Volume 2, Books 4-5

———

An Indecent Apposal Series

Something Real, Book 1 (Prequel - FREE)

Show Me Your Secrets, Book 2

Claiming The Secretary, Book 3

Second Chance Romance, Book 4

All For Her, Book 5

Better With You, Book 6

Anyone But You, Book 7

———

Get notified of new releases & free reads:

www.emmaashe.com/signup